Dear Reader,

You don't know me,
I've lived a hard life, and I get by with a few simple rules: I give a day's work for a day's pay, I mind my own business and I don't look for trouble. And until I met Cassie Grant, I'd never come across anything I couldn't handle.

She grew up in the foothills of Wyoming, but she's a rich girl now, and my boss to boot. Everything I own can fit in one saddlebag, and I've never had more than a hundred dollars in the bank at one time in my life. There's no easy future for us. We both know that.

But I can't stop thinking about her. I dream about her at night, and I see her face drawn against the sky on those long lonely days out on the range. I keep making up excuses to see her, to be around her, just to hear her voice. She's got no reason to trust me—she doesn't even know me. But when I look at her I see it in her eyes, too, this feeling deep down inside me, and it makes me think that maybe, sometimes, she's dreaming about me, too.

I don't know what's going to happen to me and Cassie. But I know that after this roundup, I won't be riding off into the sunset…not if it means leaving her behind.

Logan

Please address questions and book requests to: Harlequin Reader Service
U.S.: 3010 Walden Ave., P.O. Box 1325, Buffalo, NY 14269
Canadian: P.O. Box 609, Fort Erie, Ont. L2A 5X3

RANCH ROGUES

WESTERN *Lovers*™

REBECCA FLANDERS

PAINTED
SUNSETS

HARLEQUIN®

TORONTO • NEW YORK • LONDON
AMSTERDAM • PARIS • SYDNEY • HAMBURG
STOCKHOLM • ATHENS • TOKYO • MILAN • MADRID
PRAGUE • WARSAW • BUDAPEST • AUCKLAND

HARLEQUIN BOOKS
225 Duncan Mill Road, Don Mills,
Ontario, Canada M3B 3K9

ISBN 0-373-30153-7

PAINTED SUNSETS

Visit us at www.eHarlequin.com

Printed in U.S.A.

Chapter One

The Crossing

I

The moment a man crossed the Missouri, no one asked his name, his business, or his past. Many a man left behind in the East a wife, a family, a crime, a shame. Some came with blood on their hands; some came with hope in their eyes. In the far-reaching lands of the West where only the strong survived, a man's worth was measured not by what he had done, but by what he could do.

The man who reined his horse at the edge of Copper Gorge called himself Jim. He sat light in the saddle, a tall man and lean, his eyes sweeping the red buttes and scrublands below him with practiced ease. He had been riding for a long time and he was tired. He had in mind to move onward, to stake himself a piece of land and try his hand with a few head of cattle. There was a place, he had heard, where two streams converged into the prettiest valley one ever did see, where the grass grew tall and the winter winds passed over. The Indians called it Two Waters, and that was where Jim was bound. But there were miles of desert between that place and this.

He paused there atop the rise for another moment, still as a rock, taking in the lay of the land. His senses were attuned to every shadow, every rustle, every shift in wind and alien scent. Carelessness was a vice he had left behind him long ago, in that other place, that other life. Jim was a wanted man, and he had learned to survive.

"CASSIE, WILL YOU look at that?"

"Hmm?" Cassie Grant glanced up absently, then back at the page, then, irritated with herself, closed the paperback book and gave her attention to her niece. She didn't have time for reading, anyway—she didn't have time for anything—and it was obvious that if she was to finish the volume, it would not be done during working hours. The only trouble was that on a ranch the size of the Circle P, every hour was a working hour—as she had come to learn too well.

"Look at what, Amy?"

Amy, like most seventeen-year-old girls, was a bundle of restless energy looking for a place to happen. The novelty of the ranch had worn off in less than a week—especially since most of the hands were busy with roundup and those who had dropped by the ranch house had hardly lived up to her expectations of the rugged, exciting cowboy—and she was bored. For the past hour and a half she had been wandering in and out of the office, flipping through books, disarranging papers, carrying on mostly one-sided conversations and wishing they had cable TV. Cassie told herself to be patient, but her experiences with members of the younger generation were woefully limited.

Cassie got up from the desk to see what had finally captured Amy's attention. The young girl was kneeling on the sofa, peering out the window and using the curtain to partially hide her face. "That man," Amy breathed, and Cassie repressed a sigh. She should have known.

He had just gotten out of the ranch pickup and was coming toward them, slapping his hat against his jeans to shake off the dust—and rousing more dust from his jeans than from his hat. His jet-black hair was pressed to his head from sweat and the weight of the hat, and he ran his fingers through it in a careless motion that produced a wave of loose curls atop his head. His face was lean and nicely formed, handsome despite the dark scrub of a three-day beard. He held himself with the easy, loose-limbed grace natural to one who is more comfortable on a horse than on the ground, and he moved with the long, purposeful strides of a man to whom walking was a chore to be dispensed with as soon as possible. He wore a plaid shirt, a rawhide vest and tight-fitting, narrow-toed boots— the epitome of the old-time cowboy. All that was missing was his gun belt.

"He looks like he just stepped off a Marlboro billboard," Amy said reverently. "Isn't he an absolute hunk?"

With the greatest of efforts, Cassie restrained a chuckle. "Your taste in men leaves a great deal to be desired, Midget. He looks as if he could use a bath."

"He's coming in here!" Amy squealed. And she jumped down from the sofa, straightening the hem of her walking shorts around her slim, coltish legs, fluffing the fringes of blond hair around her face, tugging the knot of her madras shirt a bit higher on her ribs.

Cassie cast her an indulgent glance. *Oh, to be young, innocent and blond,* she thought, and just then the door opened and the cowboy stepped in.

He paused for a moment, silhouetted against the sun, and his eyes fell first upon Amy, poised expectantly by the sofa, and then on Cassie. It was to Cassie he nodded, but he did not come forward. "Morning, Ma'am," he said politely. "I'm looking for Mr. Parkington."

Cassie knew only a few of the ranch hands, mostly those who had made the Circle P their permanent residence over the years. Jonas took on a dozen or more temporary cowhands every year at roundup, and this man obviously fell into that category. Cassie had not been involved in the hiring, and she did not know this man.

"Mr. Parkington is in California for a few days," she said. Stepping forward, she extended her hand. "I'm his sister, Cassie Grant. May I help you?"

The man seemed to hesitate before accepting her hand, as though the gestures of civilized society had become foreign to him. But his handclasp was warm and strong and callused, speaking of a man of firm decision and forthright approach. And his next words bore out the impression given by his handshake. "That depends," he responded frankly, "on whether you know anything about running a ranch."

This did not sound good. Jonas had promised her everything would run smoothly in his absence. With Red in charge, what could go wrong? Red knew as much as Jonas about the ranch, if not more; he had been running it for over twenty years. Cassie had been more than happy to lend her expertise to the financial side of the Circle P, but if it couldn't be placed in a ledger column, it was out of her league. What had her brother gotten her into?

Amy cleared her throat loudly, and Cassie was prompted to say, somewhat distractedly, "Oh, this is Mr. Parkington's daughter, Amy. Mr....?"

She paused questioningly, but the man only glanced at Amy, nodded and, completely oblivious to the adoring gaze she poured on him, said simply, "Hello."

Amy was not one to lose an opportunity. "You're the first real cowboy I've met," she babbled, "except for old Red, of course, who's been here forever. I haven't been to the ranch since I was a kid. Mom and Dad are divorced, you know, and since Mom decided to marry that old chatterbox Peter Browning I had a choice between living in Europe with them and getting to know my dad. Trouble is—" she shrugged "—it's hard to get to know a man who's never around. So I've just been rambling around this big old place with nothing to do and no one to talk to."

Cassie cast her a slightly amazed look, for Amy had done nothing but talk since she had arrived, but Amy blissfully ignored her. Instead, she bestowed her most delightful smile on the man in the doorway. "I'll bet you didn't know your boss had such a grown-up daughter, did you?"

Cassie stifled a groan, but it was a point in his favor that the unnamed cowboy was not inexperienced in dealing with the raptures of teenage girls. His smile was brief, tolerant and amused as he admitted, "No, Amy, I didn't. And it's a pleasure to meet you." But then he turned back to Cassie, easily all business again. "Which one of you ladies might be in charge?"

Amy was content, for although her dreamboat had hardly indulged in the flirtation she had tried to initiate, he hadn't ignored her, either, and had even gone so far as to equate her with her aunt when inquiring who was in charge. Cassie, however, was a bit more cautious. "Well," she ventured, "I might be, if it's nothing too complicated. Won't you come in?"

She returned to Jonas's big desk and sat down behind it, figuring that if she were to be in charge, she might as well act the part. Although looking the part was quite another matter altogether.

Cassie was not certain what a partner and general manager of one of the largest ranching operations in the country was supposed to look like, but an Ellie Ewing she was not. Cassie Grant was thirty-two years old, tall, gangly and not particularly beautiful. Her long bones would have been graceful had they been offset with appropriate feminine curves and soft flesh, but Cassie's build was angular and lean, not particularly attractive at all. When genetic traits had been dispensed, Cassie had received abundantly from her father and sparingly from her mother, and although her father had been a good-looking man, "handsome" was not a term Cassie cared to hear applied to herself. But she did. A lot.

The last thing Cassie had had cause to worry about over the past few months was her physical appearance, and the freedom had been enormous. After years of dressing and acting like a fashion plate for her up-and-coming young husband, Cassie's fondest daydreams had been to cast aside the frills and furbelows and let herself age naturally. Accordingly, the first thing she had done upon returning to Wyoming was to throw away all her makeup. And the first thing she had learned was that she was no spring chicken anymore.

Greg—back during their friendly days—used to have a saying. "Sometimes you look like a fox," he would tease her, "and sometimes you look like something the fox dragged in." Today was one of the latter occasions.

She was wearing jeans and a rumpled, oversize shirt that did absolutely nothing for whatever semblance of a figure she had, and made her look even more all-arms-and-legs than ever. Her dark hair was fashioned into a neat shoulder-length braid in the back, but the top sections were just growing out of a punk cut—the result of one of her mad excursions into the taste of freedom just after the divorce—and her face was framed by a cluster of uneven spiky lengths that did absolutely nothing to enhance her facial features. The skin on her nose was peeling from her riding all week without a hat, and her dark brown eyes could have used a little cover-stick to disguise the natural circles of aging and some mascara to deepen her stubby lashes. Her nails were chipped and the cuff of one sleeve was frayed. Greg would have been appalled.

As a matter of fact, Cassie herself was fairly appalled as she thought of how she must look to this extremely rugged cowboy just in from the hills. She was hardly a sight for a starving man's eyes—no matter how long it had been since he had seen a woman. And then she was annoyed with herself for wanting to be. There was no reason in the world for her to want to impress this man who, if one went by physical appearances alone, was in even sorrier shape than she was. Except that, even dusty and sweaty and unkempt—Amy had been right—he was a hunk. And in comparison with the jogging, three-piece-suited, Perrier-drinking men of the yuppie crowd to which Cassie was accustomed, he was the most innately masculine creature she had ever encountered.

Sternly reminding herself that she was behaving more like her teenage niece than Miss Ellie Ewing, Cassie folded her hands on the broad oak desk and asked, "What's the problem?"

He came forward with that same lanky gait she had admired from the window, and Cassie couldn't help noticing that he improved with proximity. There was something about the walk of a natural horseman that instinctively drew the eyes to his pelvis. She wondered if that was why cowboys were always considered so sexy.

His voice was smooth and melodious, made fluid by
the slightest hint of a Midwestern drawl. It suited his lazy,
tough appearance so perfectly that if Cassie had never
heard him speak she could have predicted with perfect
accuracy what his voice would sound like. He said,
"There's been a bit of trouble up on the line. Red sent
me in to see what Mr. Parkington wants to do about it."

Cassie held her breath, almost afraid to ask. This was
exactly what she had been dreading since Jonas left two
days before. "What kind of trouble?"

Amy sidled forward and sat on the corner of the desk,
making certain that their visitor was treated to the best
possible view of her long, swinging legs. The gentleman
in question, however, displayed an admirable immunity to
the charms of teenage girls. He replied simply, "The cook
quit."

Well, now. Cassie released a cautious breath. That
didn't sound too bad. She had been expecting a stampede
or a range fire at the very least. She inquired, "Why?"

He lifted one shoulder casually. "Cooks are temperamental folk. Always have been."

That was better than no answer at all, but not by much.
Obviously, he didn't believe in extraneous conversation.
He stood there, waiting for her decision, and Cassie hesitated, thinking it over.

Now that he was out of the glare of the sun, Cassie
could see that he had a very nice face indeed. The rough
beard stubble was only a disguise for almost artistically
perfect bone structure, his chin nicely curved, his cheekbones high and forehead broad. His lips were full, bracketed on the left side by a faint line that would deepen
when he smiled. His eyebrows were dark and winged just
slightly, and his lashes were sinfully thick. His eyes were
gray, and the light color contrasted against the darkness

of his skin could easily be called beautiful. Cassie could certainly understand why Amy had been so quickly smitten. If Cassie had legs like Amy's, she would no doubt be swinging them in front of his face, too.

Cassie became aware of his eyes upon her, patient and polite. There was something about those eyes—not exactly cool, not precisely haunted, but a combination of both that was not quite either. There was a distance to him, a caution, an alertness, an almost indifferent tolerance. Cassie was a great believer that the eyes were the windows of the soul, but she had never met anyone whose eyes revealed less than this man's did.

She said, "Well, a cook shouldn't be too hard to replace. If you boys can fend for yourselves for a couple of nights, I'll make a few phone calls and—"

"If you'll pardon me, ma'am, I don't think it's going to be quite that easy." Still his expression was perfectly polite, but there was a firmness to his tone that made Cassie hesitate. "You've got two dozen hard-working cowboys out there with nothing to look forward to but a hot meal at sundown. They're not going to take kindly to being told to fend for themselves for a couple of days."

Cassie frowned, more in irritation with herself than with the man who had so mildly pointed out the obvious truth. He was right. It wasn't as though they could send out for pizza or anything. She had grown up on the ranch and it annoyed her how quickly she had forgotten something so basic: an army traveled on its stomach, and so did range riders. Whatever solution she came up with for replacing the cook, it would have to be put into action immediately.

"Isn't there anyone up there who knows how to cook?" she asked.

To her surprise, the eyes that were as distant as clouds took on a faint twinkle; the mouth that seemed unused to smiling deepened in one corner with amusement. "Well," he murmured, "that answers my first question, anyway."

Cassie was instantly defensive. "What question?"

"Whether or not you know anything about running a ranch."

Cassie felt heat stain her cheeks, but again it was from annoyance with herself, not him. She knew perfectly well that the protocol on a cattle drive was strict and unbreachable, and nowhere was it more sacred than regarding the cook. The head of the chuck wagon held a specific and exalted position that was not to be encroached upon by anyone; contrarily, a cowhand would consider it beneath his dignity to cook for himself, much less for anyone else. Long years of tradition had instilled within the cowboy a pride that would prefer starvation to relinquishing his place on the range for the confines of the chuck wagon. And all of that was notwithstanding the fact that none of the hired men would have the faintest idea of how to go about preparing a meal for twenty-odd cowhands, an obvious truth that Cassie had somehow managed to forget. It was amazing how much of her past had been erased by fifteen years of civilization.

Cassie caught herself chewing her thumbnail, scowled and placed both hands in her lap. This was indeed a dilemma. She was certain Jonas had made provisions for just such an emergency, but by the time she reached him in California the entire hungry crew might have ridden off into the sunset. If only she could...

Amy piped up excitedly, "Why don't we go? You can cook, Cassie, and I can help you! It'll be great fun—this is exactly what I've been wanting to do, go on a real cattle drive with real cowboys—"

Cassie saw alarm cross the eyes of the implacable man

before her, and at the same moment she was quick to interject, "Don't be ridiculous, Amy!"

Amy turned to her, her large blue eyes stubborn and persuasive. "It's not ridiculous," she insisted. "It's the only logical solution. Who else is going to do it? Daddy is fifteen hundred miles away, and he left you in charge, didn't he?"

"Your father," Cassie responded flatly, "would kill me."

"No," replied Amy, "he'd only break your legs. He'd kill you if you let anything slow down this roundup. And besides," she argued reasonably, "what else are you going to do? Even if you could find a cook—and you'd have to go into town to do it—you could never get him out there before tonight's meal. It's not like you could just call up an employment agency and send him across town, you know."

The worst thing was Amy was right. Any cook Cassie could hire would have to be prepared to pull up stakes and go on the trail for several months, and he would be required to do so with only a few hours' notice. There was no one on the ranch at all besides Cassie, Amy and the sixty-year-old housekeeper. There was no one to deal with this emergency but Cassie.

She said, stalling for time, "I think I'd better call your father."

"Come on, Cassie," Amy challenged impatiently, "you can think for yourself. Daddy wouldn't have left you in charge if he didn't expect you to. Where's your sense of adventure?"

Amy could not possibly have known what a raw nerve she had struck, but Cassie cast a swift and suspicious glance at the young girl just to make sure. Amy's eyes

were filled with nothing but the peculiarly teenage mixture
of pleading and self-assertion.

And damn it all, once again the girl was right. Cassie
had spent the past eight years living her life for someone
else, letting him tell her how to dress, how to act, what
to think, until now she was incapable of making even the
most routine decision for herself. She had crawled out
under the weight of someone else's image of her, only to
find there was nothing remaining of the Cassie she had
once known but shadows. She had come back home hoping to find the pieces of her lost self and somehow put
them together again, but so far all she had succeeded in
doing was hiding.

She looked at Amy—the symbol of the girl she once
had been—and she saw the woman she had become, and
she was appalled. The Cassie Parkington who had grown
up on this ranch was full of spit and fire. There was no
dare she wouldn't take, no rule she wouldn't break, no
challenge she couldn't meet. Danger meant nothing to her;
she lived for adventure. She had driven her father to a
premature gray and her mother to despair, and even the
rough and sturdy ranch hands used to roll their eyes and
look for cover when they saw her coming. From this she
had grown into a meek and obedient corporate wife to
whom adventure meant a shopping spree at Saks, not even
a suitable caricature of the person she had meant to be.

Amy was right. It was time she started thinking for
herself.

"It would only be for a couple of days," she said cautiously, almost thinking out loud. "Just until we could
find a real cook to come out and take over."

Amy's eyes lit up and she almost clapped her hands in
glee. Cassie could see her forcefully restraining herself
from jumping up and down like a child as, ever aware

that the eyes of the magnificent cowboy were upon her, she nodded with utmost reasonability. ''It's the only thing to do,'' she agreed soberly.

''But I'll have to call your father,'' Cassie warned sternly.

Disappointment crossed Amy's face, but it didn't last long. She considered this, shrugged and then smiled. ''What can he do from California?''

Precisely, thought Cassie, but her confidence was underscored with dread. From California, Jonas could do nothing, but once he got back to the ranch he would kill her.

Jonas had made his position perfectly clear concerning his daughter's fraternizing with the ranch hands—and he was right, to a point. Amy was reckless, eager for excitement and more than a little boy-crazy—a beautiful young girl who was easy prey for some of the less-than-scrupulous drovers who hired on for the season. Jonas's last instructions to Cassie had been to keep Amy out of trouble and keep her away from the cowboys. And so what did Cassie do at the first possible opportunity but deliver Amy directly into the midst of a pack of hungry wolves?

But the alternative—leaving Amy at the house alone—was even more unappealing. Knowing Amy, and remembering how she herself had been at the same age, Cassie knew exactly what the young girl would do. She would probably try to follow her and end up getting lost or hurt, or worse. Taking Amy out on the range with her might not be the best idea Cassie had ever had, but at least she would be able to keep an eye on her. And as long as Amy was with her, Cassie could fulfill at least one part of her promise to Jonas: to keep Amy out of trouble.

Cassie glanced at the cowboy who was waiting in front of her desk for her decision. His disapproval was evident in his eyes, but Cassie thought she might as well make it official. "How does that sound to you, Mr....?"

Once again, he declined her invitation to give his name. He said instead, firmly, "Well, ma'am, now that you ask, I think it's a damned fool notion and I don't want any part of it. The trail is no place for a woman, much less—" he glanced meaningfully at Amy "—a pretty young girl." Amy preened beneath the compliment, but the cowboy's eyes were icy as they returned to Cassie. "And if you'll pardon my saying so, ma'am, you look old enough to know better."

Cassie bristled but hid it well. She folded her hands calmly on the desk and addressed him politely but deliberately. "What is your name?"

He met her gaze evenly. "Logan."

"Well, Mr. Logan—"

"No," he corrected mildly. "Just Logan."

Cassie was momentarily distracted, and that irritated her. No first name, no last name, just Logan. What kind of saddle tramps was Jonas taking on these days?

She looked into the cool gray eyes of the man who was "just Logan" and she thought a bit bemusedly, *Yes, indeed, what kind...?* For this was no ordinary, uneducated, unwashed day laborer. For one thing, his speech, though softened by the lazy drawl and careless idioms of the far West, was not that of an illiterate. For another, he held himself with the kind of instinctive pride and natural grace that wasn't common among the men who usually resorted to this kind of work. And there was something about him—an authority, a decision, an alertness and a quickness—that set him apart from any of the cowhands Cassie had ever known, from most of the men Cassie had ever known. In short, this was a man whose every move declared he had known better days, and that puzzled Cassie.

But the answer to the puzzle was obviously not forthcoming from him, if at all. Firmly Cassie gathered her roaming thoughts and continued with a pleasantness she did not entirely feel, "Well, then, Logan, to answer your unspoken question, I am thirty-two years old. The last person who called me ma'am was wearing a Cub Scout uniform and even he lived to regret it. You see I—" she smiled a little, saccharinely, to sweeten the bite placed on the words "—have two names, neither one of which is ma'am. You can call me Cassie or you can call me Ms Grant. I'll even answer to 'hey, you.' But do not, if you want to stay on good terms with your temporary employer, ever call me ma'am again."

Amy smothered a giggle, and Cassie was gratified to see the stone face before her soften just a bit with the faintest amused twitch of an eyebrow. But his tone was still stubborn and disapproving as he said, "I still think you ought to think about what you're doing. You're making a mistake."

The trouble was, if Cassie thought about it for even another minute she would no doubt realize he was right and back out entirely. But more was at stake here than a group of hungry cowboys and a missing cook. Amy had demanded to know where her aunt's sense of adventure had gone, and Cassie was curious about the answer to that herself. Her youth, her daring, her courage, her entire sense of self—where was she to find any of them if she did not first make the conscious decision to search?

She said simply, and with what she hoped was convincing authority, "I know what I'm doing, thank you."

He hesitated a moment longer and cast a last quick glance at Amy. "All right, then. You're the boss. But we only need one cook."

Cassie was both touched and surprised by his concern

for Amy's safety—perception and compassion were two more traits that were not usually associated with men of his ilk. But on that score, at least, Cassie was not going to waste time debating. She wasn't about to leave Amy behind to concoct mischief on her own, and though Jonas would undoubtedly disagree with her most strenuously, Cassie was firmly convinced that this experience was exactly what Amy needed to cure herself of the cowboy raptures.

Amy, like most girls her age, tended to romanticize everything. It was only natural that the already romantic legend of the cowboy should be enhanced into a glowing fantasy in her mind. What she was about to discover was that modern-day cowboys, very much like their counterparts of a hundred years ago, were mostly the flotsam of an underbred society.

They had broken teeth and short tempers, shallow interests and questionable habits of personal hygiene. Few had obtained high school diplomas and many had never finished grammar school. They went to riding herd because it was the only job they could get, and the only reason most of them weren't in jail was because in a society as sparsely populated as western Wyoming there simply weren't many opportunities to commit a crime. Had they lived in the city they would have been junkies, street thugs, or just plain bums and drunks, sleeping in gutters and eating in missions. Because the environment in which they lived did not provide the opportunity for dramatic vices, they made do with what they had: drifting from ranch to ranch for thirty dollars a day during the season and taking odd jobs when the roundup was over. If there was anything admirable about the cowboy at all it was only his complete and unabashed lack of ambition.

Amy was a young woman of the eighties, educated in

the best schools, accustomed to designer jeans and snobbish cliques and status cars. From her very earliest years she had been inundated with the intrinsic values of Radcliffe, Ralph Lauren and the Republican party. At the moment, the cowboy might symbolize for her all that was romantic and exciting, but Cassie had no doubt that two days on the trail would disillusion her thoroughly. And Jonas would thank her for it. She hoped.

Cassie smiled at Logan. "We'll both go," she said.

He looked at her for another moment, and she thought he might say something more. But then he simply nodded, and turned for the door. "Yes, ma—" he caught himself with a quirk of the lips, which might have been the beginning of a grin, and amended, "—Mrs. Grant. I'll take the time to clean up, if you don't mind, while you get your gear together, and then I'll drive you back up to the camp."

Cassie stood to see him out, but he paused at the door, turning with only the mildest display of curiosity in his tone. "By the way—can you cook?"

Cassie struggled with a dimpling smile. The man called Logan was difficult, enigmatic, frustrating and, on a very subliminal level, mildly annoying, but he promised without a doubt to be the most challenging thing that had happened to Cassie in years. She was looking forward to the adventure of the next days far more than she had any right to.

"Yes," she replied. "As a matter of fact, I can."

He merely nodded and, letting his eyes linger on neither Amy nor Cassie, walked outside, closing the door behind him.

Amy jumped down from the desk and began to chatter excitedly; Cassie was making a methodical list in her mind of the things they had to do and to pack for the trip.

But she couldn't seem to move her eyes away from the window, where the rangy form of Logan moved at a lanky, unhurried gait across the yard toward the bunkhouse. Without realizing it, a faint frown began to disturb her brow, and she was already hoping she hadn't made a mistake.

Chapter Two

The Crossing

II

The wilderness was no place for a woman. A man traveling through this part of the country needed to move light and move fast; he couldn't be slowed down by responsibility, second thoughts or females. This was Comanche territory, and a white woman was a most valuable prize. Jim had seen what the Comanches did to the women they captured.

Even if she managed to escape the Indians, the renegade white men, the trail sickness, it was a long, hard ride that many a good man couldn't survive. It would be weeks, maybe months, before she slept indoors again. There would be nights without a fire, days without water. She would take sick from bad food or go out of her mind from the heat and the dust.

Jim figured a man would have to be two times a fool to undertake to escort a woman across this country. He also figured, from the moment he laid eyes on her, that he didn't have much choice.

IT WAS A TWO-HOUR DRIVE—roughly seventy miles—
from the ranch house to the campsite, and Cassie had
thought to pass the time constructively. Unfortunately,
Amy had other ideas.

She had chattered nonstop from the moment they
climbed into the truck. Cassie had gritted her teeth and
tried to lose herself in the book, but she couldn't help
pausing every few pages to cast cautious, sympathetic
glances at Logan.

All in all, he was bearing up quite well. He kept one
hand lazily on the wheel, the other elbow propped on the
open window, his eyes on the road, his expression mild.
He occasionally even exerted himself to murmur replies
at appropriate intervals throughout Amy's endless recitation of her life history and that of her family and everyone
else she knew, however casually; her preferences in mu-
sic, literature and art; her favorite rock groups and tele-
vision shows and her opinions on everything from politics
to pizza. Logan rose another notch in Cassie's esteem simply for the self-control he exhibited by not stopping the
truck and demanding that Amy get out and walk.

Amy had, of course, manipulated herself into the seat
beside Logan, leaving Cassie with plenty of room beside
the passenger door. And as powerful as the urge was to
give Amy a sound pinch, Cassie couldn't help sympathiz-
ing with her young niece.

If Amy had thought Logan was attractive when he was
dusty and disheveled, she must think he was positively
devastating now that he was clean. He had shaved, and
the distinctive profile Cassie had only guessed at before
was not disappointing. His thick black hair lay clean and
shiny against the top of his collar, brushed away from his
forehead and ears, a careless style without benefit of blow-
dryer or professional cut. He had changed into fresh jeans

and a faded blue shirt, and the smell of spicy soap was enticing. Though by tonight he would be as dusty and scrubby as he had been when he walked into the office that morning, Cassie could understand his desire to shower and change while he had the chance. There were all too few opportunities to do so on the trail, and that was one part of the adventure to which Cassie was not looking forward.

"That's right," Amy was saying now, breathlessly, "a real movie, right here on the ranch." She snatched the book out of Cassie's hand. "From this book. I've never read it, but it must be good, or why would they make it into a movie?"

"That's very rude, Amy," Cassie pointed out with little energy, and retrieved her book. Amy hardly noticed her aunt's comment.

"I mean, isn't it the most exciting thing you've ever heard? To see our own ranch on the big screen? And Daddy said they might even let me be in some of the scenes—oh, not a real part, you know, just as an extra or in the background or something, but can you just imagine? Seeing yourself in a movie? I always thought the ranch was such a dull place, and I never cared much about spending the summers here, but just look—first a real cattle drive and then a movie. No one will believe this when I tell them."

Amy chattered on, and Cassie glanced at her in affectionate dismay, wondering how long she could possibly talk without losing her voice—and knowing the question was pointless. As far as Cassie could tell, Amy hadn't given her voice a rest since she arrived three weeks before, and she was still going strong.

Cassie started to turn to look back out the window, and her eyes unexpectedly met Logan's over Amy's head.

There was such amused indulgence in the depths of those
pale eyes that Cassie was startled, and then immediately
infused by warmth that was just as real and just as pen-
etrating as a handclasp, or a touch. *There is something
beneath that face of stone,* she thought in some bemuse-
ment, *and it's very nice.* She did not know why this
should seem so strange to her, or why it should affect her
like a jolt of recognition. But their eyes met for just that
moment, sharing a secret or a joke, and it was as though
a bond—however tenuous—had been formed.

Cassie, confused, quickly turned her eyes back to the
book, but she didn't read a word. And when Amy paused
for breath, Logan surprised her by uttering the first complete sentence he had managed since they had begun the
trip.

"I guess that's why your brother is in California, then,
Mrs. Grant," he commented. "For this movie business."

"Yes." Cassie looked up, but his eyes were on the
road. They were in the hill country now, and rivers of
high green forest and low yellow meadow flowed past the
window like a painted landscape. "They're supposed to
start filming here in a few weeks."

A faint frown creased his brow. "He won't be gone
that long, will he?"

Cassie could only assume that the concern in his voice
was prompted by a lack of faith in her abilities to run the
ranch in her brother's absence, and she was instantly defensive. She lifted her chin haughtily, her shoulders unconsciously squaring. "If you're worried that I won't be
able to manage until he gets back, I assure you—"

"I'm sure you'll do just fine." His drawl was lazy, and
his glance was shielded in amusement. He turned back to
the road again with a dismissing shrug. "Just seemed
strange to me, that's all, that he'd go off just now. Es-

pecially with all the—'' He broke off, as though catching himself on the verge of saying too much, and as Cassie opened her mouth to question him, he gestured toward the right. ''The cook wagon's stopped just up ahead there. If you ladies can take the ride, I'm going to turn off and go overland. It's quicker.''

Several of the main roads through the ranch were paved as public thoroughfares; others had been trampled into neat dirt trails by the constant movement of cattle and ranch vehicles. But when Logan said overland, he meant just that, and as the truck bounced and heaved over the expanse of sagebrush and gopher holes all conversation— even Amy's—was of necessity suspended for the duration.

Cassie dodged the low branches of junipers that scraped by her open window, holding on tightly to the armrest to keep from being thrown from her seat, and by the time the truck pulled up short at the campsite she felt as though she had just survived a particularly vicious carnival ride or a bucking bronco. She climbed a little shakily out of the truck and spent a few moments regaining her land legs.

One of the reasons the production company had been so interested in using the Circle P as a location for its new film was the fact that the ranch was one of the few in the country that still ran its operation exactly as it had a hundred years ago. Out here in the vast rangeland of the valley, with the majestic mountains in the background and the campsite in the foreground, one could easily have stepped back in time.

The chuck wagon was just that—a covered wagon. It was drawn by a team of drays and had barrels of water and flour strapped to its side. The only signs of modernization were that the wagon's wheels were actually tractor

tires, to better accommodate the paved roads on which the
wagon occasionally traveled, and that a tank of butane
gas that operated the cookstove was strapped to the outside of the wagon.

The extra horses were picketed not too far away from
the wagon, for the cowboys still worked on horseback,
switching mounts every day and at night for those who
had the watch. In midsummer every year the herds were
rounded up, counted, branded and driven to the railhead
spur that adjoined the ranch, much as it had been done a
hundred years ago. Today plastic ear tags were used instead of branding irons, and the cowboys carried walkie-
talkies instead of guns, but very little else had changed.
And one thing most definitely remained the same: the
cook was still the most important part of any trail work.

Cassie looked around at the still-picturesque scene and
she was suddenly overwhelmed by the task she had set
for herself. She, who hadn't even chosen a dress for herself in eight years, had recklessly volunteered to take on
the responsibility for the feeding and care of over twenty
rough-riding men. She could cook, that much was true,
but cooking for a group like this was hardly the same as
preparing tea and sandwiches for a bridge club.

And there was more to this job than just cooking. She
would get up long before dawn to prepare breakfast, strike
the camp, hitch up the team and lead the way to the next
campsite. She would stop before noon to set up the mess
tent and equipment, care for the animals and begin the
second gargantuan meal of the day. She had handled a
wagon team only once before in her life, when she was
much younger than Amy, and then only for a few minutes
as an indulgence from the team driver who could see no
other way to get her out of his hair. She had never hitched

up a team. As for setting up the mess tent and hooking up the stove…

Logan was moving without a word toward the horses, and Cassie said quickly, "You're not leaving?"

He turned, and she was ashamed of the sudden panic that had backed both the question and her voice. She suspected he was aware, too, of just how quickly she had come to regret her impetuous decision, and he had every right to say "I told you so." Cassie steeled herself for it and was enormously relieved—and grateful—when all he replied was "I've got work to do. And I guess I'd better let Red know you're here." He did not look too happy about that last statement, and Cassie was only reminded of one more thing she was not looking forward to. Red had a temper worse than Jonas's, and from the time Cassie was three he had thought he had as much right as anyone in her family to tell her what to do. There would be an unpleasant scene when he found Cassie had volunteered for this duty and that she had brought Amy.

As Logan spoke, another figure came from around the wagon. It was a blond boy about Amy's age, thin and wiry and not very tall, with an attractive Huck Finn face and a quick, shy smile. Logan glanced at him. "This is Rodney Jeffries. He takes care of the stock and sort of acts as the cook's assistant. He'll help you get set up."

Cassie breathed a brief prayer of thanks to a merciful Creator. At least she wasn't entirely on her own. Rodney, from the looks of him, might not be much help, but he was better than none at all. Perhaps at least he could be relied upon to tell her what she was doing wrong.

"Rodney," Logan said, "this is Mrs. Grant, Mr. Parkington's sister, and his daughter, Amy. They'll be taking on the cook's job for a few days."

Rodney wiped his hands on his jeans and looked as

though he might offer a handshake, then changed his mind and simply smiled at Cassie somewhat uncertainly. "Hi," he said, and then his eyes were all for Amy. Cassie knew a case of instant puppy love when she saw it, and she had to stifle a groan as the young boy's eyes lit up. Amy, however, was far from being impressed by a mere cook's assistant, and a boy her own age at that, and became suddenly preoccupied with brushing a speck of dust off her boot.

Cassie smiled at him, her sympathies instantly reversed. If young Rodney had a crush on Amy, he was much to be pitied, and Cassie thought the least she could do was distract him before Amy broke his heart. "It's nice to meet you, Rodney," she said. "Do you want to give us a hand getting our gear out of the back of the truck?"

Rodney almost tripped over his own feet in his eagerness to get to the truck. Cassie had at least had enough presence of mind to remember that each one of the crew was responsible for supplying his own tent and sleeping bag as well as personal supplies, and she had been fortunate to find two extra outfits in the storage shed. In addition, she had filled a box at random with spices and condiments she was not sure would be in ready supply on the chuck wagon, and Amy had filled two suitcases with makeup and clothes.

Cassie lowered the gate on the pickup and Amy reached inside for her bedroll. Rodney was quick to take it from her, and Amy smiled indifferently. "Thanks," she said. "Just put the rest of my stuff wherever Cassie tells you."

She wandered off, leaving Rodney looking somewhat crestfallen.

"She's a city girl," Cassie explained to Rodney, knowing that it was small consolation for Amy's rudeness. "It'll take her some time to get used to doing for herself."

Rodney tore his eyes away from Amy's retreating fig-
ure and back to Cassie. He grinned and then blushed.
"That's all right, Miz Grant. I don't mind helping out.
That's what I'm here for."

"Well, good." Cassie stretched to tug her own duffel
bag out and gave Rodney a conspiratorial wink. "Just
between the two of us, I think I'm going to need all the
help I can get."

Logan had gone to saddle his horse while Cassie and
Rodney unloaded the truck; Amy had followed him, and
Cassie could hear her voice, continuing to try to engage
him in conversation. The girl was making an utter pest of
herself, and Cassie speculated wryly that if Logan didn't
backhand her, Cassie might be forced to do it herself.

By the time she and Rodney had unloaded all the gear
from the truck, Cassie's patient amusement with Amy had
turned into downright irritation, for so far her plan did not
seem to be working out at all. Cassie had brought Amy
out here to teach her about hardship and grit, to strip away
the glamour and show her a little of the real side of life.
So far, Amy had done nothing but preen herself and practice her flirting on a man twice her age. At the very least,
Amy was going to learn that she would have to pull her
own weight if she intended to stay. Otherwise, Cassie
would have Logan drive her back to the ranch this minute—and put a twenty-four-hour guard on her if necessary.

Cassie told Rodney to start hooking up the stove, for
the men would be coming in for the day in a couple of
hours and the evening meal was always served well before
sundown. Then, wiping her dusty hands on her jeans, she
started out in search of Amy.

The horses were picketed behind a stand of spruce
about twenty-five yards away from the wagon. The sound

of Amy's low murmur and giggles, as well as the snuffling and shuffling of the horses, led Cassie to them. She pushed aside a branch and started out into the clearing and then stood still, appalled at what she saw.

Amy and Logan stood beside his saddled horse, very close. Amy's fingers were tucked around the closures of Logan's vest, holding him, as she gazed raptly up into his face. Logan's hands cupped her arms gently, and his head bent low.

Immediately every protective, motherly instinct in Cassie's body surged into furious life. She had thought for some insane reason that Logan was different, that there might be some shred of civility within him beneath the rough exterior. Obviously she had been wrong—dangerously wrong. Amy was seventeen, for heaven's sake, and that man was thirty-five if he was a day. She was sickened and enraged, and she took an angry step forward.

The sound of Logan's voice stopped her. "I'll tell you what, sweetheart," he murmured. "You're the prettiest thing that's crossed my path in a long time, and if you were five years older, I wouldn't think twice. But a man's got to look out for himself, you know, and I'm not too anxious to come up on the wrong side of your pa."

"You're not afraid of my daddy, are you?" Amy pouted provocatively, and Cassie's hand itched to slap her.

Logan smiled. "Not afraid, no. But I need this job, real bad. And I've also got a need to stay on the right side of the law for a time, and you, pretty little girl, are the quickest way I know to a first-class tour of the inside of a jail."

Amy's eyes lowered thoughtfully, and gradually Cassie began to understand. Logan could have laughed at her and hurt her badly. He could have continued to ignore her and only worsened the problem. By pretending to be tempted he had salvaged her ego, given her credit for the intelligence of an adult and remained her friend, which, all things considered, was a pretty smart way to go.

"Well," Amy said after a time, "I wouldn't want to get you into any trouble."

Logan took her hands and gently removed them from his vest, taking a step back. "I appreciate that. And I don't want you to get into any trouble, so if any of these old rowdies start giving you a bad time, you let me know, okay?"

Amy beamed at him, fairly breathless. "Okay."

He gave her a grin that was as sweet as a caress, and then turned and mounted up.

Cassie turned away and started back toward camp, a secret smile puzzling her lips, her thoughts full of Logan. He was one surprise after another, and each one of them more intriguing than the last. She wondered how Jonas had found him, and what he was doing working a job like this. Where was he from, and what had brought him here? Who was he? And then Cassie caught herself, startled, trying to remember how long it had been since she had given so much thought to any man. That was not a good sign, she reprimanded herself with a frown. Especially when she would need all the concentration she possessed to get through this job she had so thoughtlessly undertaken.

Cassie took a second look and she still couldn't believe she had done it. There was a pile of administrative work awaiting her back in Jonas's office—that was her responsibility, her area of expertise, and allowing it to fall behind now could mean an awful tangle in the future. She had been unable to reach Jonas at the hotel, but rather than wait for him to return her phone call, she had cravenly left a message, charging him with the responsibility of hiring a new cook long-distance while she and Amy did the best they could in the meantime. Cassie had no doubt that that message would send Jonas flying back in a panic on the next plane, and all things considered she had handled the entire matter very badly.

Jonas would cut short his business trip to attend to something she should have been able to solve on her own. He would be furious at her for taking Amy away from the house and outraged that she had taken on the job herself. She had left her own work neglected while she impetuously leaped off on an adventure, and worst of all, she had let herself be manipulated by a seventeen-year-old girl. She had behaved irresponsibly, impulsively and thoughtlessly—much more like the Cassie of her childhood than the grown woman she had become. Cassie was not certain at this moment whether that was good or bad.

But she was into it now, and there was no backing off. There wasn't even much of a chance for second thoughts, for the sun was getting higher in the sky. There was much to do and little enough time to do it in.

If Cassie had learned one thing in her years of charity work, it was the skill of organization. And if there was one thing she was determined to teach Amy, it was that there was no such thing as a free ride. She quickly set Rodney to work setting up their tents and organizing the mess hall, and set Amy down in front of a barrel of potatoes waiting to be peeled. The novelty of that wore off in a matter of moments, and in no time at all Amy was whining about puckered hands and chipped nails. Cassie was ruthless. She had no time for complaints and no sympathy for Amy's spoiled holiday. She had problems of her own.

There was fresh meat stored in a locker of dry ice, but the menu was limited to hamburger. The eggs and milk were powdered, but there were fresh onions and peppers hanging by bunches from the rafters of the wagon. Cassie knew that almost everything was fried on the trail, for the simple matter of convenience, but she thought a change of menu might endear her to those who would object to her presence. She decided to turn the potatoes Amy was peeling into potato salad, and it was no easy task.

She chopped potatoes until her hands ached, peeled onions until her face was red and swollen with tears. As soon as one pot of boiled potatoes had been lifted from the burner another one was ready to be put on, and Cassie's back and arms ached from sheer physical exertion. She had found some cans of blueberries in the back of the wagon and decided, also as a form of bribery, to make blueberry dumplings for dessert. That, too, was easier said than done.

Cassie set Amy and Rodney to the task of seasoning the ground beef and forming hamburger patties while she alternated between boiling potatoes and mixing dumpling batter for a gallon of blueberries. Amy was squeamish and uncooperative, but Rodney proved to be a willing and eager worker. Not only that, but he seemed to be a genuinely nice boy, and Cassie began to wish Amy would at least be pleasant to him.

He told her he was from Idaho, and Cassie had to know what had brought him, at such an early age, to Wyoming and the life of a cowhand. He quickly asserted that he was almost twenty and his own man, and Cassie tried not to reveal her skepticism. She had placed his age at just over eighteen, if that.

"And anyway," he added with a shrug, "my grandpa was pushing cows when he was thirteen. That was back in the twenties, o'course, but the West was still a place where a man came to prove himself. And my great-grandpa used to ride the Chisholm Trail, and he was one of the first to lead a train through the Oregon Trail. You ought to hear some of the stories he handed down, about Indians and such. It's kind of a tradition with us, I guess, the open range. I never thought about doing nothing else.''

Cassie was struck then by how little separated the life-style of a century ago from the present out here, and then by how sad it was that it should be so. There were many things about the past worth preserving, but a boy of Rodney's age should have more ambition, and more opportunities, than his ancestors had.

Amy, however, showed her first signs of life at Rodney's statement and demanded to hear some of the stories his grandfather had handed down. Cassie knew this was more of a ploy for getting out of work than anything else, but she was so relieved to finally see that sullen look disappear from Amy's face that she couldn't bring herself to object too harshly. Besides, Rodney worked fast enough for both of them.

Red rode in ahead of any of the others, and Cassie went outside to greet him. She was glad for the excuse to be out of the steam room of the mess tent—even if it was only to face more hot water from Red.

He did not disappoint her. A short, bandy-legged little man whose thinning crop of red hair was now turning a washed-out gray, he swung out of the saddle and strode over to her with all the disdainful authority of his sixty-odd years. He looked her up and down, spat a stream of tobacco juice on the ground and declared, ''Well, I didn't believe it but I shoulda known better. Only you would come up with a harebrained scheme like this.''

She smiled at him sweetly. ''You needed a cook. I can cook.''

He scowled at her. "You know very well there's a damned sight more to this job than just cooking."

"I've got Rodney to help me with the heavy work."

"And what does your brother think of all this, young miss, just tell me that!"

Cassie was momentarily uncomfortable. "I don't imagine he likes it much. He's in California, and I didn't talk to him."

Red looked at her with contempt. "I mighta known. And what the hell's he doing in California without so much as a by-your-leave, do you want to tell me kindly?"

"He's taking care of some last-minute details with the movie people and he will only be gone a few more days." Cassie was getting defensive. "It's no big deal, you know, Red. I can handle what I've taken on. And even if I can't, there's nothing you can do about it, so you might as well learn to like it!"

He looked her over thoroughly once again, and there was no compliment in his tone as he declared, "You haven't changed a bit. I thought when you came back here all fancied up and citified you might have brought some good sense back with you, but it just ain't so. You haven't changed a damn bit."

But Cassie liked the way that sounded, and she smiled at him. "Do you want to watch your language, Red?" she advised, nodding toward the tent where Amy and Rodney still worked. "And pass the word along. We've got a young girl here, and I wouldn't want her corrupted by any rough talk."

Red glared at her for a long moment, then stalked away to tend to his horse, muttering and grumbling under his breath. Cassie was chuckling as she went back into the tent. That part of the ordeal, at least, had gone much better than she had expected.

THE MEN BEGAN to drift in about an hour later. They had all heard about Cassie's presence, of course, and Amy's, and their attitude was wary and curious—and not entirely pleased. Cassie understood their resentment. These men were used to being on their own, without the supervision of women; they were accustomed to doing and saying what they pleased, fighting if they felt like it, drinking too much if they could find the wherewithal. They were used to undressing and bathing in public and didn't want to be bothered with modesty or manners. The presence of women was inhibiting enough, but these women were more than just cooks—they were the boss's family. They had not only the power to cramp the life-style on the trail, but to hire and fire. It was a taciturn, self-conscious and mostly unhappy group of ruffians that filed through the chow line that afternoon.

Cassie was so busy she barely had time to look at their faces, much less sympathize with their problems. But she couldn't help but notice that Amy, who had decked herself out in fresh makeup, tight jeans and a body-sculpting sweater for the occasion, went from distaste to dismay to undisguised woe as she spooned heaping helpings of potato salad onto one tray after the other.

"They *smell*," she whispered to Cassie at one point, her small nose wrinkling with distress.

Cassie, as tired as she was, chuckled. "You've got to learn not to judge by appearances, Amy," she advised.

"But they're so old," Amy whispered back. "And rude."

"It takes a lot of experience to be a good cowhand," Cassie answered, turning to scoop up another platter of hamburger patties from the griddle. "And they're not rude. You just make them nervous."

Amy looked both disbelieving and unimpressed.

When Cassie turned back, Logan was greeting Amy while she filled his tray with overgenerous servings of potato salad and beans. Suddenly and unexpectedly, Cassie became aware of how she must look—wilted and rumpled behind the stained, oversize white apron, her hair in a shambles and her face and her clothes damp with perspiration. She made an effort to tuck a few strands of hair back behind the faded bandanna she wore over her head, and she blotted her sweaty face with the back of her hand. But then she felt foolish when all Logan did was nod to her, briefly and impersonally, and move on down the line after his tray was filled.

The men sat at long, camp-style tables, hunched over their trays, their conversation low and subdued. The tension in the room was thick and restrained, and it didn't take a great amount of perception to understand why. Occasional covert glances were cast in the direction of the serving table where Amy and Cassie still stood, and Cassie knew that she was making them as uncomfortable as the men were making her.

She calmly wiped the splattered grill, placed the serving bowls in easy reach for seconds and untied her apron. "Why don't we take our plates and eat outside?" she suggested to Amy.

"Gladly," the girl muttered.

They took a couple of folding camp chairs and ate at a worktable outside, and almost immediately after they left, the conversation inside the mess tent took on a more normal, boisterous pitch, accompanied by the sounds of knives and forks being moved more enthusiastically. Cassie had to smile at the sound of tension audibly dispersing. The afternoon sun had not yet touched the horizon, and it felt strange to Cassie, who was accustomed to dining fashionably late, to be sitting down to dinner so early.

Still, she was starved, and the meal, despite the hardships and her own uncertainty, was quite good.

"I've never seen so many ugly men in one place in all my life," Amy complained, and so earnestly that Cassie laughed. Amy did not think it was funny. "Where does Daddy find them?" she insisted. "They look like they just crawled off skid row, or like they belong on death row!"

Cassie took a sip of her coffee, chuckling, and then winced. The thick black brew was strong enough to take the paint off walls, and she was appalled. She would no doubt be getting some complaints about that, and made a mental note to weaken the mixture for the morning.

"It's not much like you imagined, I guess," she commented to Amy, and Amy grimaced, waving at an insect that buzzed over her plate.

"Not much," she agreed unhappily. "Why do they always make it sound so exciting in the movies?"

Cassie shrugged. "That's what people want to hear, I guess. A lot of things in life are like that, not nearly as much fun as they sound." She was thinking about New York, and Greg, and glamorous dinner parties and chic gowns and the in crowd. Now, sitting in the open air with the majestic mountains in the background and the rustle of the wind through the grass, she wondered how she had ever stood it for long—much less that she once could have found it exciting.

Amy picked at her food, resting her hand on her cheek. "My hair is filthy already, and I want to take a shower. There's no place to plug in my blow-dryer. And no offense, Cassie, but I'd really rather have sent out for Chinese."

"This was your idea," Cassie reminded her.

Amy sighed and stoically agreed. "Maybe tomorrow will be better. But there sure doesn't seem to be much happening around here, does there? Except a lot of potatoes and dirty dishes.''

Cassie smiled to herself, and did not think this was an appropriate time to point out that tomorrow would hardly be much better—especially since Amy's day would begin at four o'clock in the morning.

They finished their meal in a more or less desultory silence, and Cassie was both amused and gratified to see what effect exhaustion could have on Amy's usually vociferous nature. Cassie was wondering whether or not it would help the taste of her coffee to weaken it with water when Rodney came out.

"The boys are really packing away your grub, Miz Grant," he told her with a grin. "I guess they like it better than that swill old Amos used to serve up. Maybe it wasn't a bad thing after all, him quitting like he did."

Cassie smiled. At least that much she had managed to get right. "I'm glad to hear it, Rodney."

Rodney glanced at Amy. "I'm going to go bed down the horses for the night," he invited offhandedly. "You want to come along?"

Horses and Amy were a natural combination, and Cassie did not think she would refuse. But Amy was careful to disguise her enthusiasm as she pushed away her plate and agreed carelessly, "Might as well. There's not much else to do around here."

"Except the dishes," Cassie reminded her, and Amy looked crushed.

"Oh, don't worry, Miz Grant," Rodney assured her. "We'll be back long before it's time to clean up."

"Just don't leave the camp," Cassie told Amy, but she needn't have worried.

Amy spread her hands dramatically and asked with a touch of despair in her voice, "Where would I go?"

Cassie smiled after her, thinking how much like Amy she had been at that age...and yet how different. Restlessness, a yen for adventure and the lure of bright lights had driven her away from the ranch, but even as she had despaired of the isolation, the sameness, the lack of modernization, there had been something about the rugged majesty of this land that had always held her heart. At Amy's age nothing suited her better than to spend a night outdoors, with the stars her roof and the mountains her walls, camping with her father or fishing with Jonas. She needed no further entertainment than riding across the plains alone, playing the games of her own imagination.

But even then, she recalled sadly, it hadn't taken much to draw her away...and keep her away. She wasn't proud of all she had lost along the way, or of how quickly she had forgotten her heritage and all that it meant. But at least she was home now. And she was home to stay.

Sitting there in the dying rays of the afternoon sun, she was certain for the first time in many years that she had done exactly the right thing.

Chapter Three

The Crossing

III

A man like Jim learned to ride alone, and learned to like it. When every stranger could be an enemy, when every closed door and shuttered window could conceal a cocked Winchester pointed where it would do the most good, when even the empty plains and ragged buttes could contain a war party or posse, a man learned quickly that the only person he could trust was himself.

He learned to read the signs left by camp fire ashes and bruised poppies; he learned to ford the shallows and wait out the rapids; he learned the ways of the buffalo trails that wound high into the mountains, trails even the Indians had forgotten. He learned to count the miles by the sound of the coyote's wail and fetch water by the scent of it. He belonged to the land and was a part of it.

But sometimes he worried that a part of him, the good-feeling and human part, had long since been swallowed up by the land, and the life he led. Sometimes the inside of him felt as wide and as empty as the plains he rode. And sometimes, at sunset mostly, when a man's thoughts

naturally turned to things that were beautiful, he got lone-
some, and he got to thinking that riding alone was not
always the best way to go.

But for a man like Jim, there could be no other way.

THE SOUNDS FROM THE TENT were loud and masculine—
the clink of silverware against metal trays, bursts of laughter and occasional off-color phrases and inventive oaths—
the reassuring noises of two dozen hardworking men
winding down after a long day. Someone turned on a por-
table tape player and Waylon Jennings added his voice to
the cacophony. Cassie sat there for a while longer, reluctant to go inside and begin cleaning up, thereby putting a
damper on the relaxed atmosphere that pervaded the tent.

The sun slipped behind the mountains, shading the sky
with dusky twilight. She talked herself into staying a
while longer, enjoying the solitude and the much-needed
rest. She glanced up when someone exited the tent, and
her heart gave a peculiar—and uncalled for—little jolt
when she saw it was Logan. He did not notice her.

He walked a little away from the noise and activity,
past the shadow of a juniper, to a broken log at the edge
of the wood. He propped his leg up and sipped his coffee,
a peaceful, contented figure looking out over the land. For
a moment Cassie took pleasure in just watching him.

There was something enduring about the pose he struck
so unconsciously—a solitary silhouette against the vast
Wyoming sky, his long body relaxed but watchful, one
leg propped up on the log, coffee cup in hand. The fading
sun glanced off one side of his face and narrowed his
eyes, picking up streaks of gold in his hair and on his
forearm beneath the rolled-up shirt sleeves. Alone, stalwart, at home in his environment, he struck a chord of
something basic in Cassie. It was nothing she could de-

fine; rather, something to which she responded as instinctively as she would to the grandeur of the snow-capped Tetons or to the breathtaking surprise of a patch of wildflowers amid a windswept plain. He was as much a part of this environment as were the flowing meadows and the stately aspens, and she just wanted to look at him.

After a time, however, she began to feel like a spy, and worse, she had the distinct impression—though he had not turned or glanced her way even once—that he was aware of her gaze. She left her half-finished cup of tar-paper coffee on the table and went over to him.

He glanced around as she approached. "Good meal," he complimented her.

She smiled, tucking her fingers into her pockets in a gesture that was instinctual when she was nervous. "Thanks. You sound surprised."

"I was, a little," he admitted. Then he glanced at his coffee cup. "The coffee's a little weak, though. You still have something to learn about cooking for cowpokes."

She stared at him. "That coffee is strong enough to be used as shoe polish."

He shrugged. "Just trying to give you a little constructive criticism. Coffee like this will earn you a bunch of grumpy riders if you try to serve it in the morning."

"Maybe in the morning I *will* serve shoe polish," she grumbled.

He grinned, a quick and endearing gesture that was devastating for both its beauty and its unexpectedness. It lit up his eyes and transformed his face from implacable to wonderful. "Now, there's a thought."

Cassie felt a warmth tingle through her, which was from nothing more than the light of his grin, and her returned smile seemed to be formed from the inside out. When he met her smile, the spark of amusement in his eyes softened just fractionally and changed into something that seemed to want to linger. For a moment Cassie thought he found as much pleasure in looking at her as she had in looking at him. But then, as though surprised at himself and unused to dealing with whatever it was he was thinking, he moved his gaze away, easily but deliberately, and looked out over the empty landscape again.

Cassie felt a twinge of shyness and she suddenly wasn't quite sure why she had thought it was such a good idea to join him here after all. Perhaps he really wanted to be alone. He certainly hadn't shown much of a sociable disposition to this point, and Cassie didn't want to get the same reputation for a pest that Amy had.

But she couldn't just walk away. And she did have something to say to him.

Broken leaves and stubble rustled beneath her feet as she rocked back on her heels, another nervous habit. "I wanted to thank you," she said, "for what you did for Amy this afternoon. You handled that very well. Another man might not have been so gentle with her feelings."

He glanced at her, and not the faintest bit of surprise flickered in his eyes. She wondered if he had been aware that she was watching his interchange with Amy from the bushes all along.

His lips turned down at one corner in a kind of rueful gesture, and he murmured, "Gentle with her feelings. Nobody's ever accused me of being that before." He took a sip of coffee and added, "She's a good kid. Reminds me a lot of my own—" She thought he was going to say sister, but he broke off, finishing quickly, "I didn't see any reason to give her a bad time. Besides, it was better than my other idea."

Cassie looked at him curiously. "Which was?"

He glanced at her with a flash of unexpected mischief.

"Chasing her right back. It would have scared the bedevil out of her, that's for sure, but I was afraid her aunt would come after me with a carving knife. And while I'm not ashamed to say I can face down most anything, man or beast, an angry female protecting her young is one thing that'll make my hair turn white."

Cassie chuckled throatily and admitted, "You made the right decision."

His eyes crinkled with responsive mirth, and the moment between them was warm and easy. Cassie was encouraged and forgot about leaving him to his solitude. She inquired, "Logan...is that your first name or your last?"

"Both," he responded easily. "Either. Maybe neither one. Only a woman would ask a question like that."

Cassie lifted an eyebrow. "Oh? Don't the people you work for ever ask?"

He met her eyes with patience and frankness, and nothing else. "No."

Cassie was just a little disconcerted, until she thought about Jonas, who was happy to get whatever help he could for seasonal work. If a man had experience, and if he proved himself on the job, no questions would be asked. That much, at least, hadn't changed from the days of the Old West.

But other things had changed, and what she couldn't understand was why any man, in this day and age, would want to live like that.

After a moment she said, "Are you from around here?"

"No." It wasn't short, just to the point. Logan set his coffee cup on the tree stump and reached into his vest pocket, bringing out a thin cigarette paper and a flat tin of tobacco. Cassie tried to remember how many years it had been since she had seen a man roll a cigarette containing nothing but tobacco.

She commented, somewhat dryly, "I take it you don't like to talk about yourself much."

"You take it right." He shook a measure of tobacco into the paper, moistened the edge of the paper with the tip of his tongue, and rolled the filled paper deftly into a tube.

"That's funny. Most men think they're the only subject of conversation worth mentioning. They like talking about themselves almost more than they like sex."

Again a brief flare of amusement showed beneath his slanted lashes, and he struck a match on the heel of his boot. "Then the men you know must not be very smart."

Cassie laughed softly. "An understatement."

He cupped the match in his hands and brought it to the tip of the cigarette, watching her with a peculiar mixture of lazy interest and pleasure that made Cassie somewhat uncomfortable. She thought about returning to the mess tent and the dirty dishes that awaited her when he shook out the match and surprised her by asking, "So where are you from, Mrs. Cassie Grant?"

Cassie hesitated. That sounded very much like an invitation to stay and keep him company. Or perhaps he was just being polite. She was, after all, his boss. "Recently?" She shrugged. "A little bit of everywhere. Before that, Connecticut and New York mostly. Before that, here. Home."

He looked at her thoughtfully. "You've still got the ways of the city about you, you know," he commented, as though it were important. "I guess that's why I was surprised that you could cook."

Cassie was amazed. She glanced down at her faded jeans, stained and rumpled work shirt, and broken nails, and could not imagine that he could see anything citified about her at all. There was a bubble of self-derisive laughter in her voice as she objected, "I don't see what makes you say that! Just look at me." Self-consciously, she pushed a straggling strand of hair back into the bandanna. "My clothes are a mess and I haven't seen a hairdresser or a makeup mirror in three months. There's nothing left of the city about me at all."

"Sure there is," he replied calmly. "Because you still think things like that are important."

It was not meant to be an insult, but Cassie felt uncomfortable all the same, as though he did not approve of her values, or of how she had obtained them. She was only reminded once again of how she had changed, and how much she disliked the changes.

"I felt kind of bad about leaving you this afternoon," he continued in the same low, easy drawl, and he bent down to pick up his coffee cup. "Without showing you the ropes, that is. But I guess you didn't need any help after all. You managed everything just fine."

It was a low-key compliment, a simple statement of fact, but Cassie glowed under it. *Yes, I did,* she realized, for the first time allowing herself a well-earned moment of pride. *It wasn't easy, and a year ago I wouldn't even have considered doing it, but I managed just fine.*

She lifted her shoulders in a not-quite-genuine gesture of self-effacement, and responded, "I learned to cook when I was three. And I've had a lot of practice taking care of men. I know it's not a very liberated thing to admit, but it seems as though that's what I do best."

She hadn't meant to say that; she didn't like the way it sounded or the fact that it was true. For eight years she had been a decoration on the arm of Greg Grant; she had dedicated her life to making him happy, anticipating his needs, serving his purposes, until she began to hate herself and to hate him, and she simply couldn't stand it anymore.

When the marriage ended, she had promised herself freedom, self-reliance and achievement in her own right. It was painful to realize that, still, the only thing she had ever been any good at was being a wife.

Logan's gaze was quiet and accepting and far too perceptive. Cassie couldn't meet it, and she began to fidget. In a moment his eyes moved away, and he lifted the cigarette again. "Where is Mr. Grant?" he asked.

"In Connecticut. We're divorced." And then, because she didn't entirely like the turn of the conversation, she inquired, "Have you ever been married?"

"No." Again, direct and to the point, leaving more questions than answers. "What happened?"

Cassie's smile was slow and sly. "I see," she murmured. "You don't like to talk about yourself, but you don't mind at all hearing me talk about myself."

He glanced at her, his half grin an admission of guilt. "Maybe I just like to hear you talk," he confessed. "The sound of a woman's voice is a rare thing out here, and something a man comes to miss. But I didn't mean to pry. We can talk about something else, although I frankly can't think of anything half as interesting as you, and how you came to be here."

His charm was easy, straightforward and utterly devastating—perhaps mostly because it was so unexpected. Cassie had no desire to even try to resist it, and she responded with the same simple frankness. "I can. You…and how you came to be here."

He half laughed, glancing into his coffee cup. "Where else should I be?"

Cassie could not imagine. He was so at home in this environment, so much a part of it, that it was difficult to picture him anywhere else. And yet he was cut of sterner stuff than even the modern-day cowboy, and it wasn't so much that he was out of place, but out of time. She started to say as much, but doubted he would understand. It barely made sense to her.

She sat down on the log, removing her hands from her pockets and looping her arms around one knee. "My answer is easy. I thought I wanted one thing; I found out I needed another. I couldn't play the games that go along with being a corporate wife anymore; I wanted something a little more real." She shrugged. "After the divorce, I thought I was going to set the world on fire...and then discovered I didn't know how to *do* anything."

A faint heat of shame stained her cheeks and she lowered her eyes, trying to cover it. "Then my father died, and Jonas needed someone to help him on the ranch. I still don't know how much help I'm being, but at least I feel as if I'm doing something. And I'm where I want to be," she finished simply.

She looked at him, waiting for him to answer her question as honestly as she had answered his. In the brief silence that followed, she thought he would decline, but once again he surprised her. "My answer is even easier than that," he said, taking a draw from the cigarette, and without meeting her eyes. "Cash at the end of the week, solid meals, a place to sleep, something to keep busy at. I never wanted much more than that. I don't like to make life too complicated."

Cassie looked at him thoughtfully. True...perhaps. She should have been satisfied with that. But there was more that he did not care to tell her, and though she knew she should respect his privacy, she couldn't help being curious.

She asked casually, "Have you been doing this kind of work long?"

"I learned to rope and ride when I was a kid," he

replied, by way of circumventing a direct answer. He lifted his coffee cup, found nothing but dregs and tossed them out. ''The Circle P's one of the nicest outfits I've ridden for in a long time, though,'' he added. ''There aren't too many like it left.''

Cassie did not like to think about that. The independent rancher was fast going the way of the small farmer, and the Circle P, despite its size and distinction, had been operating in the red for over a year. Jonas kept it, Cassie knew, as more of a hobby than anything else, a tribute to the past and a gesture of honor to their legacy. But if they had depended upon the ranch for their income, they would have been bankrupt long ago.

The Parkingtons had always been shrewd financiers. Even in the golden age of cattle ranching, their assets had been diversified into minerals, railroads and stocks. Today the family fortune was not immense—and certainly nothing like it had been before the Depression—but it was comfortable. And it allowed them to keep the ranch, for tradition's sake.

Cassie said, smiling a little, ''Wyoming is a hell of a place to try to make a living of any kind. What amazes me is that it took people over a hundred years to find that out. It takes thirty acres to feed a cow, blizzards can wipe out half your herd overnight and nobody can understand why small ranches are dropping like flies.''

''It'll be a pity,'' Logan said soberly, ''to see it go.'' His eyes were once again sweeping over the landscape behind them—a panorama of greens and yellows lit now by the pinkish tinge of a brilliant sunset. There was sadness in his face, but his tone was matter-of-fact. ''I'll see it in my lifetime. Things just won't be the same.''

They were silent for a time, watching the sky begin to glow with pastel arcs of pink and orange and aqua, tingeing the twilight with gold and cerulean as the brilliance of the sun played out its final gentle cords. Nowhere in the world was the sunset as magnificent as here, and the sight of it never failed to make Cassie feel humbled and breathless.

"It's beautiful, isn't it?" she said softly.

"Yes." The pitch of his voice was equally quiet, and the colors of the sky whispered across his face in gentle washes of blue and rose. There was a reverence to the time when day was dying; each of them was aware of it and each of them shared it—or perhaps it was the sharing that made it reverent.

"It's funny," he said softly after a moment, "how many artists over how many years have tried to capture this scene on canvas, on film or just with words—but it can't be done. It's a quality, not a thing. It has to do with being up here all alone with your own thoughts, tasting the air and listening to the breeze, and knowing how many centuries of men before you have stood just here, and done the same thing."

There was a beauty in his words that matched the subtle glory of the scene nature had painted around them, and the poignancy of it took Cassie's breath away just as surely as did the simple sensory impact of the setting sun. The moment was captured between them, purely and cleanly, a single thought, a shared feeling. Cassie had never known such a simple, unmitigated rapport with another human being before; it was singular and it was fleeting, but all the more precious for that.

"It's sad, to think we might be the last generation to see it in just this way," she said, "with the camp in the background, and the horses picketed just a few yards away and the cattle bedded down for the night." She wasn't doing a very good job of expressing herself, but she knew he understood. She did not need to be articulate to express what they both saw in the shadows of the sunset. "It's been the same for so many years, but pretty soon it will all be gone. The ranches are breaking up, the herds are growing smaller and the cowboys are riding motorcycles. It just doesn't seem right somehow."

He smiled faintly, not looking directly at her but including her in the breadth of his vision. "Everything changes, I guess. Only pure stubbornness made it last this long. The sun will still set over the mountains, but the people who watch it won't be the same. That's what's really sad. Because the life will be gone out of it all. And what's left will be no more than a backdrop, like those painted sunsets Hollywood used to have the cowboys ride into at the end of the film. Pretty, but not real. And not worth much."

The air was cool and tinged with the faint smell of cigarette smoke. The background of voices and movement from the mess tent sounded very faint and far away, for here, on this little knoll overlooking the entire world, there were only the two of them, wrapped in the quiet splendor of a moment rare and treasured.

His boot was propped next to her elbow, his slim knee bent, his forearm resting upon it. The cigarette smoldered lazily in his other hand, and he looked down at her. The twilight made a misty mirror of his eyes, giving them the color of an opaque prism, and his gaze was gentle, thoughtful and intent. Cassie was lost in the vague and tender smile that seemed almost to linger at the back of those eyes, and wrapped in the moment of communication that seemed so natural between them. Then she realized that he was looking at her as a man might look at a woman, and she wished she were prettier. She wished he would kiss her, and then her heart started beating faster.

It was a strange, almost alien, experience for Cassie to be having such thoughts about a man, and for a moment it confused her. With the death of her marriage had come a withering and a fading away of other things—emotions, sexuality. She had been so happy to be free of oppression that she had not missed warmth. She had been so involved with herself that she had not missed companionship. And she had been in such a turmoil of an identity crisis that she had buried sexual needs and emotional yearnings so deeply she had not even been aware of their absence... until now.

She felt the nearness of wiry masculine muscles and imagined the sensation of being wrapped in them. She saw the broad, callused hands, and could almost feel their caress. She glimpsed the beard-roughened cheek and imagined its texture against her own, and she looked into his eyes and remembered tenderness. And beneath it all her heart was pounding a slow, steady rhythm of anticipation as she thought how good it would feel to be held by a man.

Suddenly—and not for the first time today—she became convinced that Logan knew exactly what she was thinking. His expression had not altered, nor had he made a move, but there was something about him—the character of his light, opaque eyes, perhaps—that seemed to imbue him with a sixth sense. One got the impression that he missed nothing, and knew far more than he would ever tell. Logan was a keeper, and a reader, of secrets.

Cassie moved her eyes away, breaking the moment, once again stuffing her slightly damp palms nervously into her pockets. It was embarrassing. She was no better than Amy, and she was crazy to think a man like Logan would be attracted to her. All he had wanted was someone to talk to, and in truth, that was all she had wanted, too. A quiet hill, a sexy stranger, a kiss in the twilight—those were all very fine things, but hardly Cassie's style. Neither, as a matter of fact, was romantic fantasizing, but it was nice to know she could still do it.

And even as she withdrew into her uncomfortable role of half boss, half trail cook, she felt a small glow inside for the moment that was passing. She was grateful to Logan for sharing it with her, and for stirring back to life the ashes of sensations she had thought long cold.

Cassie got to her feet. "Well, there's a ton of dirty dishes waiting for me. I guess I'd better get back to work."

Logan finished his cigarette and ground the stub beneath his heel. Cassie reached to pick up his empty coffee cup. "I passed the word down the line about your niece," he said. "You don't have to worry...the boys will leave her alone. They're a pretty good lot, at that."

Cassie smiled at him, touched and grateful. "Thanks."

He dismissed it. "I just don't see any need for more trouble than we've already got."

Cassie almost didn't catch that, and by the time she did, he was already turning to go. "See you at breakfast, then," he said. "Don't forget what I said about the coffee," he advised over his shoulder, and then he was moving down the hill at an easy, rolling gait toward the stream.

Cassie watched him go, puzzled, almost tempted to call out to him. "More trouble than we've already got." What had he meant by that? What kind of trouble did they have besides a missing cook, and Cassie had fixed that...hadn't she?

She stood there for a moment longer, half frowning with irritation over his persistent habit of speaking in unfinished mysteries, half musing over the sheer sensory pleasure of watching him move…even if he was moving away from her. And then, when his shoulders disappeared behind a ridge, she turned reluctantly and started back toward the tent. Her workday was only half finished.

Chapter Four

Customarily the men lingered after supper, sitting around the long tables, smoking and drinking coffee and telling tall tales in the light of the battery-operated lamps and the warmth of the canvas—the modern-day equivalent of sitting around the camp fire and relaxing at the end of the day. Tonight, with Cassie and Amy working busily in the background, no one seemed to have much to say; cigarettes were put away when Amy began to cough, and Logan was right—no one seemed to care much for seconds of her coffee. One by one the men began to wander out, setting up their tents and preparing to bed down early. That suited Cassie just fine. She was sorry to have taken the fun out of their evenings, but her job was to keep them fed, not to make them comfortable. And the work went much faster when no one was around to watch.

Cassie had never been more tired in her life, and even Amy, with her unflagging energy and seventeen-year-old enthusiasm, was looking a little hollow around the eyes. She made no objection when Cassie suggested that she go to her tent and try to get to sleep immediately—complaining only that she wished she could have a shower.

Rodney, whose body clock was attuned to early rising, promised to wake Cassie an hour before sunrise. It was a little before eight o'clock when Cassie crawled into her one-man tent, extinguished her flashlight and changed from her soiled and sticky clothes into a soft flannel sweat suit for sleeping. It was barely dark, but already the camp was beginning to settle down to the sound of occasional sporadic voices, curt grunts as boots were tugged off, the rustle of tent flaps and now and again a soft snore.

Cassie settled into her down sleeping bag and, as tired as she was, she did not know how she would be able to fall asleep. It had been many years since she had camped out, and her body wasn't as accommodating to the lumps in the ground as it once had been. Years of city traffic had made the silence of the countryside seem like a roar, and she lay awake, the events of the day racing through her head.

She was pleased with herself. She had been faced with a crisis and she had handled it. Perhaps she had not handled it in the most efficient, or even the wisest way, but she had seen the problem and taken care of it. And she hadn't done such a bad job of it, either. There weren't too many women, after all, who could take on a job like this with no prior experience and on such short notice, and actually see it through with no major disasters. She had never realized before just how shaky her own self-confidence was, but now that the test had been met and passed she felt better about herself than she had in years.

The hard work hadn't hurt Amy any, either. Jonas would still be furious with her for bringing Amy along, but in the long run the experience would leave a definite mark of improvement on his daughter. Besides, it would only be a few days. Cassie winced a little as she imagined Jonas receiving her message and making hurried arrangements even at this moment to come home. Amy would probably be back in her own little bed by tomorrow night.

Cassie turned over and tried to find a more comfortable position on the hard ground. She herself should have been looking forward to returning to her own bed, but strangely, she was not. Today, for the first time in years, she felt a sense of accomplishment. Tired though she was, she could not remember feeling more content. This evening, sitting with Logan and watching the sunset, she had at last felt as though she had come home. Really come home.

Logan. She closed her eyes and was unaware of the small smile that touched her lips as she thought of him. No, what she had felt this evening for those few moments with him was more than just comfortable. It was more than just meeting an attractive stranger and making cocktail party small talk. There was something so special about him, and so intriguing, that Cassie couldn't even define it. She only knew that it made her feel good inside. Very good.

She was not aware of falling asleep. She only knew that one minute she was thinking drowsily about Logan, the way his hair brushed his forehead and the sun shadowed his face, and the next minute someone was shaking her arm gently, prodding her to wakefulness.

"Mrs. Grant...Cassie. Wake up."

Groggily, Cassie turned in her sleeping bag and pushed her hair away from her face, forcing her eyes open and trying to make them focus in the dark. It couldn't be time to get up already. She couldn't possibly get up now. She groaned softly and tried to keep her eyes open.

"Cassie," he whispered again. "Are you awake?"

Gradually her eyes focused, and then she thought she must still be dreaming. It was Logan, crowding up her small tent with his presence and his warmth, his strong fingers light upon her shoulder, his face close to hers. She gasped, first with surprise, and then with alarm, and struggled to sit up. "What—"

He placed his fingers lightly over her lips to quiet her. "I'm sorry," he whispered, "but there's been an accident. Come outside."

Cassie's heart jumped and began to pound, but he turned and was gone as quickly and as silently as he had entered before she could question him. All she could think was *Amy*, and adrenaline pumped swift and awful wakefulness through her as she fumbled in the dark for her boots and her jacket. She pulled them both on clumsily and hastily over her sweat suit and stumbled outside.

The night was bright with starlight, and deceptively peaceful and still. Moonlight bathed the rows of tents in which the men slept undisturbed; a tree frog hummed contentedly in the background. Cassie cast around frantically, and Logan stepped from the shadows, taking her arm firmly. "Amy?" she whispered anxiously. "Is she—"

He shook his head. "No, she's all right." He spoke softly, leading her away from the camp so their voices wouldn't disturb the others. Swift and weakening relief began to spread through her but had hardly registered before he said, "It's Red. He's been thrown. He looks all right, but he took a bad rap on the head and his leg is broken. I'm going to take him to the hospital. I thought you'd want to know."

Cassie stopped in midstride, staring at him. Her heart was still pounding with emergency signals, but it was incredulity that widened her eyes and rendered her momentarily speechless. Red? Thrown from a horse? He had been riding the meanest animals on the ranch for over thirty years and had never had an accident. It didn't make sense, everything about it was wrong, and even as all her instincts flashed a warning, she knew this wasn't the time to ask irrelevant questions. She demanded, "Where is he?"

"I splinted his leg and bedded him down in the back of the pickup, as comfortable as possible."

Cassie moved swiftly through the dark toward the truck, which was parked in the shadows beyond camp. She sprang into the bed of the pickup and knelt beside Red. "You okay, Boss?" she said softly, using the nickname she had called him when she was growing up.

He scowled at her, and she could tell it was as much in an effort to subdue pain as to pretend irritation. There was a bruise on his forehead that glowed purple in the moonlight, and when he turned his head she saw a clot of blood in his thinning hair on the back side. "Hell, no, I'm not okay!" he growled. "I broke my damn leg. How'm I supposed to ride with a broke leg, I'd like to know!"

Logan had padded the truck bed with one sleeping bag and wrapped Red securely in another for the trip. Cassie could tell by the shape of the blankets that Red's leg was splinted, and she trusted Logan to have done a good job. She said, "Don't worry; we're going to get you to the hospital. You'll be as good as new in no time."

She was rewarded with an encouraging mumble of curses, and she turned and climbed over the side.

"How did it happen?" she demanded quietly of Logan. His face was blank. "He didn't say."

"What was he doing out there in the night?"

"He was on patrol," Logan explained patiently. "I'd better get going now; he's in need of some painkiller in a bad way. I just wanted you to know where we were."

"I'm going with you," Cassie said. "Wait a minute; let me get another blanket."

Logan caught her arm as she turned. His voice was

mild, but his grip was firm. And his face was decisive. "There's no need for that," he said. "It's a long drive and you need your sleep."

Cassie faced him impatiently. "How much money have you got?"

He merely stared at her.

"Do you have his insurance information or medical history?" She pulled her arm away. "I'm going."

Logan looked disapproving, but he had no argument. He merely jerked his head, shortly, back to the tents. "What about the youngster?"

Cassie hesitated, unwilling to wake Amy in the middle of the night for the long ride to town, yet certain that if Jonas were here he would not leave her alone. This kind of responsibility was alien to Cassie, but she knew an injured man took precedence over a sleeping girl. She said, "We'll be back before she wakes up." And hurried to her tent for the extra sleeping bag.

The nearest hospital was actually closer than the ranch house, although it didn't seem so to Cassie, freezing in the back of the truck and trying to protect Red from the jolts and jostles of the road. He was a stalwart old man, but after a while even his curses faded away into grim-lipped pain, and eventually he lapsed into semiconsciousness. Cassie kept Red as warm and as still as she could and silently willed Logan to hurry.

Over and over she ran through the accident in her head. Something about it just didn't sound right. She supposed it was customary to patrol the herd at night, for although attacks by wild animals were rare these days, cattle were easily spooked, and if the herd scattered at night it could mean many days of extra work gathering them again. But for Red, of all people, to be thrown from his horse hard enough to break his leg... And then she realized the other thing that did not seem right about it. Red had two head injuries—one on the forehead and one on the back of the skull. How had that happened?

The cold wind whipped through her, and the star-filled sky seemed bleak and endless. Cassie felt a shiver of despair run through her as she looked out over the straight, flat expanse of highway, the ghostly landscape flying past. Only this morning she had been safe and warm in her own house, living out her routine life, worrying about nothing but herself. A year ago her biggest problems had concerned seating arrangements at dinner parties. What in the world was she doing in the middle of this empty, untamed land in the dark of the night with an injured man on her hands and a sleeping girl left behind in a camp of strangers? She wasn't equipped to deal with this.

It was only a little after eleven o'clock when they arrived at the small county hospital, although it seemed much later. The orderlies came out to transfer Red onto a stretcher and wheel him into the emergency room, and for the next half hour Cassie was kept busy filling out forms and answering questions.

Logan was in the waiting room, leaning back in one of the uncomfortable vinyl chairs with one foot crossed over his knee, smoking one of his hand-rolled cigarettes. The little room was empty except for the two of them.

"They took him right in," Logan told her before she asked. "The doctor thinks he's going to be all right. They'll want to keep him overnight, though. Probably longer."

Cassie nodded and sank down onto the squeaky imitation-leather sofa across from him. She was suddenly immensely tired. "How did it happen, Logan?" she asked for a second time.

She noticed the way his long lashes shaded his eyes as

he moved to tap ashes into a nearby ashtray. But his face was unreadable. ''I found him in a gully when I came on duty. His horse had wandered off. Must have been spooked or something.''

That was the logical explanation, of course. What other answer could there be?

''Does everyone take a shift on night watch duty?''

''Eventually.'' He answered offhandedly, as though that was something she should know. ''We rotate in two-hour shifts.''

''Just one man at a time?''

He looked impatient with her questions, and then was spared from answering when the doctor came in. Both Cassie and Logan got to their feet.

''A simple fracture,'' the doctor explained, ''and a mild concussion. Because of his age, we'd like to keep him a couple of days to keep an eye on his injuries, but I don't expect any problems.''

''Could we see him?'' Cassie asked.

''Just for a minute. He needs his rest.''

Red looked pale and groggy with his head bandaged and his casted leg propped up on a pillow—and also very uncomfortable and out of place in the sterile, efficient hospital room. Cassie came over to him and patted his hand. ''You're a sight,'' she told him, smiling. ''I wish I had a camera.''

He managed a scowl. ''Still got that smart mouth, I see.''

Cassie's expression went serious. ''What in the world happened, Red? You've never been thrown in your life, and nobody knows the countryside like you do. How..?''

He avoided her eyes. ''Fool horse stepped in a gopher hole,'' he muttered. ''Went right over his neck. And this headache is killing me; I need some shut-eye.''

Cassie looked at him thoughtfully for a moment, and he never once glanced back at her. Then she squeezed his hand affectionately and said, "All right, you get some rest. I'll be back to see you as soon as I can. Meanwhile, don't go giving the nurses a hard time and do as you're told."

Red grunted. "That'll be the day."

Logan stepped over to him. "Take it easy, Red. We'll miss you out on the range."

Red looked at Logan, and something passed between the two men that Cassie could not read, but which she knew was exclusive and important. Red said quietly, "Thanks, kid." And there seemed to be more to that simple statement than gratitude for having taken care of him. Then Red turned his head on the pillow and closed his eyes.

The sound of their boot heels echoed loudly on the tiled floor, making Cassie want to tiptoe. No one liked hospitals, she supposed, but there was something about a hospital in the dead of night, with its subdued silence and low lighting, that made her skin crawl. She felt guilty for her anxiousness to get out of there.

Logan seemed unusually preoccupied and subdued as he walked beside her, but with him it was hard to tell. His natural state seemed to be silence and preoccupation, and he was probably just as tired as she was. She glanced at him, and his face was shadowed and unreadable beneath the brim of his hat. His hands were tucked into the front pockets of his vest, because he had not worn a jacket even in the chill of the night, and there was something strong and reassuring about his presence. Cassie tried to imagine how much more frightening this middle-of-the-night race to the hospital would have been without him, and it made her shiver. Or what would have happened to

Red if Logan hadn't found him. Logan, a man who walked alone, but who always seemed to be there when he was needed. Just like an old-time legend.

That made her smile a little, for she did not think he would appreciate, at this point, a comparison with the Lone Ranger. She said instead, "You did a good job with Red. That was quick thinking."

He did not seem to be impressed. "First aid is second nature on the range. There was nothing hard about it."

In similar circumstances, Cassie was certain she would have panicked. Certainly most of the men she knew would have made a much bigger production out of the matter than he had. But Logan, calm and authoritative, was nonplussed by nothing. He had quietly and efficiently taken care of what needed to be done, and he had only awakened her to report on it after the fact. Being in charge came naturally to him.

In the hospital lobby he paused. "Do you want to call your brother?"

At first Cassie did not understand what he meant, for it hadn't even occurred to her that Jonas might want to be apprised of this latest turn of events. A glance at the clock showed her it was after midnight, and she hesitated. She suspected that yesterday—this morning, even—she would have been quick to run to her brother for advice, reassurance and support. But she had taken so much on herself in the past twelve hours that one more responsibility seemed hardly to matter, and she shook her head.

"There's nothing he can do," she answered reasonably. "If I don't hear from him tomorrow, I'll get word to him. But there's really no reason to bother him this late."

Logan seemed to agree, and he touched her shoulder lightly as he pushed open the big glass door for her. Cassie caught a brief reflection in the glass—herself, almost comical looking in the rumpled gray sweat suit and big down jacket, her baggy pant legs tucked into her boots, her hair an undisciplined mass of tangles. And Logan, tall, slim and masculine, beside her. Never had two people looked less like they belonged together, and the image was rather depressing.

They stepped out into the night air, and Cassie did not speak until she was seated beside Logan in the truck. Then she looked at him thoughtfully, and she said with quiet certainty, "He was lying, you know."

Logan showed not the slightest bit of surprise. His face was carefully blank as he turned on the ignition. "What makes you say that?"

"A lot of things." Cassie's voice was musing as she tried to sort it out in her own head. "That bump on the back of his head, for one thing. If he went over the horse's head he would have fallen forward, which would account for the bruise on his forehead, but not the one on the back of his head. And how did he break his leg?"

Logan glanced at her, a spark of amusement in his eye. "That's quite a deduction, Mrs. Grant," he drawled. "But on mighty flimsy evidence, if you ask me."

"I've known Red all my life," she insisted. "I know when he's trying to hide something. What I don't understand is why."

Logan was silent.

She shifted a little in her seat to better look at him, determined to prove her case—flimsy though it might be. "Did you find his horse?"

His face was momentarily illuminated by a parking lot lamp as he turned the truck, and Cassie did not mistake the slight tightening of his jaw. She was certain he knew what she was getting at. "Yes."

"And it wasn't injured, was it? It wasn't limping or

bruised? If the horse had fallen, there would have been some sign.''

Logan made no denials. He pulled out onto the highway and shifted into gear, and he kept his eyes on the road. "Maybe he was confused about what happened," he said. "Something like that is bound to shake a man up.''

Logan seemed matter-of-fact and unconcerned, and of course he was probably right. Cassie did not want to be accused of being overimaginative, but she couldn't shake that strong feeling that something about this was not quite right.

But that was just what it was—a feeling. And what experience did Cassie have with such things? The night— the entire day—had been filled with high drama in unfamiliar circumstances, and how much could she really rely on her own judgment? Much less her intuition. It was just an accident, and Red had no reason to lie about it. There was nothing mysterious about any of it at all; it was simply that Cassie was overreacting to events that had no place in the quiet, protected and orderly world from which she had come.

Cassie sighed and leaned her head back against the seat. It had been quite a day. First a temperamental cook who walked off the job, then a man injured in a freak accident in the middle of the night. The Circle P had surely had its share of excitement for a while. She wished Jonas were here.

Almost as though reading her thoughts Logan said, "I guess you got a little more than you bargained for today.''

She thought there was a touch of sympathy in his voice, and his glance invited confidence. She wondered if it was in his nature to make women feel protected and cared for simply by his presence, or if it was only she who reacted to him that way. She answered tiredly, "If you mean I might have bitten off more than I could chew when I decided to solve everyone's problems and take over the cook's job this morning, I'm beginning to think you might be right. I'm not cut out for this kind of life. I should have stayed home where I belong.''

"Now, I didn't say that," he objected mildly. "As a matter of fact, I think you're handling it all pretty well, considering.''

She turned her head, still resting on the seat back, to look at him. "Considering what?''

"Considering the fact that you haven't had a lot of excitement in your life...or challenge, either. Most people, when they've had it soft for a while, forget how to cope. You didn't.''

Cassie was surprised both by his perception and by what was, for him, generous praise. The kind of challenges she had faced today were child's play for men like Logan, but for her they were an important test. He recognized that fact and acknowledged it. His sensitivity touched and intrigued her.

Still, there was a cynical note to her voice as she admitted, "You had every right to expect a hysterical incompetent, I guess. At least I didn't burn the biscuits and cry, but I'm not saying any of this has been fun. On the whole, I'd rather be curled up in my own bed right now, with real sheets and a feather pillow.''

He slanted her a glance that sparked with subdued mirth. "Wouldn't we all?''

Cassie laughed softly, and felt some of the tension in her body seep away. The hands that had been clenched tightly in her lap relaxed a fraction; the tight muscles of her back and neck began to cautiously unknot. She couldn't put it behind her, the abrupt awakening in the middle of the night, the nightmarish trip to the hospital, an old man badly hurt and the twisting fear every time she thought how much worse it might have been. But now, with Logan near, the horror of it did not seem so acute. His quiet strength was contagious.

He said unexpectedly, "You have a nice laugh."

Cassie glanced at him in self-conscious surprise, and she could not prevent a little tingle of pleasure, which only embarrassed her further. No one had ever told her that before. In fact, it had been so long since anyone had given her a compliment of any kind that she hardly knew how to react.

And then she was annoyed with herself for reacting at all. Too many years had passed in which the center of her life had focused on a man's approval; she had thought she was beyond that now. She did not need compliments from a man, or recognition, or gentle words.

No, she did not need those things, but they were awfully nice to have.

He glanced at her and seemed amused by her sudden, tongue-tied silence. "There's not much of a family resemblance between you and your niece, is there?"

"No." Cassie's tone was light but her hands began to tighten in her lap again. "I was always the ugly duckling of the family."

"That's not what I meant." There was reprimand and disappointment in his voice, and the glance he cast upon her made her feel small. "I just couldn't help noticing the way Amy knows how to drag attention out of a man whether he wants to give it or not, and you seem embarrassed when anyone even notices you."

Not anyone, Cassie thought. *Just you.* But she shrugged. "That has a lot to do with just being a teenager, I think. Amy gets most of her charm from Jonas's side of the family. You've met Jonas,'' she added, trying to change the subject. ''You know what I mean.''

He nodded. ''Seemed like a nice enough fellow,'' he agreed, deadpan. ''But I've got to say, he didn't exactly send my heart into a tailspin.''

Cassie couldn't help laughing again, and his eyes, as he smiled at her, were warm and approving. That was when she realized that he had structured the entire conversation to distract her and cheer her up. Such thoughtfulness seemed both out of character for him and instinctual, and another puzzling dimension was added to his personality.

''How long have you been working for the Circle P?'' she asked after a moment.

''A few weeks, a few months.'' A typically evasive answer. ''How long have you been back?''

''Since spring. About three months.'' Neither one of them commented on the fact that they had never met before. On an operation the size of the Circle P they might well have never met at all, if not for the cook's defection when Cassie was in charge. And when Cassie thought of how easily they might have gone the whole summer without ever meeting each other, she felt foolishly sentimental.

She asked, without meaning to, ''Will you be staying on after the roundup?''

Of course, the decision was not really up to him. He had been hired for the season, and the Circle P couldn't afford to keep on many men during the winter. Yet she knew without a doubt that Logan was exactly the type of man they needed working full-time on the ranch. Red was not getting any younger, and after this accident Cassie wanted him to lighten his duties considerably. He would need some reliable help. If Jonas didn't ask Logan to stay, Cassie would.

But the point became moot in the next moment as Logan answered easily and without qualification, "No, I'll be moving on. I don't like to stay in one place too long."

Cassie wanted to protest that that was foolish, to demand that he tell her where he intended to go and what he intended to do for the winter, to offer him a permanent job right then and there—but common sense stopped her just in time. She knew nothing about this man, and it was certainly none of her business where he went from here. She must be more tired, and more shaken by the events of the evening, than she realized. Her judgment was going steadily downhill.

As far as that went, she had shown nothing but bad judgment from the moment she had met Logan. She should have called Jonas about the accident. She should have used her brains, and not her instincts, when Logan had first approached her with the problem of the absent cook. And Amy...

She glanced at her arm in the dark and then realized she wasn't wearing a watch. The slim-banded Cartier her husband—or her husband's secretary, more likely—had given her for her anniversary had seemed tacky and out of place on the ranch. She looked at Logan anxiously. "Will it take us much longer to get back?"

"Worried about Amy?"

She nodded, biting her underlip. "That was a stupid thing to do, going off and leaving her like that. God, I'd make a terrible mother."

"I think little Miss Amy could take care of herself just fine if she had to," he answered calmly. "Probably a lot better than any of us give her credit for. As for being a bad mother...well, not that I'm an expert on such things, but it seems to me what you did for her today was a lot smarter, and a lot braver, than most mothers would have been able to do. You brought her out here to teach her a lesson, didn't you?''

Cassie was almost to the point where his reading her mind and her motives didn't surprise her anymore. She smiled a little, half guiltily. ''Yeah. From the minute she got to the ranch, she's had this big romantic fantasy about cowboys. Jonas has been terrified she'd do something foolish. I thought the quickest way to disenchant her was to give her what she wanted.''

He chuckled. ''I'm willing to bet it worked. She didn't seem quite as perky this afternoon as she did this morning.''

Cassie's smile widened, remembering. ''That's for sure. She expected rhinestones, I think, and she got trail dust.''

His own smile, in the passing shadows, was a little dry. ''I guess we all know how that feels.''

''Yes,'' Cassie agreed soberly, and silence fell.

She leaned her head back again and closed her eyes. She was trying not to think about all the dreams that had turned to dust in her own hands, or to wonder whether coming out here today had been only another in a long list of mistakes. But beyond all this she was thinking about Logan, and how peculiar it was that he had come to play such an important role in her life in such a short time. There could be danger in that, she knew, and she tried to warn herself against it. But at that point the warning seemed small and unimportant, and the only thing that really remained was how incredibly comfortable she felt with him. She could not recall ever feeling that way with a man before.

The movement of the truck was rhythmic and the sound of the motor soothing. Cassie was asleep before she knew it.

Something—perhaps the change in the movement of

the truck or the shifting of Logan's arm beneath her cheek—awakened her. She opened her eyes a little groggily to find her head leaning against his shoulder, and the feel of hard male muscles against her face was so unfamiliar, yet at the same time so strangely comfortable, that for a moment she did not move. She had a feeling she had been dreaming, and that this sensation of warmth and strength had been an integral part of it.

The truck bounced over rough ground, and Cassie sat up abruptly, passing a hand over her eyes to push the dreaminess from them. Her heart was beating rapidly and she was quickly and fully awake. "I—I'm sorry," she stammered. "I didn't mean to fall asleep."

He glanced at her, and there was gentle amusement in the corners of his smile. "That's all right. I kind of enjoyed it."

He leaned forward and switched off the headlights so as not to disturb the sleeping camp, and the truck rolled to a gentle stop beneath a lone tree. He turned off the ignition.

"Well," said Cassie, with a breath. "What a night." Her heart was still pounding a light double time, but she suspected that had less to do with the sudden awakening than with Logan, so close to her now as he turned to look at her, his body shifting slightly, his arm stretching out over the back of the seat. In that position, he seemed almost to enfold her without actually touching her at all.

But his expression in the gently shadowed interior of the truck was relaxed, and not in the least threatening. "Morning," he corrected easily. "I don't know how to tell you this, Cook, but it's almost time for you to start breakfast."

Cassie looked around in dismay. It was still serenely night outside; not even the faintest line of dawn lit the sky. In the distance she could see the vague forms of the tents where the crew slept deeply and undisturbed. But in little more than an hour they would begin to stir, and by that time Cassie must have a hot breakfast ready to see them on their way, for their workday would begin as soon as it was light enough to see.

Cassie groaned softly. "I don't envy you your choice of life-style, Logan. A man would have to be crazy to keep these hours."

"If I could think of an easier way to make a living," he admitted, "I would."

Cassie thought about the long day that lay ahead with no sleep to see her through it, and she almost groaned again. Unless she had greatly mistaken her brother, he would be arriving today, and she was not looking forward to that encounter. Not to mention breakfast and dinner for a hungry crew and the problem of replacing Red.

Determinedly, she resolved to see it through. One day of hard work with no sleep wouldn't kill her, and she had wanted an adventure, hadn't she? Besides, she had no choice.

She said, dealing with the most immediate problem first, "We'll need a new tallyman. I don't know any of these boys. Can you recommend someone for the job?"

He looked briefly and faintly surprised that she even knew what a tallyman was. And then, pushing his hat back a little on his head, he leaned back against the door with his arm still stretched out over the seat near her, and he gave it some thought. "Yes," he decided finally, almost reluctantly, and he looked at her. "Me." One corner of his lips deepened with a hint of ruefulness. "I'm the best qualified," he explained simply, and expected no argument.

Cassie wasn't about to give him one. In the old days

the tallyman's responsibilities had been limited to counting the stock as it was branded, and the only qualification for the job was the ability to count. Today the mathematics were a bit more complicated, and by tradition the tallyman was also line foreman and trail boss. He would be stepping into Red's shoes and, from this moment onward, be responsible for everything that happened on the rest of the roundup.

Cassie knew she was once again thinking with her instincts and not her brain, but what choice did she have? She would much rather trust the job to Logan than to any of the ruffians she had met today—at least she knew he could count. And if Jonas didn't like it, he could always choose someone else.

She said diplomatically, "I'd appreciate it if you'd take over for today, anyway. Jonas will make the final decision when he gets back."

The curve of his smile seemed a little playful. "I doubt if he'll be able to find anybody else, but it won't hurt my feelings any if he does. I wouldn't do this for anybody but you."

Cassie glanced down at her hands, confused and a little flustered by his unexpected teasing, and then impatient with herself for being nervous. She was the boss here, after all.

She looked back at Logan with a quick, bright and not entirely genuine smile, and answered lightly, "I appreciate that, Mr. Logan. And now, I guess you'd better get some sleep, and I'd better get to work."

She turned toward the door, and she felt his hand light upon her shoulder. He said her name softly, just once. "Cassie." And when she turned he kissed her.

It was not a quick or a sudden thing. Rather, she turned and saw his eyes, soft and colorless and gently secretive in the night, and his face with its dark, roughened planes, very close. His arms slid around her shoulders and his fingertips touched her neck lightly. It was a single smooth, unbroken and instinctual movement; her face upturned slightly, questioning, and his lips pressed hers gently, lingeringly. Still, it was the last of all things Cassie had expected, and it took her breath away.

His lips were soft, his fingers upon the bare skin of her neck warm and callused. He smelled of the open meadows and the mountains at night. He kissed her gently, not with caution or hesitance, but with a tenderness that was nonetheless backed by an instinctual masculine firmness. Surprise weakened her and made her pulses flutter, but before the surprise had even faded, other sensations were opening like floodgates, awareness poured through into every cell of her body.

It lasted only seconds, but in those few seconds a lifetime of forgotten needs was awakened in Cassie. Warmth blossomed in her skin and flowed through her veins, her breath died in her throat, heartbeats scattered through her body like startled raindrops in a sudden gust of wind. Consciousness expanded like a deep, slow breath and then faded into nothing but the sheer sensory awareness of Logan, his closeness, his lips caressing hers. So sweet. So invasive. And so powerful.

Her hand fluttered against his chest, her tingling fingertips registering the texture of smooth, tanned animal hide and then, just briefly, the thin flannel fabric of his shirt that protected warm, hard muscles. And with her touch, light, uncertain and sheerly instinctual as it was, new sparks of awareness seemed to kindle within him. Quickly—so quickly she might not have noticed—his kiss deepened and was touched with hunger, and then with the awareness came caution. He moved away.

His eyes were bright now, shaded by his heavy lashes, but deeply alert as they moved briefly across her face. His fingers touched the side of her face in a light caress and then played over her chin, holding it briefly. His breath flowed like a whisper across her lips, he was still that close. And Cassie felt mesmerized, flooded still by the sensations he had evoked, poised on the brink of discovery and yet uncertain, waiting.

He said huskily, "I shouldn't have, I know. But I guess you already know how much I've wanted to kiss you, since this afternoon."

Cassie simply looked at him, unable to speak, unable, almost, even to breathe. Yes, since this afternoon, when they had shared a moment that was unfulfilled. The kiss had completed what was shared between them, but it still felt like only a beginning.

His arm slid away from her, and he smiled at her. Cassie knew that was her signal to leave. She wasn't behaving with much sophistication, she knew, or even very sensibly, but she couldn't seem to think of anything to say. She couldn't help wondering what would happen then if she stayed.

She reached for the door handle and got out of the truck. All she was thinking was that nothing had ever felt quite so right, so simple and natural, as those few moments she had been in Logan's arms.

Chapter Five

The Crossing

V

Trouble had a way of following Jim. He didn't seek it, but he had never gone much out of his way to avoid it, either. He usually managed to hold his own against anything that came his way.

He was fast with a gun—faster than most people hereabouts had ever seen and faster than he wanted to let most people know—but that was a solution he usually found best to save as a last resort. Years of living had toughened his muscles and made him light on his feet, and there weren't many men who came up against his fists who wanted to try it again. But mostly Jim was a thinking man. He believed there was no problem that could not be solved if a person took his time and thought it through.

He had been thinking for days now, and there were no two ways about it. Trouble was heading his way, and it was not the kind of trouble he could fight with a gun, his two good fists or a cool and steady head. It was the kind of trouble he had never faced before, and it had taken him by surprise. He wasn't sure there was any way out of it at all.

It had begun the moment he looked into a pair of pretty brown eyes and the woman had smiled at him.

BY THE TIME THE MEN began to fold up their tents for the day, Cassie had mixed up a gallon of pancake batter and a vat of hot cereal, sliced and fried half a ham and a side of bacon, and scrambled what amounted to six dozen powdered eggs. The coffee was strong enough to dissolve dental work, and to Cassie, in her state of walking exhaustion, it was a lifesaver.

Word had spread with astounding rapidity about last night's accident, and even Amy had heard about it before Cassie had a chance to tell her.

"Do you mean," Amy demanded with a mixture of incredulity and dread, "that you went all the way into town last night and left me alone with these—" she glanced around uneasily at the few men who were beginning to shuffle into the tent "—creeps?"

Cassie did not know whether to smile or scowl. Amy, her face pasty, completely devoid of makeup, and her eyes puffy from lack of sleep, with her hair knotted in an untidy clasp at the back of her neck, looked almost as bad as Cassie felt. Cassie's little object lesson seemed to be working, and she did not think she needed to worry about Amy's romantic illusions anymore. Nor did she think that Amy, when she returned to her pampered, fourteen-karat-gold world, would be quick to forget this experience. That part of her plan, at least, had worked out well. She only hoped that in the final balance it would be worth it.

Cassie transferred several pancakes from the griddle to a platter and ladled out more batter. "You didn't even miss me,'' she pointed out. ''Besides, what was I supposed to do? The man had to go to the hospital.''

Amy had no answer for that. Rather belatedly she inquired, ''Is he all right? I mean, was it serious?''

''A broken leg always feels serious to the man who's got it,'' another voice replied, and Cassie turned to meet Logan.

Her heart skipped and his eyes smiled. He looked as fresh and well groomed as though he had spent the night in a comfortable bed with twelve hours of uninterrupted sleep. He had shaved and changed his shirt, and his hair, beneath the hat that was pushed back from his forehead, was freshly combed and shiny. Another time Cassie would have simply thought how attractive he was, how striking and essentially virile. Today she thought that and something else as well—how familiar he seemed to her, how comfortable and right his presence seemed to her, as though she had been waiting for something for a long time and she looked up and he was there. The strong possessive urge she felt upon seeing him was instinctive and surprising, and it even embarrassed her as an extra dimension of pleasure was added to the glow that darted through her when she looked into his eyes. Then she turned away quickly and began to serve his food.

You're being crazy, Cassie. A kiss, for goodness' sake. What was so remarkable about a trail-weary cowboy making a move on the nearest available female when the opportunity presented itself? There was nothing magical in the fact that she had enjoyed being kissed by a good-looking stranger.

Cassie was a fairly enlightened woman. She knew there was nothing mystical about sexual attraction and she was honest enough to admit to herself that she had felt nothing but attraction for Logan since the moment she had first

seen him. She had always had a healthy physical relationship with Greg—sex was one of the few things about
which they did not fight—and she had been alone for
almost a year. All of those were very logical and obvious
reasons for her present vulnerability, and for being very
careful.

Her womanhood had been quietly buried, recuperating
in peaceful hibernation, since her divorce. She had felt no
yearnings, no dissatisfaction, no emptiness, no interest at
all in beginning another relationship. And then Logan,
with his quiet, unobtrusive masculine presence, had begun
to draw her into awareness again. Naturally, the reawak-
ening would be intense.

It was normal, logical, predictable. There was no reason
to attach any special significance to the man or to his kiss.
Cassie knew all this, she told herself all this quite sternly
and calmly, but that did not stop her pulse from speeding
or her skin from flushing when he walked into the room.
She felt like a girl with her first crush, and though she
was annoyed with herself, she could not seem to do anything to mitigate the feelings or put them in their proper
perspective.

Because it did feel special to her. And she did not think
it was going to go away.

"Your aunt didn't get enough sleep last night to
count," Logan was saying to Amy, "so how about pitch-
ing in and lending an extra hand today?" He cast the
young girl a twinkling glance, which immediately and
unquestioningly won her full cooperation. "After all, it
wouldn't do for the cook to fall asleep over the stew tonight, would it?"

"What about you?" Cassie slid a stack of pancakes
onto his tray. "You didn't sleep at all."

He shrugged. "I'm used to it." His attitude was natural

and relaxed. Nothing in his manner or expression indicated that anything had passed between them during the night except an emergency trip to the hospital. He flipped the lever on the coffee urn and lifted an eyebrow as the thick black brew poured into his cup. "The coffee looks good," he commented, and then took his tray and went over to a table.

That was all. Cassie didn't even have time to feel disappointment or to tell herself there was no reason to be disappointed. The breakfast rush had begun and she was kept busy turning from the griddle to the serving trays placed before her, and she had all she could do to concentrate on not burning or spilling anything.

The men were much less subdued than they had been yesterday, and the talk was all of Red. They filed in out of the dark and into the warm, fragrant mess tent, and scraps of conversation reached Cassie that she was too busy—and too tired—to assimilate.

"I could see it coming, just as plain as day."

"Tried to tell him there was trouble on the way."

"Damn fool thing to do, if you ask me. What did he think he was gonna prove?"

"Did anybody hear how many of them there were?"

"Well, they're welcome to them, if you ask me. You'll never catch me going up against a bunch of rustlers, not on what I'm paid. That's the sheriff's job."

It was the word "rustler" that finally filtered through to Cassie. She paused in the process of transferring a stack of pancakes onto the tray of the man before her, and looked up.

He was large—"fat" would be a better word—with greasy dark hair, which straggled over his shoulders, and tobacco-stained lips. She had heard the men call him Bill. She said, "Pardon me, but did you say 'rustlers'?"

He looked at her boldly but not without a touch of respect. "Yes'm. And no offense, but the boss, that is, Red, he knew how we felt about it from the start. We'll ride your herd, but we don't aim to get ourselves hurt doing it. There's just no percentage in it. We don't even know how many of them there are, or how mean they are. And after what happened to Red, well, I don't mean to start trouble, ma'am, but I don't reckon you'll be getting too many volunteers for night watch anymore."

Cassie said nothing. She filled his tray and he passed on through.

Amy was practically dancing with excitement beside her. "Rustlers?" Her voice trilled with laughter and her eyes were bright. "Did he say rustlers? Come on, Cassie, he had to be putting you on! That's right out of the movies! That's—"

Cassie thrust the spatula into Amy's hand. "Finish up for me, will you?" she said abruptly and, tugging off her apron, she walked across the room.

Logan was just finishing up. His eyes were expressionless over his coffee cup, but he had heard the talk. He knew exactly what was on her mind.

Cassie said in a low voice, "I want to talk to you." And she pushed aside the tent flap and stepped outside.

Dawn was just beginning to wash over the sky, pale and gray-blue. The grass was damp with dew, and the breakfast smells mingled with the scent of hardwood and mountain herbs in a subtly intoxicating aroma. The air was chill but gentle; morning peace lay over everything. It all seemed jarringly inappropriate for the turmoil that was raging inside Cassie.

Logan, with his easy, long-legged stride, soon caught up with her, but Cassie kept moving away from the mess tent, where they might be overheard. She said, without looking at him, "You knew." Her voice was low and tight with anger, and she had to thrust her hands in her pockets, bunching them tightly, to regain some semblance of control.

Logan answered simply, "Yes."

She turned on him, her eyes flashing and her face blotched with temper. "Last night...I knew something wasn't right. I tried to tell you. And you knew! You knew all along Red was lying about what happened!"

His face was utterly blank. "That's right."

She felt betrayed, misused, bitterly deceived. She had not realized until that moment how totally she had trusted him, how completely she had depended on him, instinctively and without question. "Why?" she demanded, and her voice was creased with a note of pleading that she hated. Vainly she hoped there would be some reasonable answer, but she knew it was futile. The fact was she had trusted him and he had lied to her...but why?

He answered calmly, "It wasn't any of my business."

Her breath left her lungs and for a moment she could only stare at him. "None of your—A man was attacked last night by thieves, part of an illegal operation that everybody in this camp knew about but me! You didn't report it, you didn't acknowledge it, you pretended it was just an accident!"

"Red told you what he wanted you to know," Logan said, and now there seemed to be an edge to his voice. "It wasn't my place to interfere."

"You lied to me!"

His eyes darkened, and Cassie could see the muscles of his forearms bunch beneath the denim shirt as he moved his own hands to the slit pockets of his vest. "I don't lie, lady," he said quietly, and there almost seemed to be a note of warning behind his voice that Cassie was too upset, and too unwary, to heed. "I might not tell everything I know, but I don't lie."

"You were there!" she accused wildly. Her nerves were stripped raw from lack of sleep. She had coped with more in the past twenty-four hours than she had in the past ten years of her life combined; she had been wrested from her cozy, uneventful little life into a world of challenges, decisions and hard work. She had seen violence and blood. She had been frightened half out of her wits last night, and then she had let this man take her in his arms and kiss her and a part of him had lodged itself inside her mind, her emotions, and had begun to grow there and consume her. Now she discovered he had been lying to her all along, covering up an illegal act.

She remembered how smooth he had been last night, how easily he had changed the subject when she began to ask questions about Red, how charming and uncharacteristically flattering he had been. And she had fallen for it. He had wanted to lead her off the track and he had done so...but why?

"You must have seen something," she prodded ruthlessly, her voice shaking with repressed anger. "Why else would you lie about it? Hell, for all I know you were in with them! Maybe it was you who hit Red over the head and pushed him down the gully!"

The swift flare of dark anger in his face was frightening to behold, and if Cassie had been less involved with her own fury and feelings of betrayal she would have stepped away immediately; she would have turned and run. His eyes blazed, his muscles clenched, and she saw such violence in that one swift moment that she took an automatic step backward.

And then, suddenly catching himself, he turned sharply on his heel and strode away.

The still morning air echoed with the threat just past and so narrowly missed, and for a moment Cassie was held motionless by it, her heart pounding, her throat dry. And then, galvanized by the sound of his retreating footsteps, she went after him.

She caught up with him as he reached the picketed horses. "Don't walk away from me!" she demanded angrily. "I want an answer!"

She grabbed his arm, and he flung her touch away, turning in a swift motion that caught her off balance and caused her to stumble backward. His face was perfectly composed, his expression quiet and controlled, but his eyes were snapping. He said angrily, "I don't have any answers for you, Mrs. Grant." He bit out her name with bitter emphasis. His face was very close and she could see his breath frosting faintly in the damp air, his muscles straining beneath the fabric of his shirt. The long tendon in his neck was taut and prominent. "But I will tell you one thing. You're not mad about Red, or rustlers, or even my keeping quiet when you think I should've spoken up. You're mad about this."

Without any warning whatsoever he pulled her against him, hard, and his mouth covered hers.

In a surge of outrage and shock, Cassie struggled. But then, in less than a breath, she realized she was struggling against nothing. In those first moments when his fingers clamped down over her upper arms and he hauled her against his hard body she had expected an exercise in dominance, mockery. She didn't know him anymore, she had never known him at all. Wasn't this typical of the mentality of the kind of life he led, the kind of man he represented, to satisfy his own ego with a display of force?

But it wasn't force at all. It wasn't mocking. It was a

kiss, deep and sensual and frankly hungry, but pretending nothing else.

His hands were on her arms, holding her still; her hands were pushing against his chest in instinctive defense, but only for a moment. His mouth claimed hers, and any thoughts of resistance were irrelevant. His arms slipped around her, holding her close; her arms went around his back, holding on to him. They kissed because they wanted to, nothing more.

His mouth opened on hers and her lips parted for him. Shaking waves of adrenaline pumped through her as she felt the tip of his tongue tease her lips and her teeth, and then, on a breath, urge its way inside with deliberate, luxurious exploration. His hand moved over her back, tracing the shape of her spine and her shoulder blade, cupping the back of her neck warmly beneath her hair. It was not the kiss of an angry man but a needy one.

She felt the strong muscles of his back, his lean waist, the tautness of his thighs pressed against hers. She felt the sensation of being drawn into him, of losing herself within him, and her head roared. His tongue tasted the texture of her own, invaded the secret recesses of her mouth, claiming her in intimacy and demand. She was helpless against the responses he incited, as any woman would have been. And even as the heat flooded her muscles and her breath caught in her throat and her body weakened and molded itself against him, she felt the sting of moisture in her eyes, the pain of protest in her chest.

Because he was right. She had not been angry because he had deceived her about last night's events and had possibly abetted a criminal attack. She was hurt because he had lied to her and then had used his power over her senses to distract her and disarm her. Because he had awakened her to emotions that were based on deception, and he had done it for no other reason than to protect himself. And he was doing it again.

The kiss ended slowly, with a caress on her cheek that caused tears to tremble on Cassie's lashes. His face was flushed gently with a passion that had nothing to do with temper, and she could feel the carefully controlled rise and fall of his chest, which was an effort to steady his breathing. His eyes were dark and intense, and he looked at her for a long time.

Cassie let her hands fall from around his waist, but she did not move away from him. She felt stripped and weak, nerve endings exposed and alive, unfulfilled yearning tightening and aching in every cell. Her heart was still thundering, her skin tingling, her breathing uncertain.

The intensity of the gaze that searched her face made her want to bury her face in his shirt and hide from him, to wrap her arms around him and silently seek his comfort for the hurt he had inflicted. But she compressed her lips and lifted her chin slightly, letting him read in her face what he would.

He saw only the truth. The hurt and the dignity, the wanting and the strength, the acknowledgment of the breach that lay between them. He saw the faint moisture that had gathered in the corner of one eye, the softness of vulnerability and the quiet waiting.

But in his eyes she could see nothing. Oh, there were a dozen emotions, all of them as rapid as the lightening and darkening of shadows on a windy day, all of them indeterminate, none of them clear. He looked at her, examining and absorbing all of her, and giving back nothing of himself.

Then he said softly, "Damn it." He lowered his gaze and stepped away.

She watched him as he moved over to the picket line

and untied his horse, giving it an absent pat on the flank before bending to lift his saddle. He worked with swift, efficient movements, tightening the cinch, adjusting the bit, checking the stirrups. And then he said, without turning, "I don't get involved in things that are none of my business, Cassie. I figured that if your brother had wanted you to know about the trouble we were having out here, he would have told you. When Red asked me to keep quiet, I did."

For a moment confusion overcame everything else. "Red asked you not to tell me? Why?"

He turned to face her, holding the reins loosely in his hand. "There was nothing you could do," he explained simply. "I guess he thought he was protecting you. Red's from an old-time school of thinking; he figures a man handles his own problems."

"But when I asked you," she insisted, a little shakily, "you should have told me. We could have gone to the sheriff last night—"

"I don't think so." He turned and mounted in a single fluid movement.

Cassie stared at him. Her senses were still reeling and her mind was fuzzy. Nothing he told her made sense anymore. "What do you mean?"

"For one thing…" He turned his horse to face her, and his expression was once again blank and controlled. "I don't talk to sheriffs. For another, I don't think you would have liked what I would have told him."

"What?" Her voice sounded hoarse. She thought he was going to ride away without answering and she wanted to take a step forward to detain him, but she couldn't make her legs move. "What would you have told him?"

He looked down at her for a moment, measuringly. She clenched her fists, willing him to answer, and then he did.

"The men who came up on Red from behind last night," he said simply, and with no more trace of expression in his tone than if he were commenting on the weather, "were riding Circle P horses."

Cassie looked at him blankly, her mind struggling to assimilate what he said and reeling with a dozen unanswered questions. She couldn't put any of them into words. She could only look at him, so tall and straight in the saddle, and remember the feel of his arms around her and the taste of his mouth on hers, and wonder how this could have happened to her, how she could have gotten so deeply and helplessly enmeshed in something she did not understand, something that had nothing to do with cattle thieves and mysterious desperadoes in the night.

He lifted the reins and started to go, and then he turned back. The horse was restless, but Logan held him in check. He looked down at Cassie soberly and he seemed a great distance away.

"One more thing," he said quietly. "When I kissed you last night it wasn't a game, and neither was what happened a few minutes ago. I'm sorry for it and I wish it hadn't happened, but scheming's just not my style. I'm not that sophisticated."

He gave his horse a nudge with his thigh and the animal turned instantly. In another moment they broke into a gentle gallop, and Cassie stood there until the sound of hoofbeats faded away.

JONAS ARRIVED just as they were making camp that afternoon. The campsite moved according to the area in which the crew would be working, and for the next four or five days the roundup would be focused on the herd that had made the foothills and high valleys its summer home.

Having heard the story of Cassie's adventure during the night, Rodney and Amy could not do enough to lighten her work load. When the wagon was packed up, Rodney insisted on driving the team while Cassie took a nap in back. After watching a few moments to make sure that Rodney had, indeed, driven before, Cassie took him up on it. She did not think for a moment she would be able to sleep, but she was grateful for the time alone with her racing thoughts and mangled emotions. She found a place on the wagon floor between a stack of tents and a fifty-pound sack of flour and closed her eyes, going over and over in her mind what Logan had said that morning. Before she knew it she was asleep.

The few hours' rest left her restored, if not refreshed, and she awoke with Logan still on her mind. What did he mean, he didn't talk to sheriffs? And what was he implying when he said the attackers were riding ranch horses—how did he know, what had he seen? How dare he presume to keep secrets from her about her own ranch?

But even thinking about it made her head ache like an overused muscle, and there was more than enough to demand her attention. She was grateful for the physical activity that pushed worry and uncertainty to the back of her mind.

They were driving stakes for the mess tent when the sound of the Jeep reached them, and everyone paused, moving expectantly toward the edge of the clearing. Although Cassie's enthusiasm did not quite match Amy's, she was aware of a swift and shameful sweep of relief. Jonas was here. Let him handle things from now on. It wasn't her problem anymore.

He pulled to a stop at the edge of the clearing, the back wheels skidding a little on the carpet of pine straw and crushed shrubs. Amy squealed, ''Daddy!'' and ran toward the Jeep as he stepped out. He looked exactly like what he was—a wealthy rancher in crisp Levi's, tailored western shirt and hand-tooled boots. He had always been a good-looking man—his hair was a richer nut-brown than Cassie's, his eyes sparkling hazel, and on his face their father's stern features looked appropriate. He had taken care of himself, too, and age had only improved him. He was still athletic and tanned, though not in the naturally rugged way Logan was, of course, and by all accounts exactly the kind of father any girl would be proud to claim.

Amy threw herself into his arms and he lifted her off her feet, laughing and giving her a playfully affectionate slap on the bottom. Watching them, Cassie felt a small stab of jealousy—not for Jonas, but for Amy and Jonas, who had each other. And that was strange, for she had watched the two of them interact many times before and had never been plagued by this niggling awareness of how empty her own life was and had always been. She couldn't understand why it was suddenly so painful to watch two people, even father and daughter, in such an easy and open exchange of affection.

Jonas set Amy on her feet and Cassie could see him trying to make his expression stern as he spoke to her. Cassie couldn't hear the words, but she could very well imagine the lecture that was taking place. And her turn would be next. With a weary sigh, she braced herself for it.

Rodney glanced at her perceptively. "I guess you and Mr. Parkington have some things to talk about. I'll finish setting up the tent."

"Thanks, Rodney. I'll be back to help as soon as I can."

Amy did not seem to be taking her father's reprimand

in the spirit it was meant, and an impish grin tugged at her lips as she caught his hand and began to pull him forward. "No, it was great fun, honestly," Cassie could hear her lie as they approached. "And really, Daddy, you wouldn't believe how educational it's been. I mean, you're always talking about broadening my horizons, but Cassie says you can learn things out here that you could never learn from books, and I never realized how deprived I've been."

Cassie groaned silently. Had she said that?

Jonas murmured, "Deprived, are you?" And he glanced at Cassie.

"Hello, Jonas," Cassie greeted him brightly. "Have a nice trip?"

"Fair," he responded, and his bland tone did not fool Cassie for a minute. He gave Amy's braided pigtail a tug and suggested, "Well, I don't want to deprive you of your 'educational' experience for another moment. Why don't you go on with what you were doing and let me talk to your aunt for a minute?"

Amy looked reluctant, for pounding tent stakes was not now, nor had it ever been, her idea of either fun or education. Before Amy's busy little mind could think of some excuse, Cassie smiled sweetly and handed her the hammer she had been holding. "We've got less than an hour before we have to start dinner," she pointed out. "Rodney can't do it by himself."

Amy looked from her aunt to her father, saw herself trapped and accepted the situation with good grace. "Don't go away," she called over her shoulder to her father as she started off. "You wouldn't believe all the things I have to tell you!"

Oh, yes, thought Cassie heavily, *you wouldn't believe…*

She stood there for a moment, looking everywhere but

at Jonas, trying to decide whether she would fare better
by taking an aggressive stance or by standing meekly and
letting him get his lecture out of his system. He had every
right to be angry with her. She had upset his trip and
endangered his daughter. He had left her in charge for
two days and in that time they had managed to lose a trail
cook and a foreman. Paperwork—important work for
which she had been responsible—was lying neglected in
the office. She had acted impulsively and irresponsibly
and had left behind a string of problems for him to solve.

So she thought it might be better if she waited for the
lecture.

She was surprised by the note of amusement in his
voice as he drawled, "Well, well. So it's the same old
Cassie after all. I was worried about you for a while there,
you know."

She couldn't disguise her amazement as her eyes met
his. "Do you mean you're not mad?"

His own eyes sharpened with astonishment. "Mad? Of
course I'm mad. I'm mad as hell. But at least you're behaving consistently. It wouldn't have occurred to you to
simply wait for me to return your call and solve the problem over the phone. Oh, no, you have to drop everything,
drag my teenage daughter out into the wilderness with a
bunch of wild, sex-starved men and pretend to be a cook
yourself. You, who haven't done so much as make a cup
of tea for yourself in over ten years!"

He was working up a good head of steam now, and
Cassie found herself actually beginning to relax. He, too,
was behaving consistently. "What if there had been some
emergency back at the house?" he demanded. "What if
I had needed to reach you from California, or what if
Amy's mother had shown up and found out what her
daughter was up to? Did you ever think of that? Or even

more likely, what if one of you had gotten sick or hurt out here miles from nowhere...how do you think that would've made me feel? I left you in charge. For God's sake, Cassie, won't you ever grow up?''

Cassie was genuinely chagrined. In fact, she hadn't thought of any of those things, and now she was beginning to realize that her actions had not only been hasty and ill-advised, but selfish and dangerous as well. And he hadn't even heard the worst of it. He didn't know about Red or the rustlers. But she met his eyes bravely. ''I am sorry, Jonas,'' she said honestly.

''You should be,'' he answered with satisfaction.

''But,'' she continued intrepidly, ''I didn't really have much choice and I couldn't think of anything else to do, and—''

''And, as it happens,'' he interrupted mildly, ''it seems to have turned out just fine. I hear you've done a good job.''

She stared at him, robbed unfairly of her defenses and justifications by the mischievous spark in his eyes.

''I've got to admit,'' he added, ''that I was just about blown away when I got your message. You've changed so much these past years that I'd almost forgotten who you really were. I should have remembered that you always thought it was easier to take the bull by the horns than to walk around the pasture. And I'm glad to see—'' Cassie couldn't believe the light of reluctant approval she thought she saw in his eyes. ''—that you haven't lost your touch. You did fine,'' he admitted, and then quickly grew grim again. ''But don't you ever do anything like this again...and certainly not with my daughter. You were lucky this time, that's all. What would have happened,'' he demanded sternly, ''if you had forgotten how to cook?''

Cassie grinned at him. "Then, instead of congratulating me, you'd probably be cutting me down from the highest tree right now." But her humor, and her relief, were short-lived. She tucked her hands into her pockets and started walking away from the camp, gesturing with a small movement of her head for Jonas to join her. "But it hasn't all been a bed of roses, Jonas," she confessed, keeping her voice low. "Last night—"

"I know. I stopped by on the way up and talked to Logan."

She paused, her face reflecting her surprise. "Well, I hope he told you more than he told me."

Jonas reached out and absently caught hold of a protruding branch, breaking off a sprig of juniper in his hand. His expression was sober, but not unduly concerned. "We have unaccounted-for losses every round-up," he said. "I've always suspected rustlers, but it was Logan who gave me the proof I needed."

"What is he?" Cassie demanded, incredulity underscoring the cynicism in her voice. "An undercover cop?"

Jonas smiled a little. "I know; he doesn't talk much. But he's a good man, and he knows what he's doing."

Cassie released a breath of relief, not even realizing how much she had dreaded this conversation with Jonas until the worst of it was over. Obviously, he approved of her decision in giving Logan Red's job. And she was spared the necessity of telling him about the rustlers and Red's injury. Things would be much easier now that they could get down to business.

"So you've known about the rustlers," she said. And she couldn't keep the note of pique out of her voice as she demanded, "Why didn't you tell me?"

He looked at her as though the thought had never occurred to him. "Why should I?"

"Because this ranch is half mine," she said, barely able to restrain her sarcasm and her impatience. "For heaven's sake, what is this—some kind of male conspiracy? First Red, then Logan and now you! What do you think, just because I'm a woman I shouldn't be bothered with details?"

Jonas looked guilty. "It's pretty much still a man's world out here, Cassie," he confessed. "Red is used to reporting to no one but me, and I...well, hell, Cassie." He looked at her with a strange mixture of embarrassment and reluctance in his eyes. "The ranch is half yours and you like to call yourself general manager, but as far as I knew—still know, for that matter—this was just another one of your little toys. Who knows how long you're going to stay? I've been running this ranch for almost twenty years, as well as everything else, but for you it's just something to keep you entertained. I didn't see any reason for you to get involved in anything important."

That hurt, mostly because it was true. She had only been amusing herself these past months, pretending to be of help to Jonas. They both knew she was no more experienced in running a ranch than she was in anything else, and Jonas had every right to think that she would soon get bored and move on. As a child she had been flighty; as a woman she had been pampered and self-indulgent; and since her divorce she had been restless and unsettled. Of course he would think her interest in the ranch was just another passing fancy.

Her hands tensed in her pockets and her voice sounded a little stuffy as she said, "So, you've just been humoring me."

He sighed. "Cassie, don't be hurt. You know you have a home with me as long as you want, but—"

She stopped, and she looked at him. "I don't want a

home with you," she said sharply. "I want *my* home. And this—" she released one hand from her pocket and made a sweeping gesture to include all that surrounded them "—is mine, just as much as it is yours."

She took a breath and added, more gently, but with a determination that surprised her as much as it did him, "This is not a game to me, Jonas. I didn't come here for a rest stop. I *am* involved, and I'm committed to our partnership, whether you are or not. I'm all grown up now," she said simply, "and I'm staying." The strange thing was that, until she said it, she had not even realized how true that was. She had come back here seeking her self, and she had found it. And she had known so, quietly and clearly, since last night when she had watched the sun set over the mountains with Logan.

Jonas looked at her, a slow acceptance of the truth dawning through the puzzlement in his eyes. He said softly, "You really mean that, don't you?"

She nodded.

But instead of the pleasure she had expected to see, a faint scowl crept across Jonas's handsome features, a troubled expression came into his eyes. "Cassie..."

And then he seemed to think better of it. He hesitated, then smiled and flung his arm around her shoulders in a brief, affectionate squeeze. "Well, welcome home, partner. I guess we have a lot to talk about when we get back to the house."

"Right," Cassie agreed decisively, and there was a new spring to her step as they walked on. "But right now let's talk about this rustling business. You've been in touch with the sheriff?"

He nodded. "There's not much he can do. On a spread this size, we more or less have to take care of our own problems." He frowned. "This attack on Red puts a different light on it, though. We're not equipped to deal with violence.''

"Did Logan tell you about the horses?"

"Yes, which means it could be some of our own men, or anyone else in the state. They drive a truck out here, rope the cattle on horseback, lead them to the truck and take them out. It would be a lot more convenient for them to stash some ranch horses somewhere, or even take them off our own picket, than to have to carry horses *and* cattle in their truck.''

"Well, if you know all that," Cassie said, exasperated, "what in the world is stopping you from having the sheriff out here to arrest them?"

He chuckled softly. "It sounds easy, doesn't it? We're only talking about several hundred square miles here, with a million and a half places to hide a truck filled with stolen cattle. We have to catch them in the act, which may be what Red tried to do last night, or catch them with evidence, and the odds aren't too good for that.''

"You certainly are taking this well," she accused.

He shrugged. "I don't like it, but we're not talking about whole herds. Six or seven head a week...it's not worth getting men hurt over, and it's one of the hazards of cattle ranching.''

"The sheriff should talk to Logan," she suggested. "After all, he was at the scene.''

Jonas shook his head. "Logan won't talk to the sheriff.''

Cassie stopped and looked at him. She was almost afraid of the answer, but she knew it was a question she had to ask. "Why not?"

Jonas met her gaze evenly, and she knew he was thinking the same thing she was. But he answered simply, "I don't know. Sometimes it doesn't do too much good to dig into a man's reasons, Cass. All I know is Logan's a good worker and I wouldn't want to lose him. Not in the middle of a roundup, anyway.''

They started walking again. ''I take it he has a shady past,'' she said with some difficulty.

''I don't know that, either.''

Cassie's throat felt tight, very tight, but she had to say it. ''Do you think…'' She couldn't quite look at Jonas. ''Do you think he might be involved, in some way, with the thefts?''

''No.'' There was no hesitation in Jonas's answer, for it was obviously a matter he had considered before. ''For one thing, it's been going on since before he arrived. For another, he's been too helpful in tracking them down.'' And he glanced at her. ''Why? Do you have some reason to think otherwise?''

''No.'' Relief poured through Cassie at having her own instincts about Logan confirmed. ''No, I don't think that's his style at all.''

Jonas was silent for a moment, and he was looking at Cassie very peculiarly. His gaze made her uncomfortable, and she wondered what he had read in her face when she talked about Logan. She turned, as nonchalantly as she could, and started back to camp. He kept up with her.

''Cassie,'' he said quietly after a moment, and there was reluctance in his voice. Jonas didn't like to interfere in other people's business. ''I said I didn't think he was a cattle thief, but I don't know what else he might be. The men we get out here are, well, not like the rest of the population. You know that. They all have their reasons for being here, and most of them we're better off not knowing. I'd form an opinion about Logan very slowly if I were you. And be careful, okay?''

Cassie gave a self-conscious laugh and dug her hands

deeper into her pockets. "Come on, Jonas, I'm not Amy."
She changed the subject quickly. "Speaking of whom…"
She glanced at him uneasily. "I'm sorry for involving her
in this. If I had known the danger—" she tried to keep
the note of accusation out of her voice "—of course I
wouldn't have done it. Anyway, if it's any consolation to
you, all that rhapsodizing she was giving you a while ago
was just bluff. She's ready to go home."

"Good. Then I think I'll make her stay another night."
There was a sly twinkle in his eye. "Logan and I talked
about a few other things, too. He seems to think you're a
pretty smart lady."

Logan had said that to Jonas? She burned to know what
else Logan had said about her but dared not to give Jonas
the satisfaction. She shrugged it off. "I remember how I
was at her age. I thought it was better for her to see how
things really were than to keep on fantasizing."

"It seems you were right. I found you another cook,"
he continued as they approached the camp. "But he won't
be able to come out for two days." His brow knit a little
in concern. "I could find a temporary, I guess, until then,
and I don't really like to ask you to stay…."

"I'll stay," Cassie said firmly, and was surprised both
at the quickness of the decision and at the relief that lightened her as she realized she did not have to go home with
Jonas today.

She must be crazy. This was awful, grueling work; she
needed a bath; she was desperately in need of sleep and
the cold, hard ground offered no appeal. The crew resented her and there were thieves in the night who had
already put one man in the hospital. But she wanted to
stay. She needed to feel useful; she needed the physical
activity and the smell of the mountain air and the vista of
open spaces around her. This was where she belonged,

and the discovery had come too soon for her to walk away from it now.

And there was Logan…

Jonas was looking at her peculiarly again, and she shrugged and tossed him a grin. "I'm a partner, remember? It's about time I started pulling my weight."

He chuckled and dropped a hand on her shoulder, and together they walked back into camp.

Chapter Six

Cassie had many faults. She was selfish, impulsive and occasionally shallow-minded. She lacked direction, discipline and self-confidence. She had not made much of her life and she was aware of it; she sometimes wondered if she had the stamina or the ambition ever to achieve anything worthwhile.

But shyness had never been one of her vices; neither had duplicity or reticence. Cassie spoke what was on her mind because she didn't know any other way, and it simply did not occur to her to allow what had passed between Logan and herself this morning to lie unsettled.

The afternoon meal was much more relaxed than it had been yesterday, due partly to the presence of Jonas. It did not matter that he was the boss; Jonas had a way of putting everyone at ease, and the men liked him. Of course, the cheerful atmosphere might have had something to do with the fact that the crew knew the arrival of Jonas meant the imminent departure of the two women who had so infringed upon their life-style these past hours, but even with the talk of rustlers and the shadow of Red's injury still hanging over them all, everyone's mood was greatly improved.

Logan finished eating early, and when he left the camp

Cassie did not think twice about following him. With her own meal half finished—trail rations were beginning to sit heavily in her stomach anyway—she started to push away from the table.

"I don't believe it," Amy was saying, and she turned to Cassie. "Daddy's teasing me, isn't he? I'll bet he told you the same story when you were little, just to make you crazy!"

Cassie looked at her in some confusion. She, Jonas, Amy and Rodney were sitting at the end of the community table, and Cassie had been so preoccupied with watching Logan that she hadn't been following the conversation at all. From down the table another man spoke up.

"Lord, Miss, your daddy didn't make up that story. Maybe *his* daddy did, or his daddy before him!"

There was a burst of laughter, and someone else added, "People have been looking for that gold since the first wagons crossed the Oregon Trail!"

From the open flap of the tent Cassie saw Logan move into the shelter of the trees, heading toward the stream. Amy was watching her expectantly, and she answered a little vaguely, "Oh, you mean Gallagher's gold. Yes, it's supposed to be around here somewhere. Although I never believed it."

"George Gallagher," explained Jonas, enjoying his daughter's skepticism, "crossed these mountains with a pack train of Spanish gold back in 1840 or thereabouts. Seems the American government had made some kind of deal with the Spanish—there was currency speculation going on even back then—and Gallagher's job was to see the gold safely back to the States. Remember, this was all wilderness, then." And he chuckled, glancing out at the vast empty vista that was visible through the tent flap. "Not like it is now, of course."

The chatter had died down considerably, for many of the men at the table had never heard the story. Cassie had, however, and she shifted impatiently. If she excused herself now everyone would know that she had gone to follow Logan—especially Jonas. And she was still enough of a little sister to be reluctant to invite teasing from her older brother, or worse, well-meant advice.

"Well, they were moving across these mountains, or around them, I should say, not too far from where we are right now, when they noticed they were being stalked by Indians. Well, Gallagher cached that gold and found himself a place to make a stand, which was probably not the smartest thing to do, because the only place he could find to stash the gold was in a valley, and the bad thing about fighting in a valley is that you're easily surrounded. Gallagher's party was completely wiped out—horses, mules, men. All except Gallagher himself, who escaped by hiding in a stream, underwater, breathing through a cattail, until the Indians had gone." Cassie had not heard that particular refinement to the story and was certain Jonas had embellished his own version. Jonas, in the tradition of the Old West, was a great storyteller. And Amy was fascinated.

"Some even say—" he added a touch of drama to his tone as he looked at Amy "—that Gallagher himself killed the last survivors of his own party, so that they wouldn't be able to come back for the gold before he did. You see, he couldn't get the gold out of the valley without help, and certainly not without pack animals.

"So he had to leave the gold behind while he went for help. He told the men he hired the general vicinity of the place where the gold was, but not the exact location. He couldn't be too careful. And on his way back for it, he died...rattlesnake bite, I think."

"Trail fever," corrected someone else.

"Wolf attack" was another opinion.

Jonas grinned. "At any rate, he died without ever telling anybody where the gold was, and here it supposedly lies to this day."

Amy's eyes were wide. "On our land?"

Jonas scooped up another forkful of beans. "It wasn't ours back then, of course."

Amy looked at him for a long time, speculatively. And then she decided, firmly, "You're making it up."

"No, he's not." Rodney had been tautly silent throughout the entire recitation, looking not so much intrigued as uncomfortable. Now he met Amy's eyes defiantly and spoke with a force that attracted more attention than he had doubtless intended. "He's not making it up; it's a true story. My mother's maiden name was Gallagher," he said proudly. "George Gallagher was her grandfather."

Cassie did not pause to consider whether his claim was true or whether he had seized upon a particularly clever method of impressing the girl he was so obviously smitten with. It didn't matter and she was hardly interested. She took advantage of the half-scornful, half-curious attention turned upon Rodney to slip quietly away.

Cassie looked around the campsite as she stepped outside, but Logan had not returned. He could not have gone far, and she took the path he had taken through the small, sparsely wooded area that separated the campsite from a rocky stream that poured out of the mountains. She had gone about twenty-five yards, with the sound of her feet crunching softly on the carpet of deciduous leaves rising above the sound of slow-flowing water, then suddenly she hesitated. Trail conditions being what they were, a man might have more reason to seek privacy than to be alone with his thoughts. Did she really want Logan to think she was stalking him like a schoolgirl? But what other chance might they have to talk alone, away from Jonas and the others?

As she hesitated, debating whether to turn back or to call out and warn him of her presence, his voice spoke matter-of-factly. "I'm here, Cassie. Come on around."

She followed the sound of his voice straight ahead a few yards to where a huge, mossy boulder sheltered her view of the grassy banks of the stream. He was standing there, pulling on his shirt.

His hair was wet, his feet were bare and there were damp splotches on his jeans, as though he had pulled them on over wet legs. But it was his chest that drew her attention, as naturally it would.

His shoulders were lean and corded, rather than bunched with muscles. His collarbone was straight and definitive, flowing into a strong neck and a firm, taut chest. The skin below his neck was not tanned, and it gleamed with moisture. His chest was covered with a silky mat of wet, straight dark hair, a perfect inverted triangle that spanned the breadth of his chest and narrowed into his waistband. As she watched he closed two buttons at the bottom of his shirt and tucked it into his jeans in a gesture that was casual and unself-conscious, but that exuded an innocent eroticism which made Cassie's cheeks sting.

Fool, she chided herself. *You'd think you'd never seen a man get dressed before.*

"I thought a swim would clear my head," Logan said, and he seemed completely unaware of her scrutiny. "I was beginning to feel the effects of a thirty-six-hour-day." He did not even glance at her as he finished buttoning his shirt. Cassie noticed, just before he pulled the material closed with the middle button, that his nipples, brought to prominence by the movement of his chest muscles, were erect and hardened by the evening air on his wet skin.

He dropped to the ground to pull on his socks. "If you had the same idea," he suggested in the same mild, pleasant tone, "I'll be out of your way in a minute."

Cassie glanced at the stream, clear and slow-moving against the gently sloping bank. It was wide enough to swim across but not so deep that a man couldn't stand up in it, and she wondered briefly about what it would feel like to strip off her clothes, naked to the mountains and the sky and the wild creatures, and step into its depths. She hadn't done anything like that since she was a child. It would be cold, and all her nerve endings would be shocked to life. And when she stepped out the warmth of another body against hers, a strong and male naked body, would be like an electric current. Arms would enfold her; heat would penetrate her. It would be like being born again.

She was surprised at the swift, sure course her thoughts had taken, and embarrassed. She watched Logan pull on one boot, and she swallowed in a tight throat, trying to assume nonchalance. "How did you know it was me?"

He reached for the other boot. "I know the sound of your footsteps," he answered casually. The muscles of his thighs tightened against the soft fabric of his jeans as he pushed his foot into the boot, tugging it over his calf. He reached for his hat, starting to rise. "Well, it's all yours."

"No, Logan, I don't want to swim."

He glanced at her, and she thought there was a hint of gentle mockery in those placid gray eyes. "Of course. I guess the only kind of water you're used to comes out of a tap at perfect bath temperature."

A muscle in her jaw clenched in instinctive self-defense and she thrust her chin forward with unconscious belligerence. "I'll have you know I grew up in these mountains. I was skinny-dipping in these streams before it was even fashionable, so don't go acting the snob with me."

He lifted one eyebrow mildly, and amusement played with the shape of his lips. "Was that what I was being? I beg your pardon. Seems like I'm always misjudging you."

He clamped his hat down on his head and got up, starting to move past her.

"Logan, wait." She reached out a hand to stop him, but let it fall short of touching him. He stopped and looked at her questioningly, and Cassie felt foolishly tongue-tied. She hadn't imagined this would be so hard. She still couldn't understand why it should be. He was waiting, looking at her, and her heart was beating rapidly. She could see the faint dew of moisture that still gleamed on the dark hairs below the open buttons of his collar. She said, "Couldn't you stay awhile, and talk?"

He hesitated, and she could read nothing in the eyes that went over her face slowly, consideringly, yet as though from a great distance. His expression was nothing more than polite, and he said simply, "No. I don't think I can."

Cassie tried to ignore the jolt of electricity that went through her, the sudden subtle trill of recognition that was as plain between them as the sound of the stream, the chatter of the birds in the trees. His face was bland, his tone was matter-of-fact, but the unspoken truth was loud. He couldn't stay because they were alone. And every time they were alone they ended up in each other's arms.

There was another truth, just as plain, just as easy to read, but it crept up on Cassie so subtly she had no chance to defend against it. *I want him,* she thought simply, clearly. *I want him the way I've never wanted another man, not even Greg in the beginning. And he knows it.*

There was nothing surprising about that, certainly nothing unpredictable or shocking. She had been attracted to Logan from the first moment, on an instinctive level. She had responded eagerly to his kisses and she had been aware of desire unfolding its wings within her. It was just that, by making the admission to herself she had committed herself to dealing with those desires, and it no longer felt like a fantasy. It felt very real.

And Logan knew it.

Her hands went into her pockets, and she said in a rush, "I wanted to apologize for what I said this morning, and the way I acted."

His eyes were calm and quiet. But behind the screen of crystal-gray was a poised alertness and an intense perception that seemed to strip away Cassie's quickly formed layers of self-protection. He seemed to be examining her, probing her unspoken thoughts and doubting what he read there.

He smiled faintly. It was an expression that did not entirely reach his eyes. "Does that mean you don't think I'm a cattle thief any longer?"

Cassie flushed and lowered her eyes. "I never thought that, not really." And then she sighed and looked at him. "I just don't understand you, Logan. Nothing about you makes sense."

"I didn't know it was supposed to."

She took a step forward, almost as though to prevent him from moving past her, although he had made no move to do so. "Will you just tell me one more thing? And it's not an accusation or…it's not anything, really. I'm just curious. How did you know what kind of horses they were riding?"

He seemed to relax, and a smile lightened his eyes. "I thought it was going to be something hard. They left fairly clear tracks," he answered with a shrug. "And there was a moon."

She frowned a little. "You mean you can tell what kind of horse a man is riding just by the tracks?"

"There's no trick to it. There's not much to look at around here all day besides tracks, you know. You get to recognize them after a while."

"Just like you could recognize me by the sound of my footsteps?"

She had not realized before how close they were standing. He seemed to have forgotten about leaving, and his eyes moved over her face, downward to her collarbone, which lay exposed by the opening of her flannel shirt, across the slope of her slender shoulders, and rested finally and briefly on the swell of her breasts against the soft material. There was gentleness and an almost absent preoccupation in his eyes as they met hers again.

"That," he admitted, "and other things. The length of your stride, the way you move aside the brush with your hands instead of your body, the sound of the leaves against your clothes...your smell..." He lifted his hand and lightly grasped a strand of her hair where it feathered against her cheekbone, and the curve of his smile was brief and playful. "Like vanilla extract."

Cassie's laugh sounded a little choked. She was breathing a bit more rapidly than before. "No one's ever told me that before." The moment seemed suspended in expectancy. He held her hair, just a wisp of her hair, between his thumb and forefinger; he seemed absorbed by the texture. They were standing so close that Cassie could see the gentle rise and fall of his chest and smell the freshness of stream water on his skin and his hair. The smallest inflection of movement could have broken them apart or brought them into each other's arms. He did not move. And neither did she.

"I think," she added softly, searching his face, "that you are indeed a unique man, Logan."

He met her eyes, and his voice was a little husky as he answered with a half smile, "No one's ever told me that before, either."

His hand, large and rough, moved lightly over her cheek and around to caress the shape of her skull in a gentle, fluid movement that could have been a prelude to drawing her closer or stepping away. He did neither, but dropped his hand lightly and naturally on her shoulder in an impersonal, almost brotherly gesture, and the moment was gone. "Come on," he said, "I'll walk you back."

Disappointment tasted sharp in the back of her throat, for he must have known as well as she did that that was not what she wanted to hear from him. Awareness lingered like a memory, for they both knew the moment between them should have had a much different ending.

After a few steps she said, as naturally as possible, "Jonas found a new cook. He'll be out in a couple of days."

"I guess you were glad to hear that." His tone, like hers, was distant and preoccupied, as though he were reciting words that had nothing to do with what he was thinking.

"Not really." She stopped as he held back a branch for her, and looked at him. "Thanks for running interference for me with Jonas, by the way."

He looked mildly surprised, though whether or not that was affectation Cassie could not be sure. "Did I? I didn't mean to."

"Oh, I think you did. And I appreciate it." Then, instead of preceding Logan onto the wooded path he indicated, she turned and walked over to a rock that made a natural seat overlooking the stream. She wasn't ready to go back to camp yet, back to dirty dishes and noisy men and Jonas's authoritative charm and Amy's sullenness over the fact that she would not be returning to her own bed and makeup mirror tonight. Too much was fighting for attention in her head—new ideas and ideas that were not so new, and most of them had to do with Logan. She wanted to be alone and listen to the stream and try to get a perspective on what she thought was happening to her.

"You go on ahead," she told him. "I think I'll sit here for a while."

Logan hesitated for a moment and then came over to her. The action surprised her as much as did his easy grin. "This is the 1980s, you know. I don't think your brother will shoot me if we come out of the woods together. Besides—" he dropped down to the grass next to her, taking off his hat "—I don't guess it would be very chivalrous of me to leave you alone out here with desperadoes running around."

Cassie chuckled, tossing him a challenging glance. "You are also a very strange man," she told him. "One minute you talk about the 1980s, the next about chivalry and desperadoes, like a character out of the Old West. So which century are you in, anyway?"

"Sometimes I don't know myself," he admitted. He ran his hand through his damp hair, separating it into coal-black curls and waves that fell partially over his forehead and dampened his collar. "Maybe the thing I like best about living out here is that it doesn't matter."

She looked at him curiously. "So where are you—" She started to ask where he was from, but caught herself with a wry shake of her head. "Sorry, I forgot. You don't answer personal questions."

"That's right." He said it easily and without shame, and he leaned back on one elbow, watching the play of the late sunlight on the water.

"And you don't make friends, or get involved in other people's business or have relationships..." She had meant to sound casual, even playful, and was irritated with the note of accusation that seemed to underscore her voice. Perhaps, she thought bleakly, it was nothing more than his persistent air of mystery that fascinated her. Maybe it was a kind of game he played, to trap the unwary. Some men charmed with words, others with silence. But if his reticence was a calculated device, it was a very effective one, and she couldn't help resenting that.

He moved his eyes back to her, his gaze clear and steady. He said simply, "That's right." There was a very definite meaning to his tone, almost a warning.

"Then why did you go out of your way today to make sure Jonas got a good report on me?" she insisted. "Especially after..." She glanced down at her hands, uncomfortably. "Well, we didn't exactly part on the best of terms this morning."

"I didn't go out of my way," he answered. "I just volunteered a little information. I didn't think you needed any more trouble than you already had. You've done a good job out here; it couldn't hurt to let your brother know it."

"I still think it was a nice thing to do."

He chuckled, turning his gaze back to the quiet movement of the stream. "Now wouldn't that be something?" he murmured. "If underneath it all I turned out to be a nice guy?"

"I don't think I would be very surprised."

''You don't know anything about me.'' His manner remained relaxed as he lay half-stretched out there on the bank, but his tone seemed to tighten a little.

But Cassie was growing used to his fluctuations in mood and was not intimidated. ''So whose fault is that?'' she challenged mildly, and then she shrugged. ''Anyway, you don't know much more about me than I do about you, so we're even.''

He glanced at her from beneath his half-lowered lids. His lashes were incredibly thick, as black as his hair and unfairly beautiful. ''Oh, I know more about you than you realize.''

''That I grew up in Wyoming, that I own half a ranch, that I'm divorced,'' she replied carelessly. ''That could apply to half the women in this part of the state.''

''That you're stubborn and headstrong, that you're not very responsible and that you're not used to thinking out decisions before you make them,'' he elaborated effortlessly. ''You're not as confident of yourself as you used to be, and you worry about that. You worry about a lot of things. You're a drifter, just like me. The only difference is, we're drifting down two separate roads. I do it by choice; you do it because you don't know any other way.''

His voice sobered a fraction with that, and Cassie's breath was suspended, startled by his perception, touched by this secret invasion of her inner self. He had known her barely a day, yet he knew her better than did the members of her own family…better, perhaps, than she did herself. She felt as though a part of herself had been opened to him and claimed by him, yet he was a stranger. That should have made her feel vulnerable and defensive, yet, strangely, it made her feel warm. Uncertain, but right.

And then, injecting lightness into his tone, he added,

"And I know that when you're nervous you put your hands in your pockets." He captured her hands lightly between his fingers just as she was moving to hide her hands in her pockets. His eyes sparked with teasing. "Because you're trying to break the habit of chewing your nails."

His fingertip ran lightly over the broken edges of her nails, and she laughed nervously. "Very observant! Add to that the fact I smell like vanilla, Lord knows why, and you have a complete personality profile."

"And," he added softly, "the fact that you're at a particularly vulnerable time in your life right now." He held her hand lightly in his, and his forefinger moved across the backs of her knuckles down to the faint white scar of a wedding band on her third finger. He lifted his eyes to hers, and his gaze was quiet and open, poised but not expectant. "A really nice guy wouldn't take advantage of that, would he?"

Her heart was pulsing in her throat. The warmth of his callused fingertip, gently caressing her ring finger, sent a tingling stream of awareness all the way up her arm. Her voice was little above a whisper. "Is that what you're doing?"

He answered huskily, "I'm beginning to think it's the other way around."

But when he lifted his hand to touch her arm gently, there was no clear demarcation as to who made the first move. He reached for her, but already she was coming to him. His arms came around her as she sank to the grass beside him, her hands slipping behind his neck. He brought one knee up to caress her hip, encircling her with his legs as well as his arms, but he did not kiss her immediately.

Their faces were very close, almost touching. Her

breath was very rapid, and she had to part her lips. He watched the movement. She could feel his tense, coiled muscles that reflected the same expectant awareness that mesmerized her, and the moment spun out forever. Anticipation, absorption, sensation. His skin was warm against her fingers, the damp edges of his hair cool and silky on the backs of her hands. Her fingertips trembled as she moved them around to touch his throat, and she saw his pupils darken. She could feel the pulse of the vein at the side of his neck, strong and rapid. Then she could feel his breathing and her own stopped as he touched her lips, very lightly, very briefly, with his. A taste, nothing more. His fingers moved around to her spine, over her ribs, gently caressing the side of her breast.

She was trembling and her eyes closed. He kissed her fully then, with a deep and growing urgency that took her unprepared. His mouth opened over hers, tasting her, drawing her in, and his hand closed over her breast, molding her with heat and pressure. There was nothing deliberately skilled about his kiss; there was no artifice to his lovemaking. Rather, it was a simple statement of unvarnished passion. There was something raw and primitive in his touch, in the hunger of his kiss, that opened a savage response in Cassie, and the sensation was shocking, a rapid escalation of needs and responses that whirled too fast out of her control and took her outside herself, beyond anything she recognized about herself but Logan and her desire for him.

He held her cradled in his arms, her head supported in the crook of his elbow and her legs lightly trapped under the pressure of his thighs. Her throat was bared to the nip of his teeth, the sweeping exploration of his tongue, the deep and drawing kisses that penetrated far into her core. Her fingers felt heavy and feverish as they moved beneath his collar and through the heavy, damp length of his hair, then impatiently around to the few inches of exposed flesh at his chest. Distantly the stream breathed like the wind through the trees; the deepened chill of the evening did nothing to cool her heated, tingling flesh, and she could not even think anymore. Her body ached for him, simply and purely, with no explanation and no excuses, a predictable reaction like that of two explosive chemicals accidentally mixed. She arched her neck to taste the texture of his roughened cheek, the smoothness of his earlobe, and instinctively, anxiously, their mouths slid together again.

Arousal had never come so quickly for Cassie before, or so strongly. He had but to touch her, his hand slipping beneath her shirt to move restlessly over her ribs, his mouth melded against hers and telling her of all the power, all the need, all the pent-up longing that was hers. Daylight was dying around them as Cassie, in his arms, came to life for the very first time.

His fingers slipped downward, insinuating themselves beneath the waistband of her jeans, and everything within Cassie stilled into coil-spring expectancy. His fingertips caressed the soft, aching flesh of her abdomen with brief and hesitant promise, and the blossoming ache deep within her became a specific, painful need. She arched her hips, pressing helplessly into him, her arms tightened around his shoulders, and the smothered sound that came from her throat was like a sob.

Then he gathered her close, restless hands moving over the shape of her buttocks, her spine, the delicacy of her neck beneath her tangled hair. She could feel the unsteady rush of his heated breath against her ear, and he whispered, "Ah, lady…what you do to me.…"

And then, deliberately, his fingers fastened around her

arms, his lips caressed her cheek and he moved away. He freed her from the circle of his legs, her protesting arms loosened their embrace, and he turned to sit beside her on the grass.

Her head was spinning and her muscles were like rubber. Her face burned from the abrasion of his and from the heat of passion, which would not quickly die. The knot of unfulfilled longing that had tightened in her womb loosened by painful degrees, and her body registered the shock of sudden loss even as her mind throbbed with confusion.

His shoulders were strong and square and turned away from her, but she could hear his breathing, and it was as broken as her own. The quality of the day seemed to have changed from lazily sunlit to violet and subdued. The stream ran more quietly and even the air seemed bruised and heavy.

Cassie drew her legs up and wrapped her arms around them, tightening her muscles to try to stop the trembling. *I would have done it,* she realized slowly and through the veil of confusion and sensual impulses that still shrouded her mind. *I would have made love with him here on the grass in the middle of this clearing where anyone might come by and see.... And I wouldn't have thought about it once.* She was a grown-up woman; she had been married, civilized and refined. She should no longer be victim to irrational impulses and demands for instant gratification. And never, even in her wildest youth, had she looked for brief encounters that promised no more than physical satisfaction, for passion was the one area of her life that had always been tempered by thought.

But no one had ever affected her as Logan had before. And no matter how hard she tried, she could not find shame or regret. She had to ask, a little hoarsely, "Why did you stop?"

He reached into his pocket for rolling paper and tobacco, and Cassie noticed that his hands were not quite steady. He replied, without looking at her, "One of us had to."

That was not the answer, and this time it would not suffice. And he knew it.

When the cigarette was rolled and he had struck a match, he looked at her. His eyes were still dark and lit by the fire that was slow in dying, his face was flushed like hers. But his tone was steady and sober. He said, "Sex is not a game to me, Cassie. It never has been."

She tensed in instant defense. "And you think it is to me?"

"I don't know," he answered honestly. "I guess things are different for you, in the life you come from. But for me there are a few simple rules, and one of them is that guys like me don't sleep around with women like you. That's all there is to it."

Cassie's cheeks scorched with renewed heat and her eyes kindled a fire that had nothing to do with passion. Her linked hands tightened around her knees and the knuckles shone white. "I see," she said stiffly. Her throat felt raw and it wasn't until she spoke that she realized the tightness in her chest was more from hurt than anger. He had no right to hurt her. She hadn't expected it. "Women like me, who chase after any long-legged cowboy who crosses their path, out for a good time with no questions asked. Well, I can see why you would have to be careful."

"That's not what I mean," he said harshly. He brought the cigarette to his lips and inhaled deeply, his eyes narrowing against the smoke. He exhaled in a breath, and then turned his eyes back to her deliberately. "You were the one who was so anxious to rid your niece of her cowboy illusions. Maybe you ought to give some thought to the possibility that you're spinning out a fantasy of your own.''

His words were sharp and well aimed and they hit their target. They centered in her chest and took her breath away, and for a moment she could not even speak. Oh, she had had a fantasy all right, but not the one he believed. Her fantasy had been that he knew her, that he cared for her, that beneath the hesitance and the withdrawal he felt the same kind of instinctive touching with her that she had felt with him. That he understood her.

He saw the flash of brilliance in her eyes and could not mistake it for anything other than what it was—the film of tears, hated and childlike, but unpreventable nonetheless. For the briefest instant his expression softened, something crossed his face that looked like the need to hold her, to comfort her, and his eyes were shadowed with regret. But then, almost instantly, his face tightened again, and there was nothing there but bitterness—but it was directed at himself and not her.

''Damn it, Cassie,'' he said shortly, ''look at me!'' He made a brief, terse hand gesture that scattered cigarette ash on the grass. ''I'm thirty-six years old and I don't have a steady job. Do you think there's something glamorous about the way I live? When I'm not sitting on a horse behind a herd of cattle, do you think I just ride off into the sunset and wait for the next episode? Hell, no. I pump gas, I load cargo onto flatbed trucks, I dig ditches…whatever it takes to keep food in my mouth. I sleep in truck stops and roadside motels and I've never had more than a hundred dollars in my pocket at one time. I don't even own a car, for God's sake!''

He turned away from her and drew on the cigarette

again, every line on his face etched in pain and self-restraint. He exhaled the smoke slowly, in a long breath that seemed to be designed to expel tension. When he spoke again his voice was somewhat gentler, and he did not meet her eyes. "All I'm trying to do," he said, "is to live my life and stay out of trouble."

"Poor Logan!" It burst through Cassie in a sudden explosion of bitterness and hurt, and the eyes that once had burned with tears now flashed with anger. "Nothing seems to go your way, does it? All you want is to be left alone and in less than a week you've been mauled by both the boss's daughter and the boss's sister. How difficult it must be for you!" She sprang to her feet, her trembling hands bunched into fists, her voice ringing with shaky sarcasm. "Please do accept my apologies—we Parkington women will try to find our amusements elsewhere!"

She turned sharply to go and he was beside her, his fingers steely on her wrist. She whirled angrily and tried to jerk away, but he wouldn't let go. His face was so damnably calm, his eyes so quiet and gentle, that she wanted to hit him. They faced each other for a long moment, her eyes spitting fury and hurt, his absorbing and accepting blame, and then he dropped his cigarette to the ground; he lifted his other hand to caress her head. Before she knew it her face was against his shoulder and he was holding her.

His hands were gentle on her back, and she could feel his quiet breathing. She leaned against him, her arms hanging limply at her sides, afraid to touch him, desperately biting back the tears that had no place here and would only embarrass her. She whispered, after a long time, "I'm sorry. I acted like a child." She lifted her face and stepped back a little. She faced him bravely. "I didn't mean to complicate things for you. I'm not used to analyzing my emotions. I wanted to make love with you, and it's been a long time since I wanted that...maybe, not ever as much as I wanted you." It was difficult to say, but Cassie did not flinch from his steady gaze, or from the low light that was beginning to burn far back within his eyes again. "I thought you wanted the same thing, I guess...or I didn't think at all, and..." She released a short breath and had to lower her eyes. "This is all very awkward and I'm sorry."

His hands remained lightly on her waist. She could feel the heat of his fingers through the material of her shirt. Her heart was pounding slowly. He said softly, "I did want the same thing, Cassie. I still do."

She looked up at him, suddenly shy, strangely afraid. Though whether she was afraid it would begin all over between them or end now, she could not be sure.

He lifted his hand and lightly stroked her hair. His eyes went over her face, searching, and a faint smile touched his lips, as he asked, "How could you think otherwise? Not just because I'm male and you're female, but because...you're different. Special." The smile faded as slowly as he dropped his hand, and his lashes obscured his eyes. "That's what makes it complicated," he said with a sigh.

Cassie could barely hear her own voice for the pounding of her heart. Something important was happening here, something she had suspected all along but had not fully recognized until this moment, and it frightened her. Yet it compelled her. She had to strain to form the words. "I—you're special for me, too. I don't know why, but...I think we both know it's true."

He looked at her, probing and intense. She did not shy away from him but let him read in her eyes what he would. "Cassie," he asked quietly, "could you sleep with a man and then forget about him in the morning? Just walk away and not look back?"

She held his gaze. Nothing inside her was certain; everything was in turmoil. "I don't know," she admitted. "No one's ever asked me that before."

"You'd better think about it," he replied, and his eyes were deep and gray and very sober. "Because that's how it would have to be with me. You know that."

Yes, she knew that. That was another thing she had known all along.

She lowered her eyes, uncertain as to what to say or even to feel. His hands slid down to her wrists and held them gently. Then he leaned forward and pressed a light, very tender kiss on her cheek. The gesture was so sweet, so unexpected and so uncharacteristic that it brought tears to her eyes.

When he released her hands, she turned and walked quickly back to camp, alone.

Chapter Seven

The Crossing

VII

In the early days, people were always moving on or passing through, and the West was the place they came to do it. The land was synonymous with freedom, and though many came across with the notion of settling down and building a life, few ever got around to doing it. The men who came had something behind them or something ahead of them, pushing them on, and the wide, rolling plains were just an excuse to keep moving. And a man who had all he could do to keep on surviving didn't have much chance to think on building a life for himself. So he crossed that next mountain, navigated that next stream, pushed on just a little farther to see what was around the bend. And pretty soon it got to be a way of life.

But one thing no man could resist, however independent and restless he might be, was leaving his mark behind him. Those early pioneers left trails and ferries; later ones left railroads and bridges. They never meant to, nor did they realize they were doing it, but they had opened up the West.

For where there was a road, someone was sure to take it. The farmers came, cutting up the soil and building their fences. But a farmer needed sons to work his land and remember his efforts, and for that he needed a woman. The women came, and nothing was ever the same after that.

They brought with them schools and churches and table manners and dress goods. The shopkeepers followed, and the freight drivers, and the builders, and with them came law and order and government by the consent of the majority. Civilization was born.

Times were changing. Drifting used to be a way of life; now it was something to be ashamed of. The farmers used to be looked upon, not with contempt, but with a sort of haughty disdain from the height of the saddle. Now there were more plowed fields than grazing meadows, and most all the land was fenced.

Jim could see an era passing away and there was sadness in him for it. But the worst part was, Jim was afraid he was changing, too.

AMY AND JONAS LEFT the next morning, and the relief with which Amy anticipated the end of her adventure made Cassie smile in weary self-congratulation. She had made her point but was only now beginning to wonder whether it was worth it.

When Amy departed with dreams in her head of a bubble bath and color TV, Cassie felt a brief tug of weakness in her that made her resent being left behind. She wanted a bath, too, and comfortable pajamas and a soft bed. She was tired of the taste of dust in her mouth and the back-breaking, basically unrewarding work. Maybe Jonas was right about her after all—she had no staying power. Once the novelty had worn off she, like Amy, was ready to pack up and seek easier entertainment.

But then, angrily and determinedly, she rejected the notion. She was not a flighty teenager like Amy anymore, and she had worked too long and too hard for self-discovery to give up on herself now. She was too mature to indulge in self-pity simply because her lover had rejected her.

She knew that was what it was. She wanted to go home because leaving a crew of hungry men, disappointing Jonas and turning her back on her own newly acquired sense of self-worth would be easier than facing Logan again.

Throughout that long day she busied herself with preparing vegetables for the evening meal, filling out the supply requisitions, scrubbing the inside of the wagon and putting everything into shipshape condition for the arrival of the new cook the next day. She pretended to carry on conversations with Rodney—who, now that Amy was gone, had become very talkative, and most of what he wanted to talk about had something to do with Amy— and she even found some time to do some reading. But not once, not for a single moment during the entire day, was Logan off her mind.

Every time she thought about the previous evening her throat went tight with embarrassment. He was right, of course. They were talking about more than just social differences or a conflict of life-styles. They were polar opposites regarding an entire set of values. It might have been different if Cassie were the type of woman who could engage in careless, meaningless sex, or if that were all she wanted from him. She was honest enough to admit to herself that, while sexual attraction had composed the basis of her initial interest in Logan—and was still an enormous part of it—she wanted more than just physical contact from him. And that was very, very foolish.

It sounded despicable beyond belief to allow such things as money and social class to stand in the way of Grand Passion, but only in fairy tales did those factors not matter. Cassie had been raised in a certain way, taught to value certain things, and there was no possibility, at this late date, of her ignoring their reality. She had never thought of herself as a rich woman, but hers was a world of credit cards and checkbooks, shopping malls and chic diets. She had despised Greg's preoccupation with frivolities and appearances, but what could she possibly have in common with a man who didn't even earn enough to pay income tax? She knew about budgets, but she had never done without the necessities of life. She had grown up in an environment that encouraged hard work and had never painted a rosy picture about life in general, but she had never missed a meal unless it was of her own choosing. She had no idea what kind of life Logan had led or the type of man it took to lead it. They simply came from two different worlds.

She told herself all this, and she told herself again, and it was all reasonable, logical and perfectly sensible. None of it, no matter how often she examined it, made the slightest bit of difference in the way she was feeling.

Because she *wanted* to know him; she wanted to unlock the mysteries that separated him from her and to let him become a part of her. For all the very real and logical barriers that stood between them, she felt she did know him, already, on some deep and important level that neither of them was quite able to recognize yet.

It was impossible, of course. She could not become involved with him. For one thing, he would not allow it;

for another, there was no future. And the future had always been very important to Cassie.

Logan realized that, when Cassie refused to. It was precisely what he had been trying to tell her last night. They had no place together. Making love would only make them both wish things could be different.

Her life was complicated enough. She must have been insane to imagine, even for a moment, that an entanglement with a remote and mysterious cowboy would do anything but multiply her problems. Logan was right. The best thing they could do was to stay away from each other.

That was precisely why facing him that evening was so difficult.

He tipped his hat to her as he came through the chow line, a polite gesture that most of the other men performed by habit. She was a woman and she was the boss; some respect was due. There was nothing more to Logan's attitude than that, except when she smiled at him, a little distantly, a little stiffly, and she thought she saw a flicker of something strange in his eyes—uncertainty, perhaps, or regret. But she did not have time to analyze it, even if she had wanted to, for his tray was filled and he was moving away.

Cassie ate outside alone that evening for more than one reason. Being the only woman in the tent made her as uncomfortable as it made everyone else, for she had already learned the men felt as though they had to put on their Sunday school manners when she was around. She was afraid that if she stayed, Logan would feel obligated to sit with her, to make her feel at ease and to pretend there was nothing more between them than a normal employer-employee relationship. She didn't want to put either of them through that strain.

The supply truck was due the next day at the same time

as the cook, and she had scraped the bottom of the barrel
for that night's meal. The meatball stew was original and
inventive, and the side dish of beans was well seasoned
with onions and garlic, but nothing had much taste to
Cassie. Even the apple cobbler, which she had seasoned
with spices brought from home, didn't hold much appeal.
She sat on a camp chair beneath a fragrant spruce and
picked at her food.

"It's a shame to waste all that food. It's pretty good
tonight."

It was Logan's voice, and Cassie's heart lurched before
determinedly resuming its normal rhythm, though beating
a bit more strongly than before. He had come upon her
from behind, and Cassie had not even heard him. Among
his other talents, Logan had the natural stealth of a wild
animal on the prowl.

"I'm getting a little tired of picking the sand out of my
food, I guess," she replied, as casually as possible. "I
don't have much of an appetite." She set her plate aside
and looked up at him.

He reached into his pocket and took out a small black
book. "The tally up until today," he explained, handing
it to her. "Your brother said you kept the records. You'll
want to transcribe this into your ledger."

Cassie took it from him, flipping through the pages
briefly before tucking it into her pocket. She glanced up
at him. "It sounds like you know a little more about
ranching than the average laborer."

That opaque screen came over his eyes again, the withdrawal she had learned to expect whenever she tried to
pin him down to anything that made him more than anon-
ymous. Only this time it did not last. He took out a cigarette, already rolled, and he said, "I grew up on a small
spread. In Texas."

The significance of that statement, small and relatively unrevealing as it was, was not lost on Cassie. For the first time he had shared something of himself, of his past and his identity, with her. He had done it willingly, with conscious decision. It marked the tenuous beginning of a change between them—nothing dramatic and nothing promised, but a tentative step in the right direction. She accepted the offering as the highly valued gift it was, from that moment on, to accept Logan on his own terms.

She smiled up at him gently, a little shyly. "Was that so hard?" she asked softly.

His eyes reflected a moment's weary amusement and resigned tenderness, and he shook his head a little. "More than you know."

He struck a match, and when the cigarette was lit she thought he would walk away. Instead, he dropped down beside her, sitting back on his heels. For a moment he was silent, smoking and watching the mountains in the distance, and Cassie made no move to draw him out. Then he said, "I don't deliberately try to be mysterious, Cassie. It's just that sometimes looking back is not a happy thing. A man gets bogged down in his past and pretty soon he can't do anything else but look back. It's even harder when you can't ever go back."

What would you go back to, Logan? she wondered. *And would someone be waiting for you there?*

She said, "None of us can go back. Not really."

There was a note of wistfulness in her tone that she had not intended, but he caught it, and he glanced up at her. "It sounds like you wish you could."

Cassie looked down at her fingernails, and then self-consciously closed her hands. A small, self-defeating smile played briefly with her lips. "Maybe I do, in a way. I guess all of us, at times, wish we could go back to the time when we made the wrong decisions and have them to do all over again.''

He lifted the cigarette to his lips, and she thought he was thinking about decisions he had made in the past, too. And then he asked, ''What wrong decision did you make?''

She shrugged a little. She couldn't get her hands into her pockets, sitting as she was, so she folded them between her knees. ''Leaving here. Marrying a man I didn't love and becoming somebody I was never meant to be.''

He looked startled. ''I can't imagine you doing that. Marrying somebody you didn't love.''

''Well,'' she admitted, ''maybe that's not strictly true. I loved parts of him…things about him, I should say. His sophistication, his charm, his ambition, his taste…Greg always had wonderful taste. That was the first thing that impressed me about him. I loved his car and his clothes and his stylish apartment. And sex. That was nice. But none of that had anything to do with what he really *was*, you know? By the time I found out what lay underneath all that shine and polish it was too late, because he had already started to turn me into a mirror image of himself. And it wasn't until we were divorced that I realized all the things I hated about myself, about the person I had become, were the very things I thought I'd loved about Greg in the first place. But I never knew him,'' she finished softly. ''In all those years of marriage, we never gave each other anything but images, and never had a clue about the people who lived underneath.''

Logan was silent, gazing at the smoldering cigarette held half cupped in his palm. After a time he said, soberly and almost to himself, ''There aren't too many people who ever really know each other, I guess. That's why there's so much loneliness in the world.''

Except, Cassie realized slowly, with Logan she did not feel lonely. She knew nothing about him, he had been right about that. She did not know who he was or where he came from, what he had done or who his family was, whether he preferred Chablis or Cabernet Sauvignon...all those things she had thought were so important about Greg. But she knew other things about Logan. Things she couldn't define, things that were basic and simple and important. He did not feel like a stranger to her.

She asked gently, "Doesn't it ever get lonely for you, Logan?"

"I suppose." He lifted the cigarette again, and did not look at her. "I never got into the habit of opening up to people and never missed closing them out...until now." And then he looked at her. He said nothing more, but the quiet simplicity of all that was unsaid left Cassie poised on the brink of hope, hesitant to grasp the moment, yet aching for it.

And then he said softly, "Damn."

He carefully ground out the cigarette in the dirt, and the sound he made was a cross between a chuckle and an oath of self-derision. "I swore I wasn't going to do this."

"Do what?" Cassie's voice was placid, if a little breathless. She did not want him to leave.

"Sit here with you, alone like this, and listen to you." He shook his head slowly, gazing off again into the distance. "You have the prettiest voice," he murmured. "Like the wind across a faraway mountain. And when I listen to you...it makes me wish I could be different."

"You don't want to be different," she assured him softly. "I know what it's like to change for someone...or to be changed. I wouldn't wish it on anybody."

He turned his eyes back on her again; a quiet moment of recognition and acceptance passed between them like a shared breath, or a single thought. And then he smiled softly and said, "You are a lovely lady, Cassie Grant. I hope you find somebody who deserves you."

I already have, Cassie thought with a low, gentle certainty that came upon her without surprise. But she did not say it. She would never say it.

And then, as easily as though the conversation had never taken any other turn, Logan switched the mood to business again. "We lost a few more head yesterday. I thought maybe they'd let up with all the fuss over Red, but no such luck."

Cassie frowned a little in puzzlement. "I don't understand. A few head here, another few there... They can't possibly sell them for full price. Why would anyone go to all that trouble just to chip away at our herd?"

He shrugged. "Well, it may not seem like much to you, but one cow—less than an hour's work—can be sold even at cut-rate for more than a cowboy makes in a week. If he gets two a day he's doubled his month's wages, and nobody's ever the wiser. Keep it small, and the chances are nobody will notice, and you hardly even work up a sweat in the meantime. If I were to go into rustling, that's the way I would do it."

"But we know what's going on," she insisted, a little frustrated. "How can they keep getting away with it?"

"Easiest thing in the world. The men are pretty spread out when they're riding herd. They go off for hours at a time to chase a steer out of a hollow or pull him out of a mud hole, and nobody keeps tabs."

"So you think it's some of our men."

He nodded. "It has to be."

"We're paying them to steal our cattle," she clarified, indignation rising.

"As long as they're cutting the herd during the day, or

on night watch when nobody notices, there's not much chance of catching them. Though Red must've come pretty close the other night.''

''Well, that's just fine.'' Her voice was short with anger and energized with determination. ''People in our very camp are making off with our cattle one by one and we can't do a thing about it. Well, *I* can do something about it. Just as soon as I get to a phone, I'm having the sheriff out here—''

He chuckled softly, shaking his head. ''Honey...'' The word rolled out naturally. ''That won't do anything but make them laugh. They might close up shop for a few days, cover their tracks and wait it out. The law is good for subpoenas and maybe a traffic accident or two, but it doesn't know anything about the country out here, which is exactly what your brother found out when he first reported our trouble. Right now they're riding high. The best thing we can do is lie low and hope they get greedy.''

Cassie looked at him curiously. ''What do you mean?''

Absently he plucked up a blade of scrub grass, flattening it between his long fingers. ''We've got a couple of hundred head corralled at the line camp, all fat and sassy and just waiting to be shipped out. Nobody patrols the stock pens, and it's an awful temptation. I'm thinking it might not hurt if I slept in the line shack for the next couple of nights. The worst it can do is discourage them from taking any of the stock I worked so hard to tag.''

Cassie said thoughtfully, ''Why are you so concerned, Logan?'' She couldn't resist throwing his own words back at him gently. ''After all, it's none of your business.''

He considered that for a moment, then agreed. ''That's right, I guess. It's not. But...'' And he slid a slow, half-rueful grin toward her. ''It gives me something to do.''

He got lazily to his feet and tossed the blade of grass

away. "That's all I wanted to tell you. I'll be away from camp for a while and I didn't want you thinking I'd run off with your horses."

Cassie's throat jerked suddenly and she had to swallow. So, this was it. They had met, touched briefly, and now they were parting. Just as Logan had warned her it would be. She would probably never see him again.

She said, trying to keep her voice matter-of-fact, "The new cook arrives tomorrow. I'll be going home."

The sun was in his eyes, narrowing them to crystalline slits. He adjusted his hat to shade his face, but still absolutely nothing was readable in his expression. "I'll miss your cooking," he said, and it was a polite, almost careless statement. "It's been nice, having a woman's touch around the camp."

Her fingers wound themselves tightly together between her jeaned knees. It was better this way. No dramatics, no fanfare, just goodbye. He had warned her.

She tried very hard to keep her voice as casual as his. "I don't guess I'll see you again."

"Probably not," he agreed. "I don't get down to the house much."

At least they were parting friends. At least that awful embarrassment and tension of last night no longer lay between them and they could face each other like mature adults, with no hard feelings for the mistakes they had made...or almost made. It was just that she had thought they would have another day, a few more hours....

It wouldn't have made any difference. It was better this way.

God, I'm going to miss you, she thought, and a deep and swelling ache came straight from the center of her being.

She managed a little smile. "Well, this is goodbye, then."

Still, his face was impossible to read. He answered simply, "I guess it is."

She couldn't let it hang between them like that. She had to say, softly, "I'm glad I met you, Logan."

He stood there, looking down at her for a long moment. And then he turned casually and walked away.

There was nothing Cassie could do about the slow burning heaviness that filled her chest as she watched him go, a lean, easy-moving silhouette against the glare of the sun. She wasn't sorry. She told herself she wasn't sorry. After all, there was nothing between them; there never had been and there never could be. He was right; she had tried to play out a romantic fantasy that could only bring disappointment, and she was fortunate that Logan, at least, had had sense enough to put a stop to it.

But still, on an insane impulse she couldn't control, she got to her feet and started after him. She didn't know what she was going to say, or what reason there could be for saying it, but it didn't seem right to let him walk away like this.

Could you sleep with a man and then walk away from him in the morning, Cassie?

She stood there for another moment, hesitant, but there was really no reason for uncertainty. She knew the answer to that question.

She didn't follow him. She bent to pick up her plate and walked in the opposite direction, toward the mess tent, to do the dishes.

THE NEW COOK ARRIVED early the next afternoon, on the supply truck. His name was Wilson, and he was a short, genial man with a bald pink head and a ruff of white whiskers that looked like bleached corn silk on his chin. Cassie was busy off-loading supplies and placing the requisition for the next delivery, and she barely gave a thought to the fact that this marked the end of her adventure. Before nightfall she would be shampooing her hair, pulling on her own fuzzy house robe, propping her feet up and eating popcorn. It all seemed so far away that it was like another lifetime, and Cassie couldn't imagine it.

The driver of the truck offered to take her back to the ranch, but he seemed to be in a hurry and Cassie did not feel right about deserting the new cook as soon as he arrived. She had the pickup, and even if she stayed until after the evening meal there would be plenty of time before dark to drive back to the house. She was surprised by the proprietorial sense of responsibility she felt toward a job she had only held a few days. She wanted the transition to be an easy one.

Fortunately, Wilson was an easygoing man and didn't mind her advice or interference. "Of course," Cassie broke off apologetically, after a full five minutes of specific directions on the best way to arrange the supplies in the wagon, "everyone likes to keep his kitchen his own way."

"Same with a chuck wagon, Miss," he replied complacently and moved a box of canned peaches from the right side of the wagon to the left. "So while you've been telling me how's the best way to do it, I've just naturally been putting things in my own place."

Cassie grinned and wiped her hands on her jeans. "I guess you'd like me to get out of your way."

"Well, now, I didn't exactly say that. I can't say I mind the company of a pretty young woman whilst I'm working. As long as you're of a mind to help, though..." He paused and straightened to look around. "You might tell me what you did with the milk. I make a fine potato soup, really sticks to the ribs, but it ain't nothing without canned milk.''

Cassie moved a few cans and boxes. "I don't remember unloading any, do you?"

He shook his head. "Could be the last fella forgot to order it," he suggested.

Cassie shook her head, frowning a little in annoyance. ''No, it's a standing order. We must have just left it in the back of the truck.''

Cassie stood there for a moment thinking. The truck had pulled out less than five minutes ago, and she could easily overtake it if she went by horseback. It wasn't as though she had anything better to do, and despite his protests to the contrary, she was certain Wilson would be glad to have her out of his way while he got settled. Besides, she would enjoy the ride.

''Listen,'' she said, ''I'm going to try to catch up with the truck. If I can't, I'll send someone out with the milk tomorrow, when I get home.''

"Guess I'd better not plan on soup tonight, then." He looked unhappy. "Too bad. It sure does make an impression, and a new cook likes to get off to a good start."

She grinned as she jumped lightly down from the wagon. "I know what you mean. I'll do my best, but maybe you'd better make your second-best dish tonight, just in case."

He nodded glumly. "My second-best dish is hash."

Cassie was chuckling as she went to saddle a horse.

Cassie hadn't ridden in this part of the country in many years, but the landmarks were familiar to her and she had no fear of getting lost. The road the truck would have taken led east, and she set off in that direction at a mild canter.

There was no reason to hurry, for until the truck reached the paved road it would be going at a much slower pace than she was. And it wasn't as though she were riding to head off a shipment of life-saving serum or anything; the mission served as more of an excuse to feel helpful than anything else.

She did enjoy riding horseback, all alone in the midst of the vast plains and hills. It allowed her to imagine what it must have been like when the first white men came across all those years ago...except for the fact that, pausing atop a small ridge, she could see the glint of blacktop in the distance and the dust raised by cowboys as they herded the cattle toward the line camp. The land was crisscrossed with dirt roads now, and the trees were mostly new. Even out here, miles away from the sound of another voice, the evidence of man's habitation endured.

It was a stupid accident, and if she had not been riding with a slack rein, daydreaming and enjoying the view, it probably never would have happened. She was walking her horse down a small incline when the loose rocky ground, disturbed by the movements of hooves, gave way. Her mount slipped on the rolling stones and soil and instinctively Cassie jerked the reins, which was the worst possible thing to do. Confused, the animal shifted its weight to the left, lost its footing and stumbled.

There was a moment of sheer panic as Cassie felt the horse start to go down, and in swift succession a series of horrible images filled her mind—she saw herself trapped in the saddle beneath the fallen animal or, worse yet, dragged by a stirrup over this rocky ground. All she could think to do was to kick free of the stirrups and leap for safety.

She hit the ground hard and rolled over and over in the dust and stones, down the hill. Her eyes and her mouth filled with dirt and her hands were torn by the briars and rocks as she tried to catch herself. When at last she came to a stop against a clump of sagebrush, she could only lie there, dazed and gasping, wondering how badly she was hurt.

Her eyes were streaming in reaction to the amount of sand they had collected, and it was a long time before she could see. She wiped her eyes and her mouth on her sleeve, and stood up a little shakily, checking out the damage.

Her hands were scraped and her hip hurt from the collision with the hard ground, but otherwise her limbs seemed to be in working order. Her eyes still stung with remnant grains of sand and all her muscles ached, and most of all she felt like a fool. She hadn't been thrown from a horse since she was thirteen years old, and then it had been a real horse—a high-spirited stallion that her father had bought for show—not one of these stolid little cow ponies that any big-footed oaf could manage.

Irritation with the clumsiness of her mount caused her to abruptly forget her own woes and discomforts and look around sharply for her horse. She had tumbled about ten feet down the hill—it had only seemed much longer—and her horse had recovered itself much more quickly than she had. Even as she looked, he was trotting off at a brisk pace in the opposite direction.

"Hey!" She took a few running steps forward, waving her arm just as though the dumb animal could see it, or would stop if he could. "Come back here!"

The horse was already about fifty yards away and wasn't slowing down. The fall had spooked him, and there was no way Cassie could catch him if she ran. Still, she did run, closing absolutely no distance between them and quickly realizing the futility of it. She stopped and tried to whistle, but her mouth was dry with sand and exertion and she was out of breath. She called out again, and the horse disappeared behind a dip in the earth and was gone.

"Damn!" she hissed angrily and turned in frustration, looking for something to throw or to kick. Here she was in the middle of nowhere without a horse and there was nothing even to vent her fury on. She turned and yelled loudly at the absent horse, "Fool!" But that did not make her feel much better. She contented herself with kicking the ground instead, raising dust and not much else.

Scowling fiercely, Cassie stuffed her hands in her pockets and looked around, surveying the situation. She did not know how far she had come from the camp, but she did know she was closer to it than to the road. Not that reaching the road would do her much good now—by the time she got there, the supply truck would have long since passed, and no other traffic was due for days. She did not look forward to the long hike back to camp—and she relished even less walking disheveled and horseless into the midst of a bevy of grinning cowhands—but she saw no other choice. Dispiritedly, she began to trudge back in the direction from which she had come.

She had been walking for about fifteen minutes when she realized she was no longer certain from which direction she had come. The spill had disoriented her, she had gone down the hill in a different manner than she had planned, and upon rising had chosen to circle it rather than climb it again. Even before the fall, she hadn't been paying much attention to landmarks. She was moving west, toward the setting sun, but a lot of things lay to the west besides the campsite. Nothing looked familiar to her.

It was very hot out there in the middle of nowhere, unprotected from the sun. Working in the shade of the campsite all day she had never really appreciated how warm it could get here in the summer. She was thirsty and just a little scared. She was beginning to understand why they used to hang horse thieves.

The air was too thin for long periods of exertion, too, especially since Cassie was not used to it. The landscape was fairly barren and offered little in the way of shelter from the heat of the sun, but Cassie had to pause and rest, looking around, trying to think what was the best thing to do.

Of course, if this were an old-time movie, her faithful horse would return to the camp and immediately sound the alarm that something was wrong. Gallant cowboys would come searching for her and her ordeal would soon be over. If this were a movie, the stupid horse would have come when she called.

She held out little hope that her mount would have sense enough to return to camp, if he could even find his way back. The horses used for range work had little chance to develop a sense of home or loyalty to the men who cared for them; they changed location almost as often as they changed riders. It was possible that in time the animal might seek out others of his own kind, but more than likely he would head first for water, then for grass, and would graze contentedly until someone accidentally stumbled upon him, which could take days.

Cassie lifted a hand to push her sticky hair away from her face and was at first horrified, then dismayed, when her hand came away smeared with blood. She had obviously struck or scraped her forehead somehow, but her head didn't hurt any worse than the rest of her body, so she could only assume the injury wasn't serious. She didn't have a scarf, or even a Kleenex, with which to clean the injury, and that only depressed her further. Not only would she arrive back in camp—assuming she could even

find her way back—embarrassed and on foot, but looking
as if she had been the victim of a serious accident as well.
So much for the respect she had hoped to earn as a well-
qualified ranch boss.

Cassie took a deep, fortifying breath, squaring her
hands on her hips, and focused on what her next move
should be. Obviously there was no point in standing here
waiting for the hand of God to intervene. She couldn't be
that far from the camp—three or four miles at most—and
while that wasn't exactly a pleasant jaunt in this heat, it
was not impossible. Assuming she could get her bearings
and walk in the right direction, she was certain she would
come upon some signs of habitation before long. After
all, there were twenty men and several hundred head of
cattle scattered throughout the countryside; she couldn't
stay lost forever.

But it was a big country and "lost" was a relative term.
Clouds were beginning to pile up on the western horizon
like snowdrifts, and Cassie swore softly. Two weeks without a drop and she was about to be caught in a rain-
storm—or more likely, a thunderstorm. Lightning in the
mountains was nothing to joke about, and now she really
began to get scared.

The correct direction was optional at this point; her
primary concern was to find shelter. She started off across
the scrubby plain to where outcroppings of rock and low
brush would provide some protection from the storm.

She knew, of course, that in open country and clear air
all objects looked closer than they actually were. But too
many years of city living had dulled her perception and
colored her judgment, and she had forgotten how treach-
erous this countryside could be. She set her sights on a
small stand of pine near a cliff overhang, and after she
had been walking an hour her goal seemed no closer than

before. Then she had to admit, fighting back a jolt of panic, that she was really lost.

She was drenched with sweat and her head throbbed and she was so thirsty she could barely swallow. *Damn it, Cassie,* she reprimanded herself furiously, *how could you be such an idiot? You should have followed the horse. You know eventually he'd head for water, even if you didn't catch him first, and once you picked up the stream you could have followed it back to camp.* But she was not a frontiersman, and whatever outdoor skills she had once possessed had been bred out of her long since by years of easy living. What would have been only common sense to her when she was a teenager roaming these hills now was the last thing that occurred to her. She might once have been a child of nature, but now she was nothing more than an out-of-place city girl who could get hopelessly lost on her own ranch.

At least there was a slight breeze now, and it was cooling on Cassie's damp skin. Though she was grateful for the relief, she knew the wind was not a good sign. The clouds were moving faster and hanging lower, and rain would not be far away. She tried not to think about flash floods, which could wipe out a whole herd in a matter of moments as the water from the mountains swept through the lowlands. There hadn't been a flash flood around here in…well, she wasn't certain how long, but surely it was many years.

Moving toward the pine trees kept her going west—at least she hadn't been stupid enough to have turned around and gone in the opposite direction—so she kept on that track. She started scouring the countryside for signs of leafy vegetation that would mean water nearby. There was nothing as far as she could see except wind, barren ground and sagebrush. She began to wonder if it was possible to die of thirst in only a few hours and then impatiently cursed herself for her dramatics. This wasn't the Mojave Desert, after all, but the foothills of Wyoming, and there were people all around.

But there was little comfort in the knowledge, and in fact, she found it difficult to believe. Never in her life had Cassie known such a sense of isolation, of being utterly and completely alone and helpless, as she did on that endless afternoon. She had never realized before how much she depended on people, the nearness of people, the simple awareness that there were others in the universe besides herself, someone to reach out to if she needed help. The sky was huge and filled with dark rolling clouds; the earth seemed to go on forever. And against that background Cassie felt very small. Fear was too weak a word for what she felt. Awareness of her own insignificance against the enormity of the emptiness that surrounded her invaded her very soul with bleakness.

She tried to think about the brave pioneers who had crossed this land, alone for the most part, just as she was. How huge it must have seemed to them then, how unforgiving. They had survived not only the harshness of the land itself but stampeding buffalo, poisonous snakes, wild animal attacks, marauding Indians.... And some of them had not survived. She tried not to think of those who had died of starvation or heat exhaustion or a simple thing like a broken leg...or the loss of a horse.

Stupid. She wasn't going to die. Thinking such morbid thoughts was not going to get her to safety any sooner.

She reached the tumble of broken rocks that heralded her three scraggly pine trees just as the first fat drops of rain began to fall. All things considered, it was not the best place in the world to seek shelter from a lightning storm, but she was so relieved and filled with self-congratulation that for a moment she just leaned against the rocks and turned her face to the rain, tasting the cool freshness on her tongue and letting the water trickle into her eager throat.

Before long the wind began to whip up, though, and the rain fell faster. She looked around for shelter before her clothes were completely soaked. What she found was an alcove beneath an overhanging boulder. It was deep enough to protect her from the blowing rain and wide enough to allow her to sit comfortably. Squinting now against the rain, she picked up a fallen pine bough and used it to sweep the interior of the narrow cave. Nothing crawled out, so she felt it was safe to sit down.

She settled herself into the shelter just in time. The full force of the rain came with a fury, spraying Cassie's face even as she huddled far back beneath the rock and creating fast-moving rivulets on the ground she could still see. It was brief, but it was violent. The sound of it thundered against the rock and swept around her like an ocean, drowning out even the sound of her own breathing. Cassie squeezed her eyes closed and buried her face in her knees, and she kept thinking about a painting that had hung on her wall as a child...a mother bird, huddled in her nest in the midst of a furious storm, shielding her babies with her wings. That was how Cassie felt, burrowed into the ground while the elements raged all around her—as if she were a tiny bird in its fragile nest. Only there was no mother bird to protect her.

Like most mountain storms, it passed quickly, leaving only a steady patter of rain that curtained the rock and was peculiarly soothing in its steady, rhythmic sound. Thunder rolled in the distance but did not threaten. Cautiously, Cassie straightened up.

The worst was not over by any means, but she felt

strengthened and renewed, as though she had survived an enormous ordeal and was the better for it. She was still lost, of course. It was still raining and the terrain would be much more difficult to cross now that it was muddy. She was not looking forward to getting out in it, and it would be dark soon.

It was gloomy under the rock, and when she squinted at her watch she was surprised to see it was only four o'clock. She felt as though she had been out here forever.

Four o'clock. The men would be coming in from their long day's work, sitting down to the evening meal with the new cook. Surely someone would miss her by now. Or would they? She tried to remember exactly what she had told Wilson before she left. Would he think she had missed the supply truck and had decided to go on home without saying goodbye? Rodney might think it was peculiar that she hadn't told anyone she was leaving, but this was a busy time of day and it might be a long time before anyone got curious. They all knew she was leaving today. How long before they noticed that the pickup truck was still there and a horse was missing? After that, how long before they put the two together...if ever?

It began to occur to her that she could be stranded out here overnight, a notion that she rejected strenuously. Being alone out here during the daytime was one thing, but at night...

She had to face it. There was a distinct possibility that no one would realize she was lost until Jonas began to wonder why she had not come home, sometime tomorrow. And even then, how long would it take anyone to find her? How would they know where to begin to look? *She* didn't even know where she was.

And that was when she had to start facing some other unpleasant facts. Even during the daytime this was no place for a woman alone. If she were found she might wish she hadn't been. There were thieves out here who knew the countryside better than she did, and they had proved themselves violent once already. And rustlers aside, she wasn't sure how far she would trust the characters of any of the men who worked for her if they found her alone in an isolated spot like this.

There was no point in debating the matter. It was foolish to even consider waiting here for someone to find her. There was danger out here; night was coming and she had to find her way back to camp. Somehow.

The rain had slowed to a light drizzle, and she couldn't hide here forever. Grimacing a little, she stretched her muscles and started to crawl out. Then she froze. The sound she heard was slow and stealthy, movement where once there had been none. Rocks scattered; mud squished. Footsteps. They were coming straight toward her, and they did not sound friendly.

Chapter Eight

Cassie held her breath, instinctively shrinking back and then damning herself for a fool and a coward. Someone had found her! She was rescued; her terrors were over. But then she remembered what had happened to Red, and perhaps it was residual fear imbued into her by her solitary ordeal, perhaps it was an overexaggerated sense of the dramatic, but she stayed still and out of sight, her heart pounding so loudly it almost drowned out the sound of the approaching footsteps.

Then she heard the voice. "Cassie?"

Relief flooded through her in a wave so intense it made her weak, and then was immediately replaced by a surge of joy that almost choked off her voice. "Logan!"

She scrambled out of the enclosure and he bent down to help her up. His grip was rough, and his fingers, closing around her upper arms, were painful. But she didn't care. He was here. Like a happy ending to a bad dream, he had appeared from nowhere to rescue her. Logan. She should have known it would be Logan.

She stood there in the misty rain, wanting to fling her arms around him but paralyzed by happiness and relief, unable to do anything but look up at him with mute wonder and joy singing through her veins. He was wearing a dark slicker, and his hat, dark and wet, was pulled low, shadowing his face. When her deliriously spinning vision cleared enough to see his face, the spiraling relief within her faltered uncertainly. He did not look very happy.

The muscles of his face were taut, and his eyes were dark and very cold. He lifted a hand to shove her hair away from her face, and she winced as his fingers brushed against the cut on her forehead. "What happened?" he demanded flatly. There was no welcome in his voice at all, or in his eyes. He looked, in fact, as angry as she had ever seen him.

"My—my horse stumbled," she explained, and felt like a child apologizing to her parent for a momentary idiocy. "I had to kick free and I fell. The horse ran away and..." She made a small gesture with her hand, trying to smile. She could not quite manage it. "How—how did you find me?"

"I spotted your horse," he replied tersely. Everything in his face seemed shuttered and restrained. "I've got him tied up back at the line shack. Come on."

His hand on her arm was rougher than he probably intended, and when he jerked her forward she stumbled a little. He did not notice. His horse stood steaming in the rapidly fading drizzle, and when she lifted her foot to the stirrup he grasped her waist and deposited her bodily in the saddle, hard. Then he swung up behind her, and the force of his weight settling against her buttocks and thighs almost unseated her. She was pushed uncomfortably and most rudely against the pommel, and when she lifted the reins he took them from her, not speaking, and guided the horse into a turn.

His wet poncho dripped over her mostly dry jeans and his pelvis was hard and heated against her backside, but there was nothing intimate about their position. He

avoided touching her voluntarily, resting one arm carelessly on the back of the saddle while he held the reins
away from her body with the other. Tension and anger
radiated in palpable waves from him and he did not say
a word.

At first Cassie was angry, too. How dare he be irritated
with her after what she had just been through? He was
acting as though having to come out in the rain to rescue
her had been an unforgivable inconvenience with which
he had no patience. As though she were a troublesome
child.

And then she saw the direction in which he was riding,
and she did feel like a troublesome child.

The line camp was not a quarter of a mile, cross-
country, from the place at which she had taken her original spill. She had been wandering through the countryside, narrowly skirting the very signs of civilization that
she sought, for hours. She had never been in a life-and-
death situation at all. If only she had followed her horse.

The stupid horse, who was trained to work with cattle.
Naturally he would head toward the familiar—the smell
of stock pens, the sound of other horses. She felt like an
idiot.

The terrors she had endured faded into childish exag-
geration beneath Logan's anger. Now that she was safe,
now that she realized she had never been far from safety,
her ordeal seemed insignificant, embarrassingly so. Logan's irritation was not only justified, but the only real
and important thing about the entire episode. With each
step the horse took over the slippery mud Cassie's spirits
sank lower.

She heard the cattle before she saw them. They were
still huddled together against the aftermath of the storm
in several wide corrals that surrounded the small log cabin

known as the line shack. Cassie's horse was tethered beneath a tree not far away, contentedly munching on wet grass. An hour ago the sight would have seemed like paradise to her. Now it only seemed like a gentle mockery of her own stupidity.

Logan slid out of the saddle, and Cassie dismounted from the other side, refusing his help. But before she could thank him, or apologize, or even retrieve her horse and ride wordlessly away, his hand closed on her elbow and he gestured her toward the cabin. "Come inside." His tone was quiet, controlled and basically expressionless. "Let's see to those cuts."

There was no arguing with him, nor was Cassie inclined to do so. She hadn't the energy or the stamina, and all she wanted to do was go back home—home to a real house and a real meal and friendly faces—and put this entire humiliating experience behind her.

The line shack was one of the oldest buildings on the ranch, though there were several like it constructed around the perimeters. In years past, it had actually served as home to the cowboys who worked year round up here and to whom the distance to the bunkhouse was impractical. It was still used quite frequently during the winter when spreading feed for the cattle was a multiday job and snowstorms frequently made the roads impassable.

The cabin was a small, efficient one-room affair with a wood-burning stove, a small table and a narrow cot. A Coleman lantern hung on the wall and a small butane-burning cookstove was stashed in one corner. There was one window and it was covered with several sheets of cloudy polyurethane. The interior was gloomy and uninviting, and when Logan closed the door the major source of light was cut off.

He flung his saddlebags and canteen on the table and

stripped off his hat and slicker, letting both fall carelessly
to the floor. A little stiffly, Cassie made her way over to
the cot and sat down. It was made with a wool army
blanket and hospital corners so neat that she felt guilty
for disturbing it, and she sat on the very edge. She pressed
her hands close together and said tightly, "Look, I'm not
really hurt. There's no need..."

His voice was low and roughened with an emotion she
could not understand as he replied tersely, "You've got
blood all over your face."

He opened his canteen and sloshed a measure of water
onto his handkerchief before coming over to her. He sat
down beside her and Cassie couldn't help flinching a little
from the brittle darkness of his eyes as he lifted his hand
to her face. He applied the damp cloth to her face with a
touch that was startingly gentle, sponging away the grime
and the blood, and Cassie felt a stab of chagrin. How she
must have looked to him, huddled beneath that rock,
bloodied and torn. And then she noticed that his hand was
shaking.

Her eyes met his in question and uncertainty, and his
fist closed around the cloth so tightly that a few drops of
water splattered on her collar. He lowered his eyes but
could not hide the pain that crossed his face. "Damn it,
Cassie," he burst out. "What the hell were you doing out
there?"

Cassie retreated instinctively from this uncharacteristic
display of emotions she did not understand; her instant
response was defensive. "Listen," she said tightly, "I feel
stupid enough as it is. You don't have to—"

"Stupid!" He stood abruptly, turning away from her,
and both fists were clenched now, anger straining in the
muscles of his shoulders and back. "Is that what you think
it is? That's not the word for it, lady!"

Cassie got to her feet, fighting back the sudden irrational sting of tears in her eyes. She thrust her hands into her pockets, and her arms were trembling. "Look, I'm sorry, okay? I'm sorry you had to come out in the rain and I'm sorry I got lost and I'm sorry my horse happened to wander into your front yard! I'm okay now and I know my way back to camp from here, so I'll just get out of your way."

She started for the door, but his hand was swift and hard on her arm, whirling her around. She jerked away and he released her immediately. They stood there facing each other, his eyes blazing, her breath coming in quick, furious bursts. She had seen him angry once before, when she accused him of lying to her, but that had been nothing compared with this. That time his anger had only fueled her own temper; this time it made her afraid.

Then, as he looked at her, the anger faded, slowly and painfully. She saw his face tighten against a new and more difficult emotion, and his eyes softened as they went over her face—softened and filled with pain. He lifted his hand, and Cassie thought he would take her into his arms. She wanted desperately to be held in his arms, to feel his strength, his comfort, his assurance that everything was all right.

But all he did was touch her hair, very lightly, barely cupping its tangled shape, as though he were afraid his touch would hurt her or soil her. His eyes lowered, and he said, a little huskily, "Sit down. Please. You need some first aid."

She let him guide her back to the bed, and she sat very still as he lifted the cloth to her face again. But almost immediately he dropped his hand and turned away from her with a weak smile that wasn't a smile at all, but an expression that was somewhere between rueful and horrified. "I can't do it," he admitted softly, with a gentle, disbelieving shake of his head. He gave the cloth to her. "Look at my hands." He stretched out his hands in front of him. They were trembling noticeably. "I saw a man get his arm caught in a thresher once," he said, still with that distant, almost incredulous note to his voice. "I've pulled people out of automobile wrecks. I never—"

He took a breath, and dragged his cupped hand over his chin, almost as though to hide his expression. The breath he released was shaky, and he did not look at her. "When I saw your horse and I thought about you out there, maybe hurt, maybe..." He wouldn't say it but instead took another breath. "Something went through me...I'm not used to being scared for anyone but myself. I've never known the feeling before. I don't want to ever know it again. All I could think about was what the world would be like without you in it."

He caught his breath sharply, and he got up and walked over to the table. He gripped the edge of the table, squaring his shoulders, straining the muscles of his arms. But his voice was calm, almost matter-of-fact. "I'm not used to being responsible for other people...or wanting to be. I never guessed, until today, that with you, I didn't have a choice."

Cassie strained toward him, her breath, her muscles, her very soul aching to enfold him. But she didn't move. There were tears in her throat and wanting in her chest, but his back was squared against her and the battle he fought inside himself had to be fought alone. Cassie knew, because she was fighting the same inner war. Only victory, for her, was a much simpler and more final thing. She had known she didn't have a choice since the first day she met him.

After what seemed like a long time, his hardened muscles began to relax; she could hear, in the utter silence of the room, his soft expulsion of breath. Then, with movements that were easy and efficient, he opened his saddle-bag and removed a compact first-aid kit.

She knew that most range workers, unless they were very foolish, carried something of that sort with them. But the modern device in the midst of so much that was part of another century looked out of place, and she smiled a little as he brought it over to her. "I should have come here in the first place," she joked weakly, and, as feeble an effort as it was, it made him smile.

She finished wiping off most of the grime from her face and hands, and he opened a bottle of antiseptic. His hands were a bit steadier now, and she tried not to wince as he dabbed a cotton ball soaked with the liquid against the wound on her forehead. There was quick anxiety in his eyes as he glanced at her, but his tone was mild as he told her, "It's not very deep. It just looked bad."

"It hardly hurts at all," she answered.

The intensity of moments just passed still echoed between them, making their words and their movements seem awkward and self-conscious. Each of them was holding needs and emotions tightly in check, and the effort that it took to do so filled the air around them, making it heavy.

He placed a bandage over the small cut on her head and turned his attention to her hands. It was his nearness that was causing Cassie's stomach to tense and her muscles to stiffen, she realized, nothing else. His palm was warm and callused as he held one of her hands lightly in his, his ministrations with the antiseptic on her scraped skin painstakingly gentle. His thigh was close to hers, his knee touching hers, and she noticed for the first time that his jeans were water-splotched from riding through the rain. He smelled of the damp outdoors, and she could feel his warmth drifting over her like the morning sun. He seemed so large, sitting there next to her. And so strong.

She pulled her hands away in a silly, nervous gesture, swallowing on a tightening throat. "It's all right," she said. "There's not much you can do about scraped palms."

He looked at her, questioningly, hesitantly, for a moment, and that only made Cassie feel more ill at ease. Their eyes met, and there was no hiding in that moment what was in her heart, in her mind. Yet distantly, firmly and as from far away, Cassie thought, *We're not going to do this. We're not going to make love in this cozy, isolated place simply because we're both scared and there's nothing to stop us.*

And in the same instant, he seemed to know and agree. The probing intensity that once had fired his eyes now lightened into a smile, and he inquired, "Any more injuries that I can't see?"

Cassie laughed. It was a nervous, strained sound, but it did make her feel better. It was almost convincing. "None that you can treat." She gingerly touched the bruise on her hip.

He recapped the antiseptic and got up to replace the first-aid kit. With his back to her, he asked casually, "Do you want to tell me what happened?"

Cassie shrugged, glancing down at her hands. "There's not much more to tell. I made a stupid mistake and lost my horse. Any twelve-year-old would have known better. I thought I could walk back to camp, but I misjudged the distance. Then I saw the storm coming and instead of heading for camp, I tried to find shelter. I got lost. End of story."

She looked up at him. He was opening the other saddle

bag. "Do the people at camp know that I'm missing? Are they looking for me?"

"I doubt it. I haven't seen any sign of movement from that direction." He extracted a metal flask from the saddlebag and unscrewed the cap. "Guess what else I've got?" he said, tossing the words over his shoulder, lightening the atmosphere with a change of subject.

The unmistakable aroma of whiskey drifted over to her as he poured a measure into a tin cup. Cassie, following his lead, lifted an eyebrow and injected a note of astonished reprimand into her voice.

"Drinking on the job, Mr. Logan?"

He found a dusty glass and filled it, turning to her with a grin. "It's good for snakebite," he assured her. He handed her the cup and sat again on the bed—not as close this time, but still filling the small space with his presence. "I'll ride back with you in a minute," he said, sipping from the glass. "My horse needs a rest, and so do you."

Cassie glanced down into the cup, but did not drink. She didn't care for whiskey much. "How did you know it was my horse?" she asked, looking back at him. "It could have been anyone's who wandered up."

He shook his head. "I could tell by the length of the stirrups. I knew it was you." And his eyes darkened, then went opaque, as he added, "I figured you for a pretty good rider, and knew something drastic must have happened." She could see the muscles of his face tighten again as he reviewed emotions he would rather not face, and his pain was reflected in an aching within her own chest. But he kept his voice very calm. "Fortunately, I caught sight of you before the rain washed away your tracks, and I figured you'd headed for shelter, just like you did. You must have been wandering around out there for a very long time."

Now Cassie did take a sip of whiskey. It was bitter and unpleasant, but it warmed her considerably with the first swallow. She tried to chuckle, but it came out more as a self-derisive grunt. "Well, it wasn't exactly a transcendental experience, I'll tell you that."

Logan leaned his shoulders back against the wall, drawing one long leg up onto the bed, his ankle resting against his other knee. He looked at her curiously. "Did you mean for it to be?"

The faint smile Cassie had mustered faded as she gazed into the cup. "No. I don't know. I think..." And she shrugged, uncomfortably. "I think since I came back here I've been looking at the ranch as some kind of road to self-awareness, or something. Maybe I thought by recapturing my past I could come to terms with who I am, or be a better person than who I am. I found out today that I'm basically no different than I was when I arrived. Incompetent, clumsy, irresponsible. I got lost in the wilderness on my own ranch, for heaven's sake, within shouting distance from where I am right now. I fell off my own horse and then let him run away. The whole thing was an exercise in idiocy, and the things I found out about myself today I'd prefer not to know. I used to make fun of kids who made mistakes that weren't as stupid as the ones I made today."

Logan was thoughtful for a moment, and Cassie took another sip from her cup. The taste was not improving, but it gave her something to do.

Then Logan said in his calm, easy drawl, "Well, all things considered, I wouldn't say you handled it all that badly. You were smart enough to kick free of a falling horse before he crushed you, weren't you?" His eyes were clear and calm and quietly matter-of-fact. She drank in strength just looking at them. "You got away from the open ground when you saw the storm coming and you even managed to find a way to keep dry. You would have reached the camp eventually. Maybe the long way around," he admitted with a wry twist of his lips, "but you probably would have made it before dark. Not too bad for a greenhorn, Mrs. Grant."

Cassie couldn't help laughing, softly and genuinely, and from nothing more than the simple pleasure he gave her with his confidence. "You always make me feel good."

"And you always sell yourself short."

His smile met hers with nothing but gentle, simple affection, and the moment between them locked and held. She wanted to be in his arms. She wanted to lay her head against his shoulder and wrap her arms around his waist and she wanted to stay that way for a long time, listening to his heartbeat, feeling the pulse of his breath. Holding him.

Then he glanced down; he took another drink. "Which is not to say," he added in a slightly altered tone, studying his glass, "that I'd advise you to go off and do it again anytime soon. Somewhere out here there are at least a couple of men who weren't shy about tackling a full-grown man on horseback, much less a little thing like you wandering around on foot." There it was again, the undertone of tightness in his voice that bordered on anger, but Cassie wasn't hurt by it anymore. For it wasn't anger, but remembered fear, and guilt twisted inside her for what she had put him through. Would she have reacted any differently had it been him alone and in danger?

"That was the last thing I thought of," she admitted, unable to meet his eyes. "And when I heard you coming, I thought...well, I thought about it then." She half smiled, trying to deny her own residual fear. "Most of the time I was too busy thinking about other things...like the bleached-out bones we used to find when we were kids. We never found any human skeletons, but I imagine we would have, if we had looked hard enough.''

And then the lightness she had tried to force into her tone completely deserted her, and the shudder that went through her was deep and primal and unpreventable. ''God, I was so scared,'' she whispered, concentrating fiercely on her cup. ''It was so empty...and I was so *alone*.'' She raised eyes to him that were wide and filled with naked emotion. ''Oh, Logan, how do you stand it?''

She was not referring to the nature of the work he did, the long days riding alone, the open spaces in which he was so comfortable—but to another kind of isolation, the utter aloneness that Cassie had only begun to taste that afternoon, but which to him was a way of life.

Acknowledgment of her meaning was written in his eyes before he lowered them briefly. Then he answered simply but honestly, ''I never thought about it much. It gets to be a habit, being alone, and I guess somewhere in the back of my mind it's always bothered me a little, that I could disappear off the face of the earth and no one would notice, or be there to mark my passing.'' Then he lifted his glass again and his tone was matter-of-fact. ''But I've been doing it for so long I can hardly even imagine any other way. There's a kind of hardness, I guess, that grows in a man who's lived alone for so long, and after a while you don't even think about it.''

Cassie smiled vaguely, watching the absent circular pattern her forefinger was making around the rim of her cup. She knew what he was trying to say, and she understood it far too well. ''It takes a different kind of person to live out here, I think, or to be able to relate to the kind of life we live here. Maybe it's the country that breeds it into them, the bigness and the emptiness of it, or maybe it's the country that brings them here. I don't know. It just takes a special something in a person to make him live here. My dad had it, and Jonas, and even I do.'' Her smile turned dry as she lifted her cup in a small salute. "Even though I do dumb things, sometimes. But my mother..." She frowned a little, thoughtfully, as she remembered. "She never adjusted to the ranch, to the emptiness. I didn't even realize how unhappy she was until I was in college, when she divorced my dad. She was just waiting until all the children were gone."

She sipped the whiskey, no longer noticing the foul taste. Logan was quiet, waiting, listening...and understanding. "But do you know what was really strange?" She looked at him, and her smile was drawn through confusion and wonder, a peculiar truth that, even after all this time, she had not completely reconciled. "She adored my father. And he was desperately in love with her. It wasn't one of those things where your parents fight all their lives and you know divorce is just around the corner...." Her voice trailed off, and she glanced into her cup again. "My mother always used to say to me, in the kind of joking way mothers have when they're trying to give teenagers serious advice but don't want to be accused of being a square...she always used to say, 'Never date a man you wouldn't want to marry, because sometimes you don't have any choice about who you fall in love with.' I never realized that she was talking about herself. She fell in love with my father, but she couldn't live his kind of life. She left him, but she loved him until the day she died. And he never stopped loving her.'' She made a small sound that was a cross between sorrow and gentle resignation. "Even though they hadn't lived together for ten years, they died within two years of each other. Of broken hearts, I think."

The silence was as gentle as a kiss, as full of promise as an open hand. It drew them together, quietly and simply, with tender threads of shared understanding. And then Logan said, "So you tried not to make the same mistake, and you dated the kind of man you thought you wanted to marry."

She nodded. "And forgot about falling in love."

"It's a tragic story, Cassie," he said soberly.

She nodded. "Both of them." Her parents' story and her own. Who was to say who had made the bigger mistake?

She took another drink of whiskey quickly; she winced, and half laughed. She set the cup on the floor. "That stuff is making my head spin."

He smiled and toasted her. "Small wonder. At three ninety-eight a bottle, it's probably fifty-percent rubbing alcohol." He drained his own glass and deposited it on the windowsill. Daylight was fading behind the rapidly dispersing clouds, but he looked easy and relaxed, not anxious to leave at all. Cassie was glad. She didn't want to go home. She wanted to stay here and just be with him for a little while longer.

"You're easy to talk to," she said softly. "I feel as though I've known you for a long time." She could not describe it any better than that. He was familiar to her, comforting, secure. As though some part of them had touched long ago and the contact still was not broken. As though they belonged together.

He simply looked at her, and understanding passed gently between them. It was true. They both knew it.

He leaned back against the wall, smiling at her in an absent, almost sad, way. "Ah, Cassie," he said softly.

"Look at us. We're two of a kind, aren't we? You're trying to escape into your past; I'm trying to escape from mine.... And we've ended up in a time bubble in the middle of nowhere, where we can pretend to be anything we want. We wouldn't survive a minute in the real world." It was a warning, but it was also a question. The truth was: *We don't have a chance together.* The question was: *Does it matter?*

There was sorrow and confusion weighing down the fluttering wings of yearning. Because Cassie did not know the answer. And neither, perhaps, did he.

Moments throbbed off between them. She knew she should go. Jonas was expecting her back tonight. Soon someone would miss her at camp. And it was dangerous to stay here alone with him like this, feeling as she did, wanting what she did. Dangerous and unfair.

Her mother had been right. Sometimes you don't have any choice as to whom you fall in love with.

They were sitting side by side on the bed, but the distance between them seemed unbreachable. In the dusky light she could see his hand, resting lightly on his thigh, his fingers long and dark and relaxed against the damp denim. She could see the length of his forearm beneath the folded up cuff of his plaid shirt, the definition of strong bones and sun-worn skin beneath a light dusting of dark hair. His throat, shadowed by the stubble of the day's-end beard, and the half circle of a blue T-shirt that was visible beneath his open collar. His face. His hair, dark and thick, a curl circling one ear. His eyes, heavily shaded by dark lashes, quiet, calm. To touch him would be only a matter of lifting her arm, opening her fingers, stretching over the distance. A small thing but, once done, irrevocable. She did not know whether she had the courage to make the move.

Logan, don't send me away now. Let me hold you just one time before I go.

Her heart was pounding. She shifted her weight, leaning toward him. She could sense his breath stop, and his eyes quickened. But he made no move to stop her. He simply waited. Slowly, she lifted her hand and touched his face.

The texture of his stubbled cheek was softly abrasive against her fingertips; warmth flowed into her palm. She felt his chest expand for air, and his lashes drifted closed as he slowly turned his lips to the pressure of her palm. Tiny tremors of pent-up longing, of aching need—of love, just love—whispered through her. And at the same moment his hand came up and closed lightly around her wrist. "Don't," he whispered. His breath was warm on her hand. "Don't do this now."

She was close to him. Her shoulder brushed his, her folded leg connected with his. Their chests were almost touching, and she could see his eyes. There was pain there, and it reflected her own. Her voice was a whisper choked by all she wanted to say and he would not allow. "Why?"

"Because..." A gentle pressure of his hand on her wrist moved her fingers away from his face, but no farther. Her hand curled against his collar, and when he lifted his other arm she thought he would push her away, or brace himself for standing. Perhaps that was his intention. But instead, his hand came around to touch her hair, to drift to her neck, to lightly caress her shoulder blade. His eyes were moving over her face, probing cautiously into her eyes, half rejecting and half welcoming what he could not help but read there. "Because now I'm not sure I could stop. Because after coming so close to losing you, after knowing what it felt like to lose you, because we've both had a scare and I'm not sure either of us could stop.

Because nothing has changed, Cassie,'' he said quietly. "You know that."

Could you sleep with a man and then forget about him, Cassie? Could you walk away in the morning and not look back?

Slowly, she lowered her face until her cheek rested against his shoulder. His hand, just as slowly, just as cautiously, spread against her back. His arm encircled her; his fingers entwined with hers against his throat. She felt his breath, deep and unsteady. She felt her own heartbeat, slow and heavy, shaking her body. "I know," she said in a low voice. The sound of it seemed to be smothered deep in her throat.

"It makes no sense." His muscles tensed, a forceful restraint against crushing her close. She felt his fingers close around a strand of hair that straggled down her back. "You can't get involved with me. Involvement means questions that I can't answer, needs I can't fill, promises I can't make...."

"It's too late," she whispered. "I'm already involved with you."

He shifted against her; releasing her fingers, he took her chin and lifted her face to his. He looked down at her, and his eyes were dark and burning and hesitant and intense, and filled with such raw emotion and torn desires that it hurt her eyes just to look at him. "God help me," he whispered brokenly, "because I'm involved with you, too. And there doesn't seem to be anything I can do about it."

His mouth claimed hers, not greedily or violently, but with a slow breaking of barriers, a desperate opening of emotion, a raw and helpless need. It was a moment of surrender for both of them, as painful as it was sweet. They explored each other and they gave to each other, and they allowed the wild and heady need to blossom and consume them, and when he moved his mouth to her neck, to the taste of her ear and her temple and her cheek, Cassie could only cling to him, awash with trembling awareness and weak with fiery need.

"Ah, Cassie," he whispered, and his heavy breath stirred the wisps of hair around her face. "I do want to make love to you. That's all I can give you now."

Could you, Cassie? Could you walk away in the morning?

Sometimes you don't have any choice.

"Then that's all I want," she whispered, and she tightened her arms around him, pressing her face to the thud of his heart, absorbing his strength and his heat, loving him, holding him. He could not be a part of her life, he could never belong to her in any way, but if the moment was all they were offered, the moment was all they could take. It was enough. It would have to be.

His fingers, strong and heavy and ungentle with urgency, threaded through her hair; he tipped her face back so that she had to meet his eyes. She did so, unafraid. She saw the tightness in his face, the urgency and the regret that churned in his eyes, but above all, the need. A need as intense as hers, and like hers, one that went far beyond the physical. "It's not that I don't want to give you more," he said steadily, and his fingers tightened on her skull. "It's that I *can't*. Please understand that."

She looked at him soberly. She did not understand, she would never understand, but she could accept. "No questions, no demands," she promised softly. "Ever." Love on its own terms was all either could offer or accept, and it was more, much more, than she had ever had before.

She saw his eyes close in helplessness and need, and he bent and took her lips softly, adoringly, lingeringly.

And then he turned, releasing her reluctantly; he moved to the edge of the cot and began to remove his boots.

He undressed before her in the dying light of day, standing beside the bed, never removing his eyes from her. It occurred to Cassie that no man had ever undressed before she did, and it seemed to her a unique display of trust, or unity of mind. But everything about Logan, and his lovemaking, was unique. Her hands were hot and heavy as she tugged off her boots, her fingers clumsy as they fumbled with the buttons of her shirt. But Logan undressed gracefully and without shame, unmindful of her eyes upon him as his body was revealed before her... strong and lean and natural in its arousal; all sinewy arms and broad chest, long legs and flat abdomen, smooth planes and dark shadings of hair.

He knelt on the bed beside her and helped her to remove the last of her clothes, not lingering over the barriers of fabric that stood between them. Naked, Cassie was enfolded in his hard length, awash in his heat, stirred by his breath. And for the longest time he simply held her like that against him, letting his body tell her of itself and absorbing the shy secrets of her own. Closing her eyes against the mist of wondering tears, Cassie tightened her arms around him, shakily inhaling the rich and subtle masculine scent of him, and she thought that she had never known a more beautiful moment than this. Surely even their actual coming together could not be more eloquent, more moving, than the sensation of being wrapped in simple warmth and quiet adoration, his flesh against hers, held in her lover's arms.

There was no practiced skill in Logan, no artful determination to fulfill a woman's pleasure. There were no pretenses, no rules, no performance awareness. He was a man who walked alone, but in her arms he had no secrets.

Everything he gave her was genuine, unadorned, unpre-meditated. And it was all of him.

He kissed her because he wanted to, and each kiss, tender upon her lips, luxurious upon her breasts, deep and drawing against the center of her abdomen, opened up something new and vital within Cassie, and revealed something deep and unashamed of him. He touched her with gentle exploratory fingers; he stroked her body with sensual awareness of the texture of her skin, the curves and planes—even the flaws and imperfections that were uniquely hers. He took pleasure in the discovery; there was adoration in his eyes and a hazy flush of wonder on his face. Cassie filled with exquisite joy just for knowing that, for all the soaring pleasure his caresses gave her, they gave him even more.

Cassie didn't need coaching to take her own pleasure from him. She was inexperienced, and she had expected shyness, but there was none. Logan was hers, there were no secrets from him, and their familiarity only began with the physical. He did not have to urge her hand to the place he most wanted her to touch; she was eager to explore this most intimate part of his body, to caress his heated length, to know the familiarity that came with loving.

There was an unspoken harmony to their movements, their touches, their needs. Physical arousal was intense and aching, but the emotional need was even more pow-erful. When Cassie could not bear to be separate from him a moment longer, when her arms wound around his back and her muscles trembled from the twisting spirals of longing, and her throat clenched on a sob that could not begin to express her need for him, he moved over her. Without hesitation, in a motion as sweet and natural as the forces that compelled them together, he slid into her.

Cassie gasped against the sensation, the strangeness of

his full length invading her, filling her, and the instinctive, unexpected power of her own body's reaction. There was heat deep inside her, building and burning where he was, and tightening anxiety, and urgent, urgent need. She had never known it could be like this, physical sensations so intense they were blinding, emotional needs so all-encompassing they were transporting. From that moment on, the world ceased to exist except as it contained the two of them, yet from the center of them life expanded to include all the universe.

His arms slipped beneath her, gathering her close, holding her as he kissed her gently. Her eyes opened and she saw in his dark, slumberous gaze the extent of all she was feeling, words she wanted to say, emotions she needed to express. There were no secrets in his eyes. And looking into them, she saw all she ever wanted to know.

Only when the pleasure, the wonder, of their initial joining had built to an unbearable level between them did he begin to move inside her. Still, they moved, they touched, they breathed as one. They gave to each other and they took from each other, and giving and taking, too, became as one. In those suspended moments of an ending day a bond neither of them had chosen and neither of them understood was forged, and if lives were not changed, souls were.

Afterward, for a long time he stayed inside her and she held him there. She felt the thundering of her heart and the unsteady rush of her own breath; she tasted the salt of his perspiration and the sweetness of his kiss. They held each other, quietly, helplessly, while muscles regained their strength and pulses and breaths slowed, and awareness slowly reoriented itself and filtered down into reality. And then, moving away from her, Logan shifted his weight and drew her head gently onto his shoulder.

Cassie lay there, her hand curled lightly against the damp hair on his chest, her cheek against the hard pad of his shoulder. She could see her fingers rise and fall with the pulse of his heart. His arm did not encircle her, but his hand barely brushed her shoulder. Full dusk had fallen, and he was not holding her anymore.

I don't think I can do it, Cassie thought, and she had to squeeze her eyes tightly shut for the awful burning in her throat, the wetness that filled her mouth and eyes. *I don't think I can get up and walk away.*

But she had promised.

The ecstasy they had shared only moments ago had turned to a sorrow so intense she could barely comprehend it. What should have been the happiest moment of her life was now the most desolate. Yet she had known it must be like this.

No, she had not known. She could never have imagined anything would hurt so much.

Desperation gripped her and she fought it fiercely. She had known the conditions. They had shared more than just a physical act, and both of them knew it. Something deep inside had changed, yet birth and death had come at the same moment, and the future ended now.

No demands, no involvement. All she could give him was the fulfillment of her promise.

She stirred, and he did not restrain her. She left the bed and, with her back to him, she began to dress.

She pulled on her last boot; she straightened her hair. Each beat of her heart was a hope that he would call her back, but she did not expect it. This was it. All either of them had promised.

When there was no delaying any longer, when at last she thought she could trust her voice, she said, "Don't come back with me, all right? I'd rather ride alone."

There was a silence, and then he answered. His voice was low. "All right."

She opened the door and then she couldn't help herself. She had to look back.

He remained as she had left him, half covered by the wool blanket, his arm thrown over his forehead. She had never seen a bleaker expression on anyone's face, and it broke her heart. But she knew her own eyes mirrored his.

She took a breath; it took all her concentration to keep her voice steady. "Logan," she said softly, "I know you don't want to hear this…and I have no right to say it, but I love you. That's all."

She did not wait for a reply. She turned, quickly, before the tears spilled over, and then she did it. She walked away.

Chapter Nine

Jonas said, "I don't know what else to tell you, Cass." He leaned back in his chair, pushing absently at a paperweight on his desk, and then he glanced at her with a lift of his shoulders, in a gesture that seemed at the same time both guilty and apologetic. "I don't want you to think I've been going behind your back or anything, but I'd made this decision long before I had any idea you'd want to come back here to stay."

They were in the ranch office. Amy was sitting across from Jonas, her feet on his desk, flipping through a fashion magazine. Cassie was on the sofa, one leg curled beneath her, absently gazing from time to time out the window and wondering how it could possibly have been less than two weeks ago that she had glanced out this window and seen a lanky form step down from the pickup truck, long legs striding toward her....

Cassie had been barely paying attention to Jonas's words. She had been barely paying attention to much of anything lately, and though she knew it was irrational, weak and foolish, she couldn't seem to help herself. She had been prepared for some depression, self-doubt and sense of loss. Nothing could have prepared her for the pervading sense of emptiness that had filled her the moment she turned her back on Logan.

Every day she awoke telling herself she would not endure the misery a moment longer. She would invent some excuse to ride out to camp; she would find a way to convince Jonas that Logan was needed at the house. She wouldn't bother him, she told herself; she wouldn't demand or cajole or even approach him in any way. She just wanted to see him. Was that too much to ask, just to see him?

But every day she resisted the temptation, knowing all along that it was only a daydream to allow her to get through the motions of living. There was much Cassie was unsure of about herself, much she wasn't proud of and much she regretted. But she did have integrity. She had bargained with life for a moment out of time, and she would not go back on her deal.

Did Logan miss her as deeply and painfully as she missed him? Did he think of her at all? Was he, perhaps, regretting his own conditions and terms now?

But she knew, without self-pity or blame, that he was not. Logan was a strong man who had come to terms with himself and his life long ago. He would not allow himself regret. He simply knew how things must be.

But none of that kept her from wondering, over and over again—sometimes angrily, sometimes from the depths of sorrow—*why*. Why must it be this way; why must they both live by his rules? Didn't he know, as surely and as deeply as she did, that they belonged together? She did not want to change him; she did not want to cage him. She only wanted to be with him.

But he did not want to be with her. And that was the part that was not only the most difficult for her to accept, but also the most impossible to surmount. She wanted to share her life with him, and he wanted only to be left alone.

It was Amy who first comprehended the meaning of Jonas's words, and the thud of her feet hitting the hardwood floor as she sat forward abruptly brought Cassie out of her self-indulgent reverie. Amy stared at her father. "Do you mean...are you saying that you're moving to South America? That you're going to live there?"

He smiled at her. "That's pretty much the size of it, Midget. This group of private ranchers needs a consultant, and they think I'm the man for the job."

"Well, I like that!" Amy's explosive hurt was genuine. "I decide to come live with you and you decide to move out of the country! I would have thought you could have found a subtler way than that to get rid of me, Daddy."

"Nobody's trying to get rid of you, Midget," he told her gently. "As a matter of fact..." He looked at her hesitantly. "I was kind of hoping you'd want to come with me. I think it would be a good experience for you, and while it took some persuading, your mother agrees. There's an American school nearby, and—"

Amy's eyes were wide. "But *South America*! Don't they have revolutions there? And snakes? And cocaine smugglers?"

"Snakes, yes," he admitted. "But there haven't been too many revolutions in Brazil lately, and I'm not sure about the cocaine situation. I'll check up on it. Mostly what they have is cattle. I don't want to influence you one way or another," he told her fairly, "but, to be honest with you, Amy, I never thought I'd get a chance like this at my age." He grinned a little, embarrassed. "The old pioneer spirit still runs pretty strong, I guess, and I thought my adventuring days were over." And he sobered. "I can't turn it down, Midget. Having my grown-up daughter along would be a bonus I never expected, but I'm not pressuring you into anything. You're old enough to make up your own mind, and whatever you decide will be fine with your mother and me."

Amy sat back, stunned. She murmured, "South America." And said nothing else.

Cassie said, uncertainly, "But what about the ranch?"

Jonas looked at her, and she knew then that she was asking him to repeat himself. But Jonas had grown accustomed, in this past week, to Cassie's hearing only half of what was said to her, and though his puzzlement was obvious, he made no comment. He merely explained patiently, "I'm sorry, Cass, I don't see that you have much choice. You can't run the place by yourself, and the oil company's offer is a good one. You've seen the books; you know the situation. This place has lost over a million dollars in the past three years—"

"A million dollars!" Amy's eyes grew round again. "I didn't know we had that kind of money!"

He smiled a little. "We don't," he admitted. "That's why we can't afford to lose it."

"Paper money," Cassie explained absently to Amy. "A ranch operates a lot like a government does, in book figures, not cash. You'll learn about it in college." And, at Amy's blank, disbelieving stare, she turned back to Jonas. "Look, we all know there's not the profit in cattle that there used to be, but…"

"We were lucky to hang in there this long, Cass," he said simply. "Now's the time to bail out. This place is turning into a dinosaur, and they're not cheap to feed. With the profit we make on the sale you could live in comfort the rest of your life, go anywhere, do anything you want to. You know you like the easy life, Cass," he persuaded gently. "Hell, we all do! And I don't see any reason why we shouldn't grab it while we have the chance.''

Cassie stood up and thrust her hands into her pockets, letting her footsteps take her aimlessly across the room. Of course what he said made sense. She knew the ranch was financially unsound, but no business was one hundred percent profitable all the time, and the slump had been going on for some time. Even when she looked at the figures with her own eyes she hadn't read their meaning, hadn't really grasped the consequences. The Circle P had been in operation for over a hundred years; it was beyond imagination that it could end now, so simply, so finally.

The summer day that spilled through the window was so bright she could see the dust suspended in the air. The world outside was brittle and poised, and inside, Cassie felt stunned, a little numb. Her chest was tight and her brain felt fuzzy. For the past week she had been walking on the edge of a nightmare, and this seemed no more than another part of it.

She said at last, a little uncertainly, ''But...selling the ranch.'' She released a long breath that reflected her own inability to grasp the concept. ''It's our home.''

''Cassie, what are you going to do?'' he asked plainly, spreading his hands. ''I never meant to put you on the spot, but I can't stay and you can't run this place by yourself. I thought you'd be glad about the profit, and you will be, once you've had time to think it over.''

He got up and came around the desk, embracing her shoulders with one arm. ''Look, Cass, I know you're attached to the place. Hell, you couldn't be any more attached to it than I am. But there comes a time when sentiment has to step aside for sound judgment, and you just have to let go. We have a couple of months before we have to make anything formal,'' he told her, and squeezed her shoulders briefly. "You think about it; I know you'll see it's for the best."

He started to leave but at the door turned back. "Oh, don't forget the production company is arriving tomorrow. They want to ride out and scout some locations; I thought you might like to show them around." He smiled, waiting for her enthusiasm, but all she could return was a blank and preoccupied gaze. He hesitated, then shrugged and left. Amy followed quickly in his footsteps.

You have to let go.

She knew about letting go. But why had it happened that she had to let go of everything at once?

Cassie brought her fingers to her temples, pressing gently, and then a little more firmly, as though by that action she could instill reason, decision, calm. But there was no reason to it, no rhyme, no great karmic significance. She had come home only to find home was going to the highest bidder. She had found love only to walk away from it. The pattern of her life was random and senseless, as much now as it had ever been, and she didn't even know what she wanted anymore.

There was no arguing with the facts. They were losing money every day, one of the last strongholds in a failing industry. The big oil companies were taking over land all over Wyoming, and the ranchers—the smart ones—were glad to sell. It was the long-overdue end of an era, and who was she to hold back the hands of time?

She should have seen it coming. She had known it must come. She simply hadn't expected it to be so soon.

She would be a fool to turn down the chance to salvage a business that gobbled up money by the handful and turn it into cash. The profit from the sale would greatly expand her own options, and Jonas's portion needed to be invested in Amy's future. Maybe Jonas was right. Maybe she did belong to the world of sit-down dinners and taxi-cabs, of polyurethane and painted sunsets. Maybe she should have known that all along.

What were her options? Jonas had a chance at something important to him, the chance of a lifetime; she couldn't deny him that. But what was she supposed to do, run the ranch herself?

She could try.

But the brief flare of self-resolve was short-lived and dissolved into apathetic resignation. Who was she kidding? She hadn't the faintest idea how to manage an operation this size, much less how to keep it from going bankrupt within the next year. What she didn't know about cattle alone would fill several textbooks, much less the day-to-day management techniques, the keeping of a crew, the marketing of beef. She had spent her youth in reckless abandon and her young womanhood chasing a hollow dream, and she had nothing to show for it at all, not even the courage to keep on looking.

Logan had said it. They were living in a time bubble, all of them, escaping into a little piece of what might have been. The cowboy, tall in the saddle, silhouetted against the sky. The vast prairies, the rolling hills, the livestock fattening on the land. Simpler times, sterner times, more real and more rewarding times…they were dying out, and so were the men and women it took to live in them.

Hugging her arms, Cassie leaned warily against the windowsill and stared blankly out. Nothing stirred in the hot, still air, and the day looked as though it would go on forever. She had been a fool for coming here, for thinking that anything of her future could be molded from her past. For one brief moment she had held love and home and certainty in the palm of her hand, but now they were sifting like dust through her fingers. Perhaps because, as usual, she had grasped the wrong things.

She didn't know what she was going to tell Jonas. She did not know how she could walk away from this place, all it had meant to her and all she had wanted it to mean. She had intended to build a life here. If she left, she would have nothing.

But she didn't see that she had much choice. She didn't have the courage or the energy to seek alternatives. And strangely, as she stood there alone in the sturdy little office with memories of a distant stranger haunting her head, she didn't feel as though she had too much more to lose.

SHE FOUND AMY sitting on the steps of the main house about an hour later. Silently, Cassie dropped down beside her, and the two women were solemn in thought for a while.

"What are you going to do?" Cassie asked, squinting a little against the glare of the sun.

Amy studied her fingernails. As always, they were perfectly shaped and glossily polished, today with a pale pink sheen. "I don't know...South America." She shook her head a little, as though she still couldn't quite believe it. "And I thought camping out on the range was an adventure."

Cassie smiled, linking her hands around one knee. "Sometimes thinking about an adventure is a lot more fun than having it," she pointed out gently.

"Yeah." Amy was thoughtful, and not very happy. "I always thought...I don't know. That it would be different. Everything looks so easy in the movies, you know? But there's nothing very exciting about sleeping in the dirt and peeling potatoes."

Cassie's laugh was a little forced. "Well, that's life for

you." *No one rides off into the sunset anymore; no one really lives happily ever after. That's just life.*

She glanced at Amy. "You should think about this carefully, Amy. It's not just a different country you'd be moving to. It's a different culture, a whole new way of life. No Duran Duran, no fashion magazines, no styling mousse. The only American TV programs you'll get will be at least six months out of date with subtitles, and most of the kids you meet will speak a different language, literally. It's going to be unlike anything you've ever known."

Amy nodded soberly. "I know. It's a chance not too many kids my age get." She turned to Cassie, her eyes confused and torn. "I try not to be spoiled, Cassie, and I don't want to sound selfish.... I love my Dad, and I want to be with him, and I know I should take advantage of this opportunity. It's just that..." She sighed, and looked away. "I wish I were braver."

Cassie reached out and patted the young girl's hand. "I know what you mean," she said quietly.

Amy looked at her. "Are you going to let Dad sell the ranch?"

Cassie withdrew her hand and tried to keep her face expressionless, her tone mature. She certainly hadn't intended to bring her problems to Amy. "Your father's a smart businessman, Amy, and he's right. It's the best thing to do."

"But you don't want to," Amy observed perceptively.

Cassie could not answer. Her throat was too thick.

"And I don't blame you," Amy went on, with a quiet energy that surprised Cassie. "I mean, it's not that I'm in love with the smell of cow manure and dust or anything, and heaven knows this place is hardly the entertainment capital of the world, but it's something, you know, to belong to a place like this. I mean, it's the last of its kind. People want to make movies here. It just doesn't seem right to sell it after all these years."

Cassie smiled at her in affection and gratitude. The girl was growing up fast. "But we've got to be practical, too," she pointed out. "What we need is a money-making operation, not a white elephant. And with your father leaving, well, we just can't afford to run it too much longer."

Amy was quiet for a moment, uncharacteristically so. Cassie could see her mind working and was both amused and touched. The Parkington blood ran strong in Amy, as much as she might doubt it.

Then Amy demanded suddenly, "What's the current market value of gold?"

Cassie blinked, a little taken aback. "I'm not sure. Around three hundred an ounce, I guess."

Excitement was growing in Amy's eyes, her busy little mind working quickly. "And let's pretend, I don't have any idea what it was, but let's just pretend, that a hundred and fifty years ago gold was a dollar an ounce, not to mention the antique value—"

Cassie could not prevent an incredulous bark of laughter. "Amy—"

Amy turned to her, her eyes alive and sparkling enthusiastically. "Don't you see? You're sitting on a literal gold mine, right here! Millions, we're talking about millions! And since it's on our land and if we found it…we'd have to share with Rodney, of course, but if we found it it would be ours! It would solve everybody's problem!"

Cassie tried not to laugh. She half thought Amy was serious. "Whoa now," she said. "If you're talking about that treasure legend—"

"It's more than a legend!"

"All right," allowed Cassie reasonably, "assuming it

is…it's not that I don't appreciate the thought, Midget, but let's not get carried away here. People have been looking for that gold for years.''

"But no one ever had a map before," Amy insisted firmly. At Cassie's skeptical look she asserted, "It's true; Rodney showed it to me! It's a real map, Cassie, with old-fashioned writing and funny little squiggly lines for streams and trees, and it shows *exactly* where the money is!"

Cassie looked at her patiently, hoping her niece wasn't really as gullible as she sounded. "Then why hasn't Rodney already picked it up and taken it away?"

"Because," Amy explained with a touch of exasperation, *"he* doesn't know where it is. I mean, he's looked, but he doesn't know the ranch or the landmarks, but Dad has maps in his office. Maps that show every little dip in the ground for miles and miles around!" She was becoming avid. "If we could get those maps and compare them with the one Rodney has—"

"Oh, Amy." Laughing softly, Cassie slipped her arm around Amy's shoulders and hugged her briefly. "You're a sweetheart and I don't know what I'd do without you. You've cheered me up. But I think it's going to take something a little more negotiable than Gallagher's gold to solve my problems."

Amy considered this for a moment, and gradually her face fell. "Maybe you're right," she admitted reluctantly. "I guess you and Dad looked for the gold when you were kids, too."

"Everybody in the world looked for the gold when they were kids," Cassie assured her.

Cassie got to her feet, and Amy rested her chin glumly in her hands. "If you sell the ranch, the oil company will have all that gold. It doesn't seem fair."

Cassie had started to go into the house; with her hand on the screen door she turned, and her smiled was a little sad. "A lot of things aren't fair, Amy," she said, and went inside.

Chapter Ten

The advance film crew, consisting of a director, an assistant director, two cameramen, a sound man, a set consultant and various assistants—complete with two vans of equipment—arrived early the next morning. Cassie was amazed to learn this was only a skeleton crew, barely representative of the contingent that would invade their land when the filming began in earnest. Jonas took the set consultant, one van and half the personnel to scout locations for their headquarters and temporary sets; Cassie was left in charge of the film crew and the director.

The director's name was James Barnes; he was young, intense and eager to get to work. He wore his hair in a ponytail and had one long, dangling earring, and looked more like a rock star than the man in charge of this creative success of a multimillion-dollar motion picture, but he left no room for doubt about his authority or his competence. Cassie was immediately intimidated.

One of the reasons the Circle P had been so highly sought after for this shoot—aside from the fact that it provided an authentic background and required little set design—was that the script called for the opening and closing scenes to depict a modern working ranch of the 1980s. The film would include documentary-type scenes of the Circle P at work, without the expense of training and costuming extras, and because the Circle P operated so nearly to the way a ranch did a hundred years ago, the fade-in into the fictional story would blend without a seam. It was all quite artistically concepted, and Cassie was impressed.

Jonas had given the production company free run of the ranch, with the stipulation that ordinary operations of the ranch not be interfered with. There would be no posing, no retakes, no rearranging of the work schedule for the sake of the cameras. This, Barnes assured Cassie adamantly, suited him perfectly. He wanted authenticity, and he promised no one would even know the cameras were there. This Cassie rather doubted, but she returned a promise to hold him to his word.

He wanted to begin filming footage today, before the ranch hands got word of the crew's arrival and began sprucing up for the cameras. Jonas had told her she would be showing them around, but Cassie had had in mind something more along the lines of a scenic tour. She had not realized they would be going right into the thick of the roundup...where Logan was.

Amy was starry-eyed with all the activity and had no intention of being left behind. Cassie steeled herself for another teenage crush and a twelve-hour day of nonstop chatter, but Amy surprised her. She sat quietly in the van beside the glamorous Hollywood types and barely said a word all the way out to the campsite—either she had decided a more mature approach was desirable in the presence of such figures of sophistication, or she, too, was completely lost in the technical jargon that was tossed back and forth, and didn't know what to say.

They arrived at the campsite shortly after ten, and Barnes quietly began to set up camera shots and give directions, murmuring superlatives over the covered wagon, the picketed horses, the cook at work. True to his word, he didn't disturb a thing, and Wilson didn't even know what was going on until Barnes asked permission to film the inside of the wagon.

Cassie had expected Amy to be pestering to get into every scene, but once again the young girl surprised her. She had gone over to talk to Rodney as soon as they arrived, and Cassie hadn't seen her since. Cassie could hardly blame her. There was nothing very exciting about filming a movie—it was, in fact, rather boring and took far longer than Cassie would have imagined. Amy's attention span just wasn't long enough to support a whole day of this and neither, Cassie was beginning to suspect, was her own.

After an hour or so, Jonas drove up with the rest of the crew. They carried with them their own commissary— fortunately for them, for Wilson was none too kindly disposed toward any of them and had no intention of preparing rations for a half-dozen extra men—and began to spread a picnic lunch over the campsite. Cassie was glad to see her brother and thought this might be the perfect time to ask to be relieved of odious duty. She told herself she had better things to do than serve as guide for half-grown men in sandals and earrings, that there was no reason for both her and Jonas to be away from the ranch house all day, that she was bored, hot and hungry. She knew the real reason was that, if she stayed any longer, she would be bound to run into Logan.

Day after day she had dreamed of doing nothing but that; she had longed for it; she had forcefully restrained herself from inventing reasons for seeing him. And now that he was minutes away, within touching distance, she found herself suddenly gripped by a chilling attack of cowardice.

She did not want to see him. She did not know what to say to him. He had nothing to say to her. They would look at each other and find nothing but awkwardness between them, and she did not want to remember their last encounter like that. Their parting had been clean and swift. She had kept her bargain. It had been painful, but at least she had known it was necessary. At least she had known, in walking away, that she would never have to do it again. She didn't want to meet him now, to try to act distant and polite, or to try to pretend she didn't see him at all. She didn't want to face the embarrassment and regret in his eyes—or worse, the resentment. She didn't want to watch him trying to think of things to say to her, and she didn't want to put herself through the same thing. He didn't want her, and it was over. There was no point in seeing him again.

Seeing him again would break her heart.

She spent a few minutes in small talk with Jonas and was just about to tell him she was going home when Barnes walked up. He had a sandwich in each hand and a quick, authoritative look in his eye. "We've got about all we can get here," he said. "How about taking us out to the real action? If we wait much longer we'll be getting into bad light. It won't take long," he assured her. "I just want to get a feel for it today, shoot what happens along."

Cassie cast an anxious glance at Jonas but he gave her no chance to object. "Go ahead, Cass. They're working out near the Twin Fork today. I promised Mr. Landeau I'd sketch some of the locations we went over, and we'll be here when you get back."

And the decision, like so many pivotal ones in Cassie's life, was taken from her. She could have protested, but

Jonas would have wanted to know why. They had promised full cooperation, and she didn't want to put her
brother on the spot. The chances were she wouldn't even
see Logan at all.

She should have known better.

She directed the van to the Twin Fork—a branch in the
valley where the herd was being gathered for driving to
the nearest line camp, and from there to the rail spur. She
directed them to park well away from the cattle and the
action, and warned them of how close they could get with
their cameras.

"Don't worry, Ms Grant," replied Barnes absently,
getting out of the van. "We've done this before."

"Not with my cattle you haven't," she returned with
asperity, but he ignored her.

"God, would you look at that? It's beautiful, isn't it?
Remington couldn't have painted it any better! It's perfect, just perfect."

His eyes were glowing as they swept over the scene—
the restless, lowing livestock shifting and kicking up dust
before them, the cowhands circling and calling lazily to
them, the sturdy ponies going about their jobs by rote. No
one had noticed their arrival as yet, or if so, did not think
it cause for comment.

"We can use the sound," Barnes said, brisk and enthusiastic. "Levine, get set up—no, I want to use a hand-
held camera on this reel; walk up as close as you can—"

"Now wait just a minute," Cassie protested.

"And get me a zoom lens. I want to see some faces.
This is great, just great."

"Not so great, Mr. Barnes." Cassie caught his arm.
"You're not going to go walking out there in the middle
of a herd, spooking my cattle—"

"Not to worry, little lady." He patted her hand but

barely glanced at her. She mightily resented being referred to as "little lady" by a man ten years her junior. "We're not going to disturb a thing, not a thing. You just sit back and watch."

Cassie had no intention of sitting back, but she did definitely watch. They set up only far enough away to allow the smallest possible margin of safety—and the best possible camera angle. The dust was thick enough to taste—but not thick enough to mar the shot—and the sounds of shifting hooves and groaning cattle were loud enough to drown out the normal speaking tone of the human voice. It was, as Barnes kept saying, perfect.

Cassie hovered close, wondering how she was possibly going to be able to stand it for the months it took to complete the filming...and then realized that she probably wouldn't have to. The oil company would honor their contract, but there would be no reason for Cassie to be here after the sale was final. No reason, and no place for her. She looked out over the familiar scene—the dust clouds, the fat herd, the cowboys on horseback—and a poignancy gripped her throat that was hard to subdue. She would never see it again. This scene was being played out for the last time, and an era in history was coming to an end before her very eyes.

No, she thought fiercely, instinctively. *I don't want it to. I can't let it. I can't be responsible for letting this all go.*

But what could she do about it?

Barnes said excitedly to the cameraman next to him, "Wait—look. That one there, on the red horse."

Cassie cast him a derisive look—the term was "roan." Then she turned to follow his enthusiastic gesture.

It was Logan.

He was circling in the foreground, and he was not yet

in position to look their way. No doubt he had noticed the van—Logan was too keen an observer to allow anything that unusual to pass him by—but its presence had apparently sparked no curiosity in him, for he was intent upon his job and nothing else.

"Will you look at that?" Barnes was saying. "It's beautiful! My God, I could have looked for weeks and spent a fortune and never had such luck. Just look at him! Whatever you do, Levine, don't blow this shot. We're using it."

Cassie, for a moment, was held just as mesmerized as were the strangers. Logan on horseback was a magnificent sight to behold. He sat tall in the saddle, the reins held daintily in one hand, a coiled lariat in the other. It occurred to Cassie that she had never seen Logan at work before, and the experience was such an integral part of the whole man, it spoke so explicitly of Logan and all that he was, that merely watching him from a distance brought a tightness to her chest, a glow of fierce possessive pride to her eyes. He was beautiful.

Horse and man worked as one as his mount responded to the slightest shift of his weight or nudge of his heel—relaxed, comfortable, poetry to watch. Fringes of his dark hair could be seen beneath his hat and the wind ruffled them as they fell against his collar and the folded edges of the bandanna that he sometimes wore over his mouth and nose when the dust became too thick. He wore vest, jeans, denim shirt and a leather glove on his roping hand. He was strong, confident and at ease, and Cassie could understand the excitement experienced by the men behind the cameras. Logan, a single figure against the backdrop of the Wyoming landscape, epitomized everything that was worth saying about this place. Independence, strength, self-reliance, competence. He was the last living remnant of a dying era, and the embodiment of something that would never come again.

Cassie had to close her eyes. *I can't,* she thought. *I can't let him go.*

But there was nothing she could do about that, either.

She heard Barnes swear under his breath beside her. "He's seen us." Then, "No, wait, it's okay—he's coming this way. Keep that camera on him. Get me a close-up. God, that's beautiful! You see, Ms Grant, I didn't interrupt your precious routine; I didn't give a single direction and I got what I wanted, anyway! Keep that camera on him, Levine, keep moving! I want his face!"

But Cassie didn't even glance at the excited Mr. Barnes. Her eyes were on Logan and her heart was in her throat, pounding heavily.

Logan cut away from the herd and approached them at a canter. She did not know why she hadn't been prepared for this. He was still holding down Red's job while Red recuperated grumpily in the bunkhouse, and as trail boss it was in his purview to inquire what was going on—or to come over and politely greet his employer when he noticed her presence. She had almost convinced herself that she would get out of here without ever having had to speak to Logan at all; she should have known better. Of course he would come over.

Everything within her was turning to rivulets of pleasure and yearning as he drew close. Another thing she had not been prepared for was the sheer physical reaction the sight of him would generate within her. His hands, light on the reins, the muscles of his arms outlined by the fabric of his shirt, his strong back, his taut denimed thighs... His presence, even when far beyond touching distance, evoked a powerful aura that enfolded Cassie against her will, a flood of memories she was helpless to control. She looked at him, and she did not know how she would be able to speak. She looked at him, and all she could think was *Logan, I don't think I can do it. I don't think I can walk away from you again.*

He drew up very close, so close that the startled cameraman had to keep walking backward to keep him in view. Cassie found her voice; she managed to say, "Logan, this is—"

But Logan was not even looking at her. His eyes were on the cameraman and his face was grim, as grim as Cassie had ever seen it, and he demanded in a low voice, "Turn that camera off."

Alarm and confusion became entangled in the sweeping emotions that were turning and leaping in Cassie's chest, and for a moment she couldn't speak. Barnes snapped, "Keep it rolling; we'll edit later. This is great!"

Cassie said hesitantly, "Logan…"

And Logan quietly, deliberately, walked his horse forward. His face was a taut mask, his eyes hard. Cassie took a confused step toward him; the cameraman began to back up frantically. Barnes shouted, "Damn it, Levine, watch what you're doing!" Logan gave his horse a gentle nudge with his foot; the animal obediently bumped the cameraman with his shoulder. Man and camera went sprawling in the dirt.

Incredulity flashed through Cassie and momentarily obscured all else. She cried, "Logan, what in the world—"

Barnes rushed toward his fallen man, who, miraculously, had held on to his camera. Logan dismounted.

"Give me the film," he demanded, walking over to the cameraman.

Levine stared at him, and Barnes exclaimed, "Now listen here!"

Logan shoved him roughly aside and bent over the fallen man, grabbing the camera out of his hand. Cassie could only stare as Logan fumbled roughly with dials and knobs, switches and levers, and finally located the film compartment.

"What the hell do you think you're doing?" the cameraman said, struggling to his feet and grabbing at the camera.

Barnes cried, "Don't open that, you'll expose—"

Cassie couldn't believe it for a long time afterward. She saw Logan's face and it was the face of a stranger, his eyes like ice, his face dark and furious. He opened the film compartment and Barnes shouted, "Are you out of your mind, you ignorant cowboy! Get your filthy hands off—"

Levine grabbed Logan's arm, trying to wrest the camera away from him, and in one smooth, almost effortless motion, Logan brought his fist around and connected it hard with the side of Levine's face. Levine sprawled on the ground with a cry, blood dripping from his nostrils; Barnes stared in motionless horror. Cassie felt her breath leave her lungs and she took a halting step forward, and Logan turned calmly back to his work. He removed the film and tossed it high in the air, a celluloid streamer glinting in the sun before it caught on the branches of a tree. Then he turned and handed the camera politely back to Barnes.

Among the little group there was no sound whatsoever except the crunching of Logan's boots as he walked slowly over to Cassie. Levine cupped his nose with his hand and Barnes stood staring at the empty camera, and Cassie didn't even breathe until Logan stood before her. His face was completely blank. His eyes hardly seemed to see her.

"Where's your brother?"

Somehow, Cassie found her voice. "At—at the camp."

He nodded and walked back over to his horse.

He had gathered the reins before Cassie's stunned and whirling brain allowed her to demand, "Where are you going?"

He looked back at her calmly. "To pick up my pay. It's time I was moving on."

LOGAN, ON HORSEBACK, arrived sometime after Cassie and the two horrified members of the production company did. By that time Barnes and Levine had told their story many times and with many outraged inflections, and as many times as she heard it, Cassie could not believe it. Jonas, calm as always in a crisis, finally convinced Barnes that he had bargained for authenticity and authenticity was what he had gotten—he had been warned to stay away from the cattle and the cowhands. Somewhat grudgingly, Barnes agreed he could have handled the situation better, but nothing could console him for the loss of his film.

Cassie shook her head slowly when they were alone. She felt as though the fist that had bruised Levine's cheek and bloodied his nose had landed right in the center of her stomach. "It makes no sense," she said softly, and it pained her even to speak. "It's not like Logan. He's not a violent man. Why should he get so upset with perfect strangers? It scared me, Jonas. Something is wrong with him."

Jonas was sitting at the camp table he had set up to sketch designs with the set consultant, and the shadow of sunlight through the spreading branches of a nearby juniper made dappled patterns on his face. He answered simply, "We don't know anything about the man, Cass. I tried to tell you that before. These people aren't bound by the same set of rules that govern conventional behavior. That's what makes them so good at what they do.''

Again Cassie shook her head, this time more violently. She would not accept that. She knew Logan; she knew something was wrong with him. All she wanted to know was the answer to the same question that had plagued her over and over since meeting him. "Why?" she demanded. "Why would he do such a thing? There was no reason for it."

Jonas's gaze went mildly over her shoulder. "Do you have an answer for that, Logan?" he asked.

Cassie turned sharply, and her heart lurched once and then went very weak. Logan had come up behind her without her hearing him, and now he stood next to her looking down at Jonas, his hands in the pockets of his vest. She could smell the scent of dust and perspiration that emanated faintly from him; she could see the streaks of dirt on his jeans and sense the residual tension in his muscles. Everything within her seemed to flow to him, to be absorbed by his nearness, and suddenly she didn't care why. She didn't want to know why. She only wanted him to say he was sorry, and not to leave.

Logan did not look at her. His manner was very relaxed, and there was no sign of that awful fury in his face any longer. He answered Jonas's question simply and quietly. "No, sir, I don't."

Please, Logan... It was all Cassie could do to keep from reaching out to touch the arm that was so close to hers.

Jonas looked at him for a long time. And then he said with a quiet casualness that belied the depth of his perception, "You didn't want to be filmed."

Logan answered with the same matter-of-fact tone, "That's right."

Cassie stared at him.

Jonas was silent for just another moment, looking at him. "I don't suppose you want to tell us why."

"No," Logan replied simply, "I don't."

Jonas sighed, and after a moment he lowered his eyes. Cassie wanted to scream at Logan, to scream at them both, for it made no sense. He had risked his job in a rare, uncalled-for display of temper because he objected to being immortalized on film? He had assaulted a perfect stranger with his fists because he didn't want to have his picture taken? That was stupid, and Logan wasn't a stupid man. There had to be another reason. Why wouldn't Logan defend himself?

Jonas said at last, "I'm not going to fire you, Logan. I can't afford to lose you."

There was a moment of silence in which something very important seemed to be going on, something that the two men silently understood already but that Cassie couldn't even fathom. And then Logan said, simply and finally, "I appreciate that. But I can't afford to stay."

Jonas did not look surprised. Cassie's whole world seemed to be dissolving under her feet. He was leaving, just like that, no explanations, no goodbyes.

Jonas said, "You'll have to come back to the ranch with me to settle up accounts. I'll see if I can get you a ride into town in the morning."

Logan nodded. "Thanks."

And he didn't hesitate. He didn't glance at Cassie once. He walked away.

Cassie stood there and listened to the sound of his retreating footsteps, and shock went through her like a dull knife. She had imagined a dozen endings to this day, but none of them had been like this. She could feel Jonas's eyes upon her, puzzled and sympathetic, and she thought vaguely, *Imagine that. Jonas is feeling sorry for me because my feelings were hurt by a drifting cowhand.* Everything seemed at loose ends, unstable, not quite real. Even her own emotions were viewed under a clinical detachment and she thought, *So this is it. Not even a goodbye.*

He had forgotten, just as swiftly and as surely as he had advised her to. She had only been fantasizing when she thought what they had shared had meant something to him. Who was she kidding? She had thrown herself at him, practically begged him to make love to her—what was he supposed to do, say no? He was out on the range for months with nothing but men and cows; was he really supposed to refuse an opportunity like the one she had offered him?

He hadn't even *looked* at her. Even the cheapest one-night stand would have had the decency to say goodbye.

She wasn't hurt anymore. Jonas could save his sympathy. She was angry. Cassie did not get angry often, and when anger came it was with a low, rolling fury that obscured reason and pride and even her own best interest. Jonas could see it building and he opened his mouth to say something, but Cassie had already turned sharply on her heel to stride away.

She almost bumped into Wilson, who looked as if he wanted to talk to her. She brushed past him, barely seeing him, and he called after her, ''Ms Grant—'' But she didn't stop.

She caught up with Logan midway across the compound. He was headed toward the chuck wagon to gather his gear, and she planted herself directly in front of him. He looked down at her, and his face was so impassive she wanted to hit him. Her arms trembled with the effort not to.

''So,'' she said tightly, ''that's it?''

When she spoke, his face wasn't impassive anymore. For just the briefest of moments something flashed across his eyes—a flicker of pain, a quickly squelched regret or even words, perhaps, that he forcefully restrained. All he said was, quietly, "This doesn't concern you, Cassie."

"Like hell it doesn't." Her voice was shaking, but she kept it very low. "You work for me, mister, or had you forgotten?"

The chill mask was firmly in place again. "That's between your brother and me."

He started to move past her and her hand shot out to grab his arm. Her nails dug into his wrist and the action, and the ferocity of it, surprised him. He looked at her. "You owe me an explanation," she hissed.

The explanation had nothing to do with why he resorted to fistfights or why he chose to walk off the job in the middle of a roundup, or even why he was so afraid of having his picture taken. They both knew that. But Logan was the only one brave enough to admit it.

There was a gentling of his face, another brief glimpse of that shadow of pain in his eyes, and then he lowered his lashes, obscuring his expression. "I owe you more than an explanation," he said softly.

Cassie released his arm and he did not move away. But neither did he meet her eyes. She stood there with love and hurt and frustration welling up inside her like tears unwilling to be shed, and he was so close that a half step would have laid her head upon his chest. She was no longer angry. She was no longer hurt—not unless one could call the awful bleakness that seemed to be spreading through every pore of her body hurt. She was simply in need. Desperately in need of Logan, of his strength, his comfort…of the truth.

Don't go, she thought. *Please, Logan, not like this. Be-*

cause if you go it will really be over, and I know I promised but I didn't know it would be so hard.... Just please don't go. Not yet.

She knew if he lifted his eyes to her the answer to her plea would be there. Moments stretched between them like suspended heartbeats, and then he started to look at her.

"Cassie." It was Jonas's voice, tense and agitated behind her, and the moment was shattered. Logan stepped away from her, and both he and Cassie turned to meet her brother. Jonas hardly glanced at Logan but demanded of Cassie, "Where's Amy? Didn't she come back with you?"

"Come back with me?" Cassie parroted foolishly. She hadn't given Amy a thought since they had arrived at camp that morning. "I thought she was here."

Jonas jerked his head sharply toward Wilson, who was approaching at a more reluctant pace. "Wilson said she rode off this morning with Rodney, but I thought surely she had come back and had gone with you out to the range."

Cassie's heart started beating a little faster, in dread anticipation of what she knew had come. "She didn't." Her throat was dry. "I didn't even know she was gone. Are you sure—"

She turned to Wilson, who looked miserable and concerned. "I'm sorry if I did wrong, Mr. Parkington, but I didn't see any harm in letting the boy have time off. And I figured the girl had asked your permission to go riding. It's just that they've been gone so long, and it's about time to get supper on."

Cassie glanced at her watch. She tried not to think what she was thinking. If Amy had left with Rodney as soon as they arrived this morning, the two of them had been gone a little over five hours. That was more than a pleasant ride through the countryside. She looked at Wilson, half pleading. "Hasn't anyone seen them since they left?"

He shook his head adamantly. "No'm. I checked around. It just ain't like Rodney to go off and neglect his duties like this. He's a good boy; that's why I don't mind if he takes his little rides now and then. But he's never been gone this long."

Logan stood beside her listening, and she could sense his alertness...and his worry. It hung over all of them like a pall, but it was heaviest on Cassie. She tried to tell herself not to jump to conclusions. Surely Amy hadn't done what she thought she had. Why hadn't she kept an eye on her? Amy was her responsibility, how could she just let her disappear like that? And Cassie should have known.

She looked at Jonas. The skin had tightened over his cheekbones and his eyes were dark with anxiety. Amy had gone off with a boy, she had been gone far too long, she hadn't reported her destination to anyone. He had a right to be concerned. But he didn't know the worst of it.

Cassie asked, hating it, dreading it, yet knowing what the answer would be. "Jonas, do you know the ranch maps you keep in your office? Did you happen to notice if any of them were missing this morning?" *Oh, Amy, no, you wouldn't be such a fool.*

Jonas's attention sharpened when he saw Cassie's expression. "Amy asked to look at them last night. I gave them to her. Why?"

Cassie released a long, unsteady breath. "That's it, then," she said, hardly above a whisper. She made herself meet her brother's eyes. "Amy has gone off to look for Gallagher's gold."

For a long time Jonas looked as though he didn't believe her, but it must have been the stunned belief in Cassie's own expression that convinced him. And then he didn't waste time with questions. "I'll round up the men and form search parties," he said. "There's still a chance we can catch them before dark." He turned quickly and started to walk away, but Logan's quiet voice stopped him.

"I wouldn't count on it, Mr. Parkington," he said. "They've got a good start on you." He turned to Wilson. "Did you happen to notice which way they rode off in?"

Wilson gestured toward the mountains. "West. Rodney likes to ride out there."

"Did they take any provisions?"

Again it was Logan's question, and a good one. Wilson answered, "I didn't notice. Do you want me to check?"

Jonas said harshly, "Yes. Hurry." Wilson took off at a gallop, relieved to have something constructive to do.

"That Rodney's no fool," Logan said thoughtfully, looking off into the distance. "I'm thinking he wouldn't have gone off on something like this without being prepared."

Jonas demanded of Cassie, "Are you sure? Are you sure that's what they were up to?"

Cassie nodded miserably, wrapping her arms around herself against a chill that seemed to come from deep inside her and spread its way out. "She was talking about it yesterday. I should have known. I never should have let her out of my sight."

But Jonas had no patience with her self-pity. "We'll comb the area. We'll find them."

Cassie looked bleakly toward the mountains. There were hundreds of square miles out there, and all they had to go on was a general direction. Amy was a good rider, but she had no experience with the outdoors. Rodney might be a good kid, but he was just a kid. The area they were riding into was rugged and deserted. They could be lost for days, for weeks.

Wilson ran up, puffing. "A couple of bedrolls, some canned goods," he reported. "Looks like they was planning to be gone a while."

Jonas swore sharply and Cassie felt her stomach clench tight. Up until now she had hoped she had been wrong.

Jonas took a breath. "All right. I'll put every man on it. Maybe they didn't get far. If we don't find them by dark…" Clearly, the idea was horrifying, and he lost some color around his lips. "Then I'll call out the sheriff's helicopter. They'll be okay. We'll find them."

He was gone, Wilson jogging to keep up. Some of the men from the film crew looked up curiously, obviously wondering what all the excitement was about. Logan turned and walked toward the picket line.

Cassie stood there for only another moment, weighed down by the beat of her own heart. It was her fault. If only she had taken Amy seriously, if only she had listened to what the girl was thinking instead of what she was saying. She should have seen this coming.

She caught up with Logan just as he was stripping his saddle off the roan and transferring it to a fresh horse. "I'm coming with you," she said. Her voice was a little breathless from running, and strained from her own inner turmoil, but the determination within it was unmistakable.

He glanced at her. "How do you know where I'm going?"

"You're going after Amy and Rodney."

"It could be I'm just lighting out of here. I don't work here anymore and this isn't my problem."

Her fists clenched and her voice shook. "Damn you," she said. "You're not going to do this to me. You're going to find them and I'm going to be with you when you do. Amy…'' She swallowed hard. ''Amy might need me.''

He paused in tightening the cinch and looked at her. Their eyes met for what seemed like a very long time, though it was actually little more than a glance. Then he checked the cinch, straightened up and commented merely, ''We're going to need some supplies. If I pick up their trail, I'm not coming back till I find them.''

Cassie swallowed hard and didn't hesitate. She started quickly toward the chuck wagon, and she and Logan were riding out of camp within fifteen minutes.

Chapter Eleven

The Crossing

XI

Back east the women were different, it seemed. Or maybe it was just that they were thought of differently, and Jim was beginning to learn that women, above all the creatures on the earth, had the ability to rise—or fall—to what was required of them. In the civilized world a man needed a woman who would look pretty in his parlor, set a nice table and make pleasant conversation with those he wanted to impress. It appeared to Jim that a lot of men back in the States wanted wives for the same reason they'd want a show horse, or one of those fancy European dogs with all the spunk bred out of them. Not that there was anything wrong with show horses, mind; they were mighty fine to look at and faster than lightning on the short haul and a dry track. But if a man had to climb mountains and outdistance Indians and shoot from the saddle, the last thing he wanted was a horse whose pedigree was longer than his own.

Besides, it struck Jim as almost indecent, not to mention impractical, for men to try to keep women as pets. Most of them would have probably been better off with a lap-dog.

Out here a man couldn't afford such luxuries. He needed a woman who could walk as his equal, who could catch him when he stumbled and stand watch on the long nights when the sounds from the hills moved closer with the dawn. When he was sick he needed more than nursing; he needed a partner who could bring in game and fend off enemies until he could get back in the saddle again. Out here a man was mighty careful with whom he rode, for it took more than a good heart and fine intentions to make a partner. The woman who shared his camp at night had to offer more than just loving; there would be times when she would be the difference between life and death. She had to understand that, and be equal to it.

And when it came time to build, she would cut and haul the logs, same as he would. She would clear the ground and he would hunt the meat, or sometimes it would be the other way around. They would stave off the winters together, and her birthing time might come upon her in the middle of the plains with nothing but a rough lean-to to keep off the sun, or in the pine forest with a cave for shelter and nobody but her man to see her through it.

There weren't many women in this world who could survive a life like that, and until he found one, a man was better off riding alone. But if it happened—if a miracle came along and he happened to meet up with that one woman in a million who could know his mind and share his life and who was willing to do it—then a man would be a damn fool to let her go.

And that, as he rode along the empty trails with this woman by his side, was what worried Jim.

THEY RODE NORTHWEST at a mild canter, not wanting to tire the horses prematurely. But it was a steady ride, and tiring, and not until they had left the camp and all signs of civilization were left well behind did Logan slow his horse to a walk.

Jonas was organizing search parties to fan out in a wide half circle toward the mountains, but he knew as well as anyone else that unless the kids had stopped—unless one of them was hurt or in trouble and had been forced to stop—there was no chance of finding them before dark. Furthermore, the direction in which they were headed was untamed country, and it would be as easy for the search party to get lost as it would be for the two young people. No one but Logan was willing to risk going much more than five or ten miles outside of camp.

Each team was equipped with a wide-range, two-way radio, and after an hour Cassie checked in with Jonas.

"Not even a sign of them," his voice cracked back over the device. The sound was faint and disguised with static, but nothing could hide the fear that backed it. "I've covered about all I can in the Jeep, and the riders aren't reporting anything, either. How are you doing?"

Cassie glanced at Logan.

"Tell him I've picked up a trail, but I don't know how far it will lead." Those were the first words Logan had said to her since they started out.

Cassie repeated the message, and her own relief was as great as Jonas's. She had been following Logan because she believed instinctively he knew where he was going. She had seen no signs of a trail of any sort.

"Do you want any help?" Jonas sent back.

Again Cassie glanced at Logan and he shook his head. "Too many riders will only confuse matters. Tell him we're staying out overnight."

Cassie pushed the transmit button again. "Logan says

no. We're staying on it, Jonas. Don't expect us in tonight.''

There was a pause, then more static. "Check in with me again before sundown. I'm going back to the ranch tonight and call the sheriff."

"Don't worry, Jonas," Cassie said, and she meant it. "We're going to find them."

She signed off and replaced the radio, and she rode beside Logan in silence for a while. He said, "It's not too late for you to go back to camp, you know. You can still see the landmarks, and there's no point in your being out after dark."

"No," she replied firmly. "I'm staying with you."

He slanted her a glance, but beneath the shadow of his hat she could not read it. She kept her horse in pace with his, watching him, wondering for the first time how he could possibly be so confident. He said he had picked up a trail, but Cassie could see no hoofprints in the scrubby ground below them. Yet he was not riding aimlessly. He scouted the ground, he nudged his horse a little to the right or the left, he seemed to know where he was going. And he had found her, hadn't he? That awful day she had been lost in the wilderness herself, rain had obscured her tracks and she had deliberately hidden herself—but he had found her. He would do the same for Amy and Rodney. She was sure of it.

But the countryside was so vast, so very empty. Patchy grass, scrub brush and broken rock stretched as far as the eye could see in one direction; deep mountain meadows and evergreen forests in another. If they were headed for the mountains—did they have any idea how far away the mountains were? Cassie remembered her own experience, how easily she had misjudged the distance and gotten lost, how she might have wandered around for days within walking distance of the camp without ever knowing where she was.

An involuntary shiver, which she tried to subdue, gripped her. It was a faint thing, barely noticeable, but Logan glanced at her. "You okay?"

She nodded, unsurprised at the sixth sense that allowed him to read her mood—almost her thoughts—from across the saddle. "I was just thinking how scared I was when I got lost. And Amy…" Her voice tightened there. "She's just a kid."

"She's not alone," he pointed out mildly, and the sound of his voice—nothing more than that—had the power to instill enormous confidence. "And they have maps. They seem to know where they're going. As long as they stay with their horses, they'll be okay."

Cassie nodded, but her throat still felt tight. She kept thinking, *What if they don't? What if they lose their horses or there's an accident? What if they can't even read the damn maps? What if…*

And Logan, with his uncanny mind-reading ability, interrupted, "Rodney's a smart kid. He wouldn't have started out on something like this, much less have taken the girl along, if he didn't think he could do it. He thinks things through. He'll be careful."

Cassie was not as desperate for reassurance as she was for the simple sound of his voice in the emptiness. As long as he was talking, as long as he was telling her things were all right, it was easier not to think how very wrong everything was. She said, "I didn't know you knew Rodney that well."

"I don't. Not to talk to, anyway. But I've watched him; I know how he thinks. Sometimes knowing how a person's going to behave is the most important part about tracking. For instance…" He slowed his horse to a stop and spent a moment glancing over the ground. "Right about here he would have been thinking about water for the horses. See." He gestured to the ground below. "They pulled up here for a minute, looking around, talking it over."

Cassie followed the direction in which he pointed, which led to a patch of ground about three feet from where their own horses stood. She could see nothing to distinguish that portion of the countryside from any other except that the weeds might have been crushed down a little, and if one looked closely, the ground underneath was broken a little in places.

She inquired, "How do you know it was them? And what makes you think they stopped?"

He nudged his horse a little closer to the place he was inspecting. "You can tell by the pattern of prints that they were standing, not moving. And where the grass is broken here…it hasn't had a chance to dry out. These tracks were made today." He looked at the ground a moment longer, then lifted his gaze to the tangle of hilly green not far in the distance. "Good boy," he murmured. Then, to Cassie, "They headed toward the stream, over there. Looks like one of them does know how to read a map, after all."

They reached the stream in less than fifteen minutes, and it was exactly where Logan had predicted it would be—nestled into a rocky incline and feeding sparse ground cover and a few deciduous trees. It wasn't much of a stream, to be sure, barely a trickle that ran out of the mountains, but it was a relief from the glare of the western sun, and the horses appreciated the drink.

They dismounted to let their horses have their fill, and Logan walked carefully around the area, reading whatever the ground could tell him. Cassie knelt beside the stream and splashed water on her face, which, despite the protection of her hat, was beginning to burn. She tried to remember whether or not Amy had been wearing a hat this morning. Her fair skin would blister under this sun, and she was so proud of her complexion.

A wave of guilt and helplessness overcame her, and she sat back on the bank, her knees drawn up to her chest, her fist pressed against her lips. "Damn it," she whispered fiercely, and she felt the hot tears thicken her throat. She fought them back viciously, and said again, only, *"Damn it."*

Logan dropped silently down beside her, sitting on his heels. Furiously, Cassie struggled to control herself, refusing to give in to self-pity, to weaken herself with tears. She tightened her fists against her lips, compressing them grimly, and took several calming breaths through flared nostrils. Logan didn't look at her, or speak to her, but his presence was quiet and strengthening. He let her work it through for herself.

When at last she was able to speak, she said, as calmly as possible, "I should have listened to her. I should have known, I should have remembered what it was like to be her age."

Logan absently turned a broken twig over in his hand. "Was there anything you could have done to stop her?" he asked reasonably.

That gave Cassie pause to think. If she had known, could she have talked Amy out of it? If she had watched her more carefully, wouldn't Amy have simply found a more clever way to get away? Cassie did remember what it was like to be Amy's age, and no one could have stopped her, had their positions been reversed. But she shook her head firmly, as though denying the absolution he offered, and she said, "She was trying to help me. She had some stupid idea that if she found the gold... Jonas wants to sell the ranch," she told him with a soft breath. "I knew it was the only logical thing to do but I...well, I didn't want to, and Amy knew that. She thought she was being helpful."

Logan smiled at her slowly and gently. And with that quiet gesture, a simple smile, all the distance between them was erased, the stress and confusion of the past hours, the unanswered questions, the hurt. He smiled at her and it was as though, from the beginning of time, they had always been together. And he asked, "Is that such a bad thing to be?"

Cassie had to look away. She couldn't believe how her pulse had speeded, how everything within her had begun to go soft, to dissolve into quiet yearning with one look into the depths of his pale eyes. She said, "It's not like Amy to go off like this. I can't understand why she would do such a thing. She doesn't like the outdoors; she hates camping out. She must have known it was a one-in-a-million chance. I can't understand why she would do such a thing."

Logan was silent for a moment, and then he said, thoughtfully, and almost to himself, "Sometimes one-in-a-million chances are the only ones worth taking." He wasn't talking about Amy anymore. Cassie could tell by the tone of his voice, the way his eyes were lowered on his own hands. "And I guess when a person has something to do, it doesn't matter who understands why except himself."

What, Logan? she wanted to plead. *What do you have to do that I can't understand? Why won't you share it with me?*

Then he looked at her, and that vague expression that had so briefly withdrawn him into himself was gone. "My guess is that Miss Amy was trying to prove something to herself even more than she was trying to help you. So don't go taking the responsibility for other people's dragons, okay?''

Before she could question or contradict, he got to his feet. ''They were here for quite a while,'' he said, looking around. ''I found a candy wrapper over there, where they sat down to rest, and the horses were at the graze for a good forty-five minutes. We're closing in on them. We can take some time to get our breath, too, if you want.''

At that moment Cassie wanted nothing more than to sit with him by the stream, to talk to him, to be near him, to try, for whatever moments they could grasp, to recapture something precious out of the horror of this day. Nothing would be lost, no harm would come of resting awhile; even Logan seemed to be advising it. But Cassie got to her feet, readjusting her hat.

''No,'' she said. ''Let's go on.''

He looked at her carefully. ''Are you sure? That sun's pretty mean, and you're not used to it. It won't hurt to rest here a bit.''

Cassie thought about Amy, in the same sun, without a hat, tired and scared and probably already regretting her impetuosity. She wanted to stay. She felt weak and wilted and totally dispirited. But she shook her head firmly. ''No,'' she said stubbornly. ''We're going on, as long as the horses can take it.''

Logan hesitated, and she thought it was surprise she saw in his eyes. But then he merely nodded and turned toward his horse. ''They crossed the stream and went on due west, trying to stay near the trees. It'll be more comfortable riding for a while.''

Cassie gathered up her own reins, but then she had to ask. ''How can you possibly know that? Where did you learn so much about tracking?''

She knew she had made a mistake the moment she asked it, for once again she was prying into his past—and she had promised no questions. There was the smallest hesitation of his foot in the stirrup, and she saw his face go blank. Then he swung astride his horse, and the next thing she knew he was answering casually, "I was with the Border Patrol back in Texas for a while. The job was to keep illegal immigrants from crossing, but mostly what we did was track them and run them back." He nudged his horse across the water, and Cassie mounted to follow. "You have to be at least as cagey as the people you're trying to outsmart in a job like that, and learning to read the signs was a part of it. In desert country, there's not much else to read."

Cassie followed in silence, and she determined to ask no more questions. But her pulse had speeded and confusion left her stunned, for with those few sentences Logan had told her more about himself than he had ever done before—and the picture he painted was quite different from the one she had imagined. She could place him now in the real world, with a real background and a solid life before he had come here.

Logan had once been an officer of the law. Then what had led him to a remote Wyoming ranch, pushing cows for thirty dollars a day? Why did he refuse to talk about it?

When a person has something to do, it doesn't matter who understands why.

The sun was full in their faces as they rode toward the mountains, climbing higher and higher into the foothills. Sweat trickled down Cassie's back and stung her eyes, and mirage heat waves radiated from Logan's horse, the only clear focal point in her range of vision. She checked in once more with Jonas, and his voice sounded very heavy as he reported nothing new. Logan gave him a fair estimation of their location and where he thought the kids were headed, and Jonas promised to have a helicopter up in the morning as soon as he could. Cassie and Logan rode on.

They stopped several times to drink from the canteen, and once Logan made her eat a candy bar. It only made her thirstier, but she did feel a small amount of energy returning. They didn't talk, except once in a while, when Logan pointed out signs of their quarry's passing.

Cassie watched him very carefully, and to her amazement began to learn from his technique. The hoofprints were not as easy to read as if they had been made in desert sand or snow, but they were definitely there, if one looked closely enough. And in land like this, where no one passed for months—sometimes years—at a time, a small sign was all that was needed. A pebble overturned, a leaf bruised, a tree scraped by a stirrup. Once they even got lucky and saw the glint of something silver in the distance, and it turned out to be the foil lining of a gum wrapper. Cassie was intensely grateful that Rodney's upbringing had not included admonitions about being a litterbug.

As they rode higher into the hills the air grew cooler, and as glad as Cassie was of that, she was also worried. She didn't think Amy had taken a jacket this morning, and it would be chilly tonight. She couldn't believe Amy would actually consent to go through with this. Surely as darkness approached she would see her folly; she would insist upon returning to camp. Cassie kept waiting for Logan to tell her he had seen signs of their turning around, but he never did.

The sun was barely an aura of radiance above the tops of the mountains when Logan pulled up and dismounted. He scouted around the ground for a while, and Cassie relieved her own mount of her weight, standing beside her horse and out of Logan's way.

"They stopped here," he said, gesturing to some flattened grass. "And got down. Looks like they were having some sort of argument. See, Amy's footprints are going one way, Rodney's another." Cassie's heart stopped. Surely they hadn't left their horses; they hadn't separated.

"Then they mounted again, and they rode off together." Cassie started breathing again. "But they were riding far apart, and it's hard to tell which way they went."

Logan looked around, squinting into the sun. "It would have been easier riding if they had cut to the east. But if they're really heading straight into the mountains, it would have been quicker to go west. I wish I knew who won that argument."

Cassie lifted her hat and passed her sleeve over her sweaty forehead. "I wish I had that map of Rodney's."

Logan began to go over the ground again carefully, looking for something he had missed, and Cassie cut a wide circle around him. She did not know what she could see that an experienced tracker like Logan could not, but she looked for anything...and then she saw something.

"Logan!" she called out. He came over and she pointed to the side of a partially embedded rock. It showed a white scar, as though the surface of the stone had been chipped away by something. "Could that be anything?"

"It sure could," he agreed. "It could be a chip left by a horseshoe. And—" he stepped over the rock "—there's another one over here. They went this way."

He turned back to her, and his grin was of surprise and pleasure, the spark in his eyes was one of pure admiration. "Where did you learn that, lady?"

"From you," she admitted, and she glowed under his approval.

He touched her waist lightly, and there was appreciation in his smile but something much deeper in his eyes. He said softly, "You're really something, aren't you?"

And that was all. He suddenly seemed to become aware that he was touching her, and that his eyes revealed more than he had meant them to. He stepped away easily and returned to his horse, and Cassie followed. But the moment lingered, and Cassie felt changed.

The route they followed took them over rocky ground, higher into the hills. They had barely been riding half an hour when Logan pulled up, turned in his saddle and looked around. "We'll camp here," he decided. The area in which he had stopped was near a stand of pine, and high enough up to give a panoramic view of the land below. "There's water for the horses, and under the pines there it's flat enough for sleeping. We won't find a better spot."

"Do you mean stop now?" Cassie objected incredulously. "There's still a good hour of daylight left."

"And we'll need it for gathering firewood and making camp," he returned implacably. "The horses need the rest, and so do we. There's nothing more we can do today."

And without giving her further chance to protest, he nudged his horse in the direction of the pines. In silence he began to unsaddle his horse, and Cassie, grating inwardly all the time, followed suit. She had a nagging feeling that he was stopping much sooner than he would have if he had been alone, and she could not afford to sacrifice Amy for her own comfort. She was tired, the heat had drained her and every muscle in her body ached, but she wanted to ride on. She would have gone on through the dark if necessary.

"I'll do that." Logan reached for her saddle just as she did, and their hands brushed. Cassie felt the quiver of electricity go through her with the simple careless contact, but she determined to ignore it. She had promised.

"That's okay." She braced herself and heaved the saddle off in a single motion, staggering a little under the weight. She had been saddling and unsaddling her own horses since long before Logan arrived, and it was nice to know that, for all the skills she had lost during her years of luxury and pampering, the ability to perform that simple task for herself was not among them.

The curve of his smile was indulgent as he watched her. He rested his elbow on her horse's back, soothing its mane with his fingers. "They're okay, Cassie," he said gently.

"You don't know that," she said shortly. She lowered her saddle to the ground and began to unfasten her bedroll and saddlebags. "We should have gone on. They could be in trouble—"

"But they're not," he replied mildly, and the confidence in his voice made Cassie look up at him. "I caught a whiff of their camp smoke a minute ago," he explained. "My guess is if we were to move on around that bend a little we could see their fire."

She stared at him. "Then let's do it! Why are we standing here? We could—"

He shook his head. "Because we'd never reach them before dark and I don't want to take any chances with the horses on this rocky ground. We've gained some time on them, they were moving slow and stopping often to rest. They knew where they were going, you see, and weren't in any hurry, while I—" and the quirk of his eyebrow was relaxed and endearing ''—had to contend with a stubborn woman who doesn't know the meaning of the word 'stop.' So we made a lot more progress today than I expected. But it still will take a couple of hours to reach them over this rocky ground, and it would be suicide to try to go in after them tonight.''

The debate within Cassie was strong, but finally common sense won out. It tore her apart to think they were so close. But it would be even worse if they tried to continue tonight and lost the trail, or worse, lost one of their horses. Logan was right. It was just that waiting had always been the hardest part for Cassie.

Logan gathered dried wood and built an efficient campfire; Cassie unrolled her sleeping bag and used it as ground cover while they heated cans of franks and beans over the coals and made instant coffee in tin cups. The sun was dying into pastel grays and pinks over the mountains when they sat side by side on her sleeping bag and took up their plates.

Cassie had eaten very little all day and she was starving, but the food had no taste and she ate only because she knew she had to. She wondered what Amy was having for supper. The child was so unprepared for this.

Logan said easily, ''So tell me about this movie they're making. What's it about?''

Cassie knew he was trying to distract her, and she cast him a brief, grateful glance. ''It's about…growing up, I guess. The changing West, and the people who were caught up in the times. It's a good book, and I think the movie is going to be good, too.''

She knew he had to be thinking about what had happened this afternoon with the cameraman. She thought there was something he wanted to say about it, for she could see it in his eyes—a disturbed apology, perhaps, or an explanation. She did not push, and after a moment he turned his attention back to his meal.

They finished eating in silence, and slowly the atmosphere of their surroundings began to creep into Cassie's consciousness and beyond, and she was surprised by what it was doing to her. Here they were, two people on a lone hillside with emptiness all around them, nothing but the sky and the mountains and the grass for companionship— but it did not feel empty. Their provisions were crude; they had no protection against the elements or the creatures that made this mountainside their natural habitat. It was a far, far cry from luxurious town houses and satin pajamas, but it felt right, somehow. There was a sense of eternity about this place that brought back to Cassie all she had ever been, that brought out strengths she had never known, and she thought suddenly, *I belong here.* Until this moment she had not been sure. Now she had no doubt.

The day had turned to twilight, and Logan fed a few more sticks into the coals, building up a blaze. His face flickered orange in the glow. There was a cry in the distance—Cassie could have told herself it was a bird, but she knew perfectly well it was a mountain lion—and her eyes followed the sound.

Logan glanced at her. "Nervous?"

She shook her head, cradling her coffee cup with both hands. "I was just thinking about Amy. I'll bet she's scared to death."

Logan piled a few more twigs around the edge of the small fire and leaned back, one elbow resting on his upraised knee. He looked at her thoughtfully, and the soberness in his eyes caused Cassie to look at him curiously. He said, "You surprise me, Cassie Grant." It was a simple statement of fact, quiet and unembellished. "From the very first minute I met you, you haven't stopped surprising me. I thought you were a spoiled city girl who was too quick to jump in over her head. You turned out to be a strong woman." And he lowered his lashes briefly. "Stronger than I ever expected, or counted on. I'm not just talking about the fact that you can sit a saddle almost longer than I can, or learn to read signs just by watching someone else do it." He met her eyes in a gaze that was clear and open and quietly honest. "But other things. You do what you have to do. You keep your word. You find a way to get through."

Cassie swallowed hard. Did he have any idea how hard it had been for her to keep her word, to let him go, to find a way to get through when her heart was breaking a little more each day? But in that moment, she thought he did.

He glanced down at the residue in his coffee cup, swirled it around a little and tossed it away. Then he set his cup on a nearby rock and looked back at her. "I guess what I'm trying to say is that Amy will surprise you, too. I think she takes after her aunt in a lot of ways, and maybe she's stronger than she looks."

Cassie lowered her eyes, and the swell of gratitude and love within her was so intense it choked her voice for a minute and made her eyes burn. Because of him, she had been forced to learn to be strong. She had come home to Wyoming looking for the nebulous shreds of self-respect and self-reliance she had left behind with childhood; she had ended up giving her heart to a man who could not accept it. She had found the place in which she belonged, only to discover that it did not belong to her any longer. She had found the man to whom she belonged, but he did not want her. And she had found herself...only to lose everything else. And the sorrow was, she could do nothing about that.

The touch of his fingers, light upon hers, caused her to look up, startled, and the tears evaporated in her throat. His eyes were so tender, his smile so gentle, that everything within Cassie was lost beneath it. "Do you know what else I think?" he said softly. He turned his hand over, letting her fingers lie against his palm, while his thumb lightly stroked the back of her hand. "I think you're not going to follow your brother's very good advice and sell this place. I think you're going to find a way to stay here, because you know that's what you have to do."

She smiled at him, and though the gesture was uncertain, the quiet determination that backed it was not. "I think you're right," she answered.

The moment between them was sweet and pure, a simple joining of minds and a sharing of souls. They both knew what was going to happen next, and they both knew it should not. And neither did anything to stop it.

His fingers traveled to her face, cupping it gently. His eyes, open and vulnerable and no longer fighting need, moved closer to hers. They kissed, and in the simple joining, plain in its need, inevitable in its destiny, the outpouring of emotions was unstoppable. They turned on the sleeping bag, and with the pine-straw-covered earth their bed, the darkening sky their canopy, they made love.

As natural as the rising stars, as silent as the wind through the trees, they came together in joy and wanting, yet it was more than passion that drove them. They joined like two parts of a whole unnatural in its separation; they shared because they knew no other way. And afterward they lay together, wrapped still in the cocoon of each other's embrace, and both knew that from this moment forward, nothing would ever be the same.

Cassie felt his heart beat beneath her cheek, the silky dampness of his chest hair against her fingers. His arms held her so tightly that there was a tremor in his muscles, and she knew the desperation that filled her was not hers alone. She ached for him; she tried not to cry. They had tonight, and tonight had never been meant to happen. It would never happen again. He had made the rules clear, and she could not hold him. But after tonight, how could she let him go?

You were wrong, Logan. I'm not strong.

She felt his lips on her hair, and there was a fervor to his touch, an intensity and desperation that pierced her tenuous hold on resolve, that caused something vital to crumple inside her. She whispered, tightening her fingers against his chest, "We can't go on like this, Logan. You know it's not right. I promised, no demands. I'm not asking for forever, I don't want you to marry me. But we can't just pretend this isn't happening between us."

Her voice almost broke and she had to stop. She felt the fierceness of his tightening embrace, and then its slow, deliberate loosening. His voice was hoarse, and very quiet, as he said, "I was wrong, Cassie. All the time I was telling myself that I had to stay away from you because I knew I would only hurt you. But that wasn't really it at all. What I was afraid of all the time was hurting myself. Because…" And with his hand he smoothed back her hair, making her lift her face to look at him. There was dark and distant agony in his eyes, a raw yearning in his face. He said, barely above a whisper, "I want to marry you. I want forever."

The words, once said, seemed to echo forever. The gentle light of the first stars threw back their reflection, the whisper of the pines returned the message. And there was a curious suspended uncertainty in Cassie, a paused breath, a wonder that did not dare to be born. For there was no joy in Logan's eyes, and he simply looked at her with a quietness to his expression that gave no warning that the words he was about to utter would cause Cassie's world to end. "But I can't," he said simply. "I can't marry you; I can't stay with you; I can't have forever. I can't have any of the things a normal man would take for granted. You see—" and there was not a breath, not a flicker of his eyes, just a quiet statement of fact "—I'm running from the law."

He sat up, and every moment seemed curiously attenuated, in slow motion, drawn out to its fullest possible extension of agony. Even the crackling of the fire seemed slower, out of step, and the chirping of the night insects out of tune, dropping and fading. He stood up to pull on his jeans, and Cassie could see his shadow, but not the man. Her heartbeat sounded slow, too slow. She said nothing.

He took papers and tobacco from his pocket; he squatted in front of the fire and began to roll a cigarette. It took a very long time. "It was back in Texas," he said. He spoke into the flames, his voice detached now, and emotionless. "They had been moving some stuff, drugs, across the border in our sector. My partner and I had the operation staked out; we were ready to make the bust." He told it briefly, matter-of-factly, ignoring the painful details that would make no difference. "The next thing I knew the local officials were in on it and my partner was arrested. I guess I should have been grateful it wasn't me, but all I could feel was fury because I hadn't seen it coming. It was a perfect setup, and we all knew that county was crooked. But it got worse. It turns out this wasn't just

local corruption we were dealing with. The feds wanted
the big man, and it suited their purposes to let my partner
take the fall while they stalled for time. It was a beautiful
frame. They even had the perfect witness, me. I was called
before the grand jury, and I wouldn't testify. They didn't
want the truth; they only wanted to hear the script. They
slapped me in jail.''

With very careful, deliberate movements, he brought
the cigarette to his lips, took a glowing twig from the fire
and lit the cigarette with it. He inhaled deeply. The silence
ticked on.

''I stayed there for two weeks, and every day they'd
bring me out and every day I didn't say a word. And then,
the next thing I knew, I was being charged with traffick-
ing. They'd found some stuff in my car.'' He drew again
on the cigarette, and his voice was still perfectly toneless.
''So I did the only reasonable thing…I broke out of jail.
That in itself wouldn't have been so bad, I guess, but I
assaulted a couple of guards in the process. That's a federal offense, Cassie. As if I didn't have enough trouble.''

He stared at the glowing ember of his cigarette. The
low flames of the camp fire cast gentle orange shadows
on his planed face. He did not look at her. ''The next
thing I knew I was in New Mexico, looking at my face
on a 'wanted' poster.'' He shook his head slowly, as
though still in disbelief. There was a low note of something almost like bitter laughter in his voice as he added,
''I guess you understand now why I'm not too crazy about
the idea of appearing on film for thousands of moviegoers
across the country.''

Cassie began to dress, and she did it with slow and
dreamlike movements that seemed to have nothing to do
with her at all. He did not look around, but sat staring
into the fire, smoking. The sky darkened, opening up a

brilliant, ever-increasing canopy of stars. Inside, Cassie felt numb, but reeling. Her thoughts chased themselves around and around in her brain but could form no conclusion, no words. She had not expected this. She had lived too long in the world of minor troubles, of paper difficulties, of invented problems that took no great ingenuity to solve. She had come to believe that nothing could stand in the way of her and Logan unless they let it. But she had not expected this.

It was a long time later that she found her voice. It sounded strained, even a little raspy, but the calmness that backed it surprised her. "You're innocent," she said. "You were always innocent. Surely if you went back..."

He shook his head, studying the low-burning cigarette. "I thought about that, once. I even checked up on it. The original case, after the furor that followed my escape and the warrants sent out on me all across the country, died quietly within a year. They let my partner go, and God knows where he is now. But they never dropped the charges against me. Why should they? I escaped federal custody. I'm guilty of assault. If I should ever be picked up, the paperwork alone would keep me in jail until it doesn't matter anymore."

Her heart was still pounding loudly, for no reason and with no provocation; it was just as though a valve had suddenly been turned on and horror was rushing through her and she couldn't stop it. "If you got a lawyer—"

But he hardly seemed to hear her. He seemed to find the stub of his half-smoked cigarette absorbing. "It gets to be a habit, you know." He spoke in a low voice, and not really to her at all. "I got sucked down into something I couldn't stop and all I could think to do was to keep moving, to try to get some control back over my life. And I guess I never realized that the one thing running never gave me was control. It only kept me away from the things I needed to stay alive.''

He took a deep breath, and he tossed his cigarette into the fire. ''I've been living like an outlaw in an old-time western for three years. I can never stay too long in one place. I can't even have a bank account or sign my name to a legal paper. My driver's license expired two years ago and I'm afraid to get a new one. And everywhere I look I'm afraid someone will recognize me. They wouldn't, of course, but fear is like a cancer; it eats away your reason.''

And then he turned to her. He looked at her solemnly, and even the pain in his eyes did not disguise the absolute truth of what lay between them. ''I can't go back, Cassie,'' he said simply. ''I don't know any other way of life anymore.''

She reached for him, blindly, and wordlessly, and he came. They wrapped their arms around each other, holding each other in helpless silence, and that way they stayed throughout the night. Perhaps each of them knew, even then, that it would be the last night they would share.

Chapter Twelve

The Crossing

XII

It came to Jim that rivers meant different things to different people. For some, like him, a river was a thing to be crossed, a barrier to be forded, something to be put behind and gotten out of the way. To others, rivers were a wealth of opportunity, a place to build a trading post, to cut logs for a home, to cultivate crops in the rich bottomland. A place to settle. For Jim, who had seen so many mountains and so many rivers, one more was not much of a challenge. It was only something else to get across on his way to whatever awaited him. But to these others, the river was the end of the road, the place to make their stand.

Jim had been on the run for a long time. He had seen the prairies and the deserts; he had climbed the mountains and followed the buffalo trails into wilderness few men had crossed. He had seen the times begin to change around him and, perhaps, in some small way, he had been a part of them. He had never made it to his pretty valley, between the Two Waters.

*They camped that night on the riverbank. Out in the
darkness somewhere, men waited who would like to kill
him. Beside him slept the woman he had never expected
to love. Tomorrow they would cross over, and he would
leave her behind. And no matter how far he rode, his
enemies would follow.*

*Jim lay awake all night, thinking about it. And by morn-
ing's light, he knew this was the place he would have to
make his stand.*

He was tired of running.

THE MORNING CAME too early. Cassie awoke in Logan's
arms with only dying coals of the camp fire shadowing
his face, and she found him looking at her. There was no
sorrow in his eyes, no reluctance. Just the truth they knew
they both must face. Without a word they got up and
began to break camp.

How strange that, with all that was dying so desperately
inside her, the very real crisis of the outside world went
on as strongly as ever, demanding her attention, forcing
her to be strong. There were still two kids out here in the
wilderness somewhere who needed her. There were still
fears to be dealt with, problems to be solved, real and
present demands pressing down on her. And yet in some
strange way that entire morning never seemed real to her;
even looking back over it in the months and years to come
it would always have an aura of dreaminess, of unimpor-
tance, almost of redundancy. She had sought adventure;
she had craved drama. That and more was unfolded before
her eyes on that chill, misty morning but none of it
seemed worth noting. The only thing that seemed real for
her was Logan's form, tall and straight in the saddle beside her, his eyes intent upon the distance, his face shadowed with the silence they both understood.

The sky was barely pink when they picked up the trail again. An hour's riding, and Cassie could smell the smoke of a camp fire for herself. They came around the curve of a hill and fifty feet below them were Amy and Rodney, cooking bacon in an iron skillet over the open fire.

Cassie stood in the stirrups and called out. Amy looked up, spotted her and waved joyfully. Cassie and Logan rode down to them.

There was confusion. Amy, looking none the worse for wear despite rumpled clothing and tangled hair, flung herself into her aunt's arms the moment Cassie dismounted. Cassie hugged her fiercely, swept by such intense relief that she hardly heard Amy's excited babble. "I'm sorry if you were worried and I know I probably shouldn't have, but wait until you hear—"

And Rodney, who had hung back reluctantly, suddenly spoke up. "Miz Grant. Mr. Logan." He stepped toward Logan, who was still astride his horse. "I know you're mad and you've got a right to be, but before you lay into me there's something you ought to know."

But Logan had already seen, and as Amy disentangled herself from Cassie's arms and began to point excitedly, he said, "It looks like tire tracks." Cassie followed the direction of his gaze, and her heart lurched sickeningly almost before she understood the significance of the large, perfectly formed vehicular tracks not twenty yards away. Amy and Rodney had not been alone last night.

Logan looked back at Rodney. "A truck?"

Rodney started to nod, but Amy interrupted. "We saw them. They drove right past and never even looked at us. We think it's the men who were stealing—"

"It's Amos," Rodney put in, obviously irritated with Amy for stealing his thunder. Amos was the ex-cook, the man whose job Cassie had taken. "And that fellow Bill.

They're the ones who've been stealing your cattle, Miz Grant."

Cassie said hoarsely, "You were out here all night with those men—"

"Oh, they went away," Amy said airily. "I wanted to follow them, but Rodney wouldn't let me. But I don't think they went very far."

"From the sound of the engine," Rodney put in, "I guess they're parked just on the other side of those cottonwoods over there. I'll be glad to show you—"

Cassie turned on Logan. "You knew," she accused. "You knew it was Amos all along."

Logan nodded soberly. "Figured it was, with him quitting the way he did. Red thought the same thing. But we couldn't do much about it till we caught him with the goods."

Logan turned his attention to Rodney, and his voice was stern. "You stay here. Cassie, take care of the kids. I'm going to ride over and take a look."

Cassie said quickly, anxiety springing to her eyes, "Be careful."

His smile was faintly wry as he turned his horse. "I always am."

As his hoofbeats disappeared, Cassie turned back to Amy, knowing she should form a fierce and furious lecture but suddenly lacking the words. Amy saved her the trouble. She took Cassie's arm, her face contrite. "I know," she said softly. "I know it was wrong and I know you're mad but... I know Dad wouldn't understand, but maybe you will." Her eyes were troubled with the difficulty of putting her thoughts into words, and shaded with pleading. "I had to do this...to see if I could, you know? It was crazy. But is it crazier than going off to South America to live with snakes and bugs when I could be in a nice little condo with Mom and that old chatterbox Peter Browning on the Riviera? I was scared, Cassie," she confessed. "Especially when that truck came right past us, and it was so quiet at night… But I'm not scared anymore. I know I'm going to be punished," she finished bravely, "and I deserve it. But it was worth it. Do you understand what I mean?"

Cassie took the young girl into her arms, and she had to close her eyes against the thickness of tears. "Yes," she whispered at last. "I understand."

And then she pushed Amy away, smoothed the tangled blond hair away from her niece's dirt-smudged face and managed a smile. "Well," she demanded, still a little huskily, "did you find the gold?"

Amy cast a glance toward Rodney that was brilliant with excitement, and Cassie stared at the two of them. She didn't believe it. Things like this only happened in fairy tales.

And then, receiving unspoken consent from Rodney, Amy said, "We found it. That is, not yet, but we found the place. There's a cave under that rock over there. See, where everyone made a mistake was in looking for a cave on the bank of a stream. But the stream changed course!" Her eyes were brilliant with excitement. "The cave is still here, but the water is gone. No one could ever find it if they didn't have an old map to compare with the new one."

She paused for breath. "We've been digging all morning, moving rocks and stuff. It's a mess, but we're almost through." Then anxiously, "Cassie, you're not going to make us go back now, are you? We've almost found it!"

Cassie heard the faint beat of helicopter rotors overhead, and she glanced up. The helicopter was not yet in sight. "That's your father, and the sheriff." Then, quickly to Rodney, "You'd better hurry. I'd say you have less than fifteen minutes to find that gold."

The two young people scampered off, and Cassie tried to raise the helicopter on the radio. It was not yet within range. She went to join Rodney and Amy.

She arrived just as Rodney lifted aside a rock large enough to allow him to peer into the cave. "This is it." His voice sounded muffled, and he withdrew his head. His face was flushed and his eyes were brilliant as he grabbed the flashlight from Amy's hand. "It's not but about three feet square, just large enough to hold a cache of gold."

He wiggled inside, and Cassie knelt on the ground beside Amy. She didn't believe it for a minute, but her heart was pounding with contagious excitement. Amy kept demanding, "Well, what do you see? Rodney, hurry up! Is it there?"

At last Rodney backed out, and the expression on his face told them both what they wanted to know. He said heavily, "It was there."

He opened his hand and revealed a single tarnished, dirt-encrusted coin. Cassie took it from him slowly, brushing away the grime until she could read the Spanish inscription, see the unfamiliar engraving. She couldn't believe it. The legend had been true, the gold had been here all along.

"Somebody got to it before we did," Rodney said glumly. "Who knows how many years ago. And they left this as a souvenir."

Cassie looked at the two of them, grimy, dispirited, looking ready to cry. Their grand adventure had come to nothing...but not really to nothing. They had lived a part of history; they had experienced an adventure that most people weren't even imaginative enough to fantasize about. She knew that soon, when the story was repeated to their friends, their relatives, and eventually their children, they would come to realize that. But today all they felt was the loss.

Cassie handed the coin back to Rodney. "This is very old," she said. "When it's cleaned up I think you're going to find it's not entirely worthless. It might even be worth thousands. And it's yours."

Rodney opened his hand, looking at the single remnant of a lost dream with new respect. Just then the radio on Cassie's belt began to crackle.

She opened her transmitter. "Jonas?"

"Cassie, I'm with Sheriff Keys." His voice was choppy and far away, and greatly distorted by the noise of the helicopter. "Where—"

"We've found them, Jonas. They're okay. We're located at—"

She glanced at Rodney, who hastily repeated the landmarks from the map. "We're about half a mile due west from the Old Spring Trail." She squinted into the sky. "I have you in sight, just barely. If you swing northwest, you should be able to see us."

Jonas exclaimed something, but it was unintelligible. Cassie signed off and hoped that he had heard her transmission. She would try again in a few minutes.

She saw the dust from Logan's horse, and she felt the anxiety quicken again. She hurried to meet him.

He pulled up before her, and he looked as easy and relaxed as ever he was as he pushed his hat away from his forehead and smiled down at her. "Well, lady, quite a day, hmm? Two lost kids and a couple of rustlers."

"Did you—"

"They've got about six of your cattle in a makeshift corral just where Rodney said. The tracks from the truck will lead you right to them. There's no one around now, probably out rustling a few more head for the shipment, but they'll be back. And they're going to be mighty irritated to find their truck's missing some ignition wires. If the sheriff's waiting for them, I guess they'll go along peacefully enough.''

The beating of helicopter rotors grew closer and Cassie looked up, distracted.

"Cassie." Jonas's voice came from the radio. "We've got you in sight. We're coming in."

Cassie spoke into the instrument. "Tell the sheriff we've got a couple of cattle thieves waiting for him, too."

A silence, then Jonas's voice, rich with astonishment, "Right!"

And then the entire dreamlike morning dissolved into a pinpoint of reality as she looked up at Logan. Her throat went dry and her chest was pounding. "The sheriff will want to talk to you."

There was a slight tightening of his lips, but no other expression obscured his face. His voice was mild. "I guess he will."

"You can't do that, Logan." The pounding in her chest became harder and faster. "You can't take that chance."

He looked at her, and what she saw in his eyes she couldn't begin to understand. Denial, reluctance, regret…courage. If she asked him, would he stay?

She would never ask him. How could she?

Her hands tightened into fists. Her next words were the hardest she had ever had to utter. "You have to leave, Logan."

He looked at her for the longest time. The pulsing sound of the approaching chopper grew closer. And then he said, quietly, "Yes. I do."

Cassie swallowed. She said, "Go back to camp. Get

one of the men to drive you into town. The sheriff will be busy here for a while.''

He nodded. His horse, alarmed by the noise of the approaching helicopter, began to dance restlessly, but he held it effortlessly in check with one hand. They stood there, looking at each other, for a moment that seemed to go on forever, for the time that encompasses a breaking heart, the end of hope, the fulfillment of a promise. Every nerve in her body cried, *Go, Logan!*

And her heart cried back, *Logan, don't go!*

He turned his horse slightly, and his eyes swept briefly over the horizon. Then he looked back at her, and smiled. It was a faint and forlorn expression. ''No sunset to ride off into,'' he commented simply.

Cassie could hardly make her throat work. ''No,'' she whispered. *I'll go with you. Ask me, and I'll go with you.*

He said, ''You've got your work cut out for you here, Cassie. You're going to do fine.''

She nodded mutely, and his figure blurred before her. She blinked furiously. She couldn't even tell him goodbye. She had no voice.

We're both going to be fine, Logan.

He lifted the reins, and his horse took a few prancing steps away. That was it. He was leaving. It was over.

And suddenly he pulled up; he turned in the saddle. Cassie wanted to run to him; she wanted to beg him to stay, to let her go with him. And her feet were rooted to the spot.

''I love you, Cassie,'' he said quietly. ''I just wanted you to know that.''

Then he nudged his horse and rode away.

Chapter Thirteen

It was spring at the Circle P, and Cassie thought there could not possibly be anything more beautiful in all creation. Perhaps it had something to do with the terrifying harshness of the winters in Wyoming, those long, dark months when everything lay dead or waiting to die. But when spring finally took its first tenuous hold upon the ground, there was no feeling more glorious in the entire range of human sensation. It was like being born again.

Cassie sat at her desk amid a stack of income tax forms, trying to concentrate, spending most of her time gazing at the small patch of crocus just outside the window. She hadn't been a victim of spring fever in a long time. But then, it had been a long time since she had spent spring at home.

The temperature still dipped below freezing at night, and patches of snow lingered in the shade. But the sturdy mountain grass was cropping through as strong and as resilient as ever it had been, and the thaw was starting in the foothills. Soon it would be time for spring roundup, and Cassie could hardly wait. She would be driving the chuck wagon again, as she intended to do every spring and fall for as long as she was physically able.

Things had changed at the Circle P. Jonas and Amy

were in Brazil, reporting with monthly letters that were almost book-length. Amy was learning Portuguese and adjusting well in school. Their house, according to her reports, was palatial, but she had killed a snake in the kitchen. She was in love with a cowboy who was twenty years old and the most beautiful thing ever to walk the earth, and her father was ready to pull his hair out. Some things, after all, hadn't changed.

Red still lived in the bunkhouse and complained daily about wanting to retire but refusing to leave a helpless woman in charge. Rodney had decided there was something to be said for enriching one's station in life and had enrolled in the vocational school in Jackson. The proceeds from the antique coin he had sold had given him the inspiration he needed to further his ambition. And the Circle P was now owned and operated by KalCo Oil.

There had been a time, after Logan had left, when something inside Cassie had gone into hiding, a kind of death of the soul, and she did not think she had the courage, after all, to do what had to be done. It hardly even seemed to matter, and through the vale of numbness and loss all she wanted to do was to follow the course of least resistance. But some genetic code, some deeply inbred spirit of challenge and stubbornness, seemed to make it literally impossible for any man or woman of Circle P stock to do anything the easy way. They had been survivors for too long.

Cassie emerged from her long, dark winter of the heart like the stubborn grazing grass that died beneath layers of soil every year and emerged ever stronger for the crucible. She discovered that nothing is ever really lost, just sometimes misplaced, or, more often, ignored.

And when the time came to make a decision, she did what had to be done.

She had sold to the oil company at a satisfactory profit most of the acreage and livestock. She had retained three thousand acres to do with as she pleased and a royalty on mineral rights. Even Jonas was impressed, for she drove a hard bargain. With her percentage of the royalty Cassie was able to run a small herd of mostly breeding stock, and to preserve in her small corner of Wyoming a way of life that had endured for centuries. There were fences now where once there had been open range; there was economy where once there had been grandeur. But when the sun set over the mountains there were men on horseback silhouetted against the skyline; rugged cattle grazed the hills and valleys, and the tradition, for one more generation, thrived.

She knew, of course, that she had only bought time. An era had passed like so many before it, and all she had managed to do was create a token remembrance, a sort of living museum. But some things were worth saving, and whatever small tribute she could make to the life that once had been on this frontier was well deserved.

The film crew had been on the site through the fall, wrapping just before the first heavy snows fell. The experience had not been one Cassie wanted to relive, but when she received a videotape of the first cut—on demand, for the production company, too, had learned that Cassie Parkington Grant was one tough customer—that, too, had been worth it. *The Crossing* was beautiful, yet for all its authenticity, it was only a reflection of the life Cassie lived every day, the life that was part of her heritage and in her blood. In its own way, the film was a monument, too, but Cassie had the real thing. She watched the reel fade out with tears in her eyes, and she knew she had made the right decision.

Jonas thought she was crazy. She was relying on the

Circle P—what was left of it—as her only source of income; she was learning a trade and building a career in the middle of her life, and none of it was easy. Everything she earned went right back into the ranch. She made mistakes. She was learning about budgets and management and income tax; she was part veterinarian, part businesswoman, part cowhand. None of it was easy. But for the first time in many years Cassie felt alive, and she was surviving.

Cassie was drawn out of her reverie by the sound of tires coming up the muddy drive. She caught a glimpse of a dusty red Mustang, circa 1970, and then the car turned off to park beside the office. She was expecting the veterinarian to bring over some information on a new vaccine, and she was glad of the interruption. Visitors had been rare during the winter, and spring brought more than flowers and restlessness. Company was cause for excitement—and a much-needed excuse to get away from tax forms.

She started to get up to greet him, but then she saw Red crossing the lawn toward the car. Guiltily and reluctantly, she sank back into her chair. Months ago she and Red had made a deal: She handled the paperwork; he handled the cattle. She had been looking for a way out of that bargain diligently, but she knew better than to push Red. He would take care of the veterinarian—probably talk his ear off—and then, in his own good time, would bring him in to Cassie.

She heard the car door slam and the murmur of male voices, and with a sigh she switched on her calculator. It was best to let Red feel he was in charge. As it was, he was anxious enough for an excuse to leave, and if she ever let him guess how much she had learned from him already, how well she was beginning to do on her own...

She heard footsteps on the outside stairs and was surprised that Red had decided to bring their visitor in so soon. Then she realized there were not two sets of footsteps but one. She switched off the calculator, and the door opened. He stood silhouetted in the glare of the sun, a tall, lanky figure in jeans and boots and a Stetson hat, and she did not know why she had ever expected anyone else.

She felt her heartbeat, slow and strong and certain. She felt her breath, thready in her chest. Somehow she managed to get to her feet but could go no farther. She could only stand there, filling her eyes with him, flooding her senses with him, and the smile that radiated from the depths of her glowed in her eyes but barely touched her lips. She said softly, "Hi there, cowboy. Looking for a job?"

Logan took off his hat and stepped forward. He smiled at her. "Just passing through, ma'am."

His hair was shorter and he was clean-shaven. He was wearing a tan corduroy jacket and a sweater vest over his jeans, and his boots had not seen a stirrup in a long time. But his eyes still held the depths of her soul, and his smile was still connected to her heart.

I always knew, she thought. *I always knew it would be like this. That one day I would just look up and you would be there, because we've never really been apart.*

But she did not say it. She didn't have to.

He stood a few feet in front of her desk, and she couldn't move. The time and space between them was heavy and rich, filled with touching and welcome and promises that were hanging by a thread, waiting to be spoken. For the longest time they simply stood there, absorbing each other, renewing each other, and it seemed as though they had all the time in the world.

Logan said at last, moving his eyes around the room, but only briefly, and then back to her, "I see you found a way to do it."

She nodded. "You knew I would."

His eyes deepened with a quick, intense glow that was pride and approval and love. He said simply, "I'm glad."

Moments spun out. She had to speak, but words were rushing up through her throat so quickly she didn't know how any of them would ever come out properly. "What—what about you, Logan? Where have you been? How have you—"

His eyes crinkled, and he nodded toward the window. "I have a driver's license now. And a car. I would have a bank account, but I don't have anything to put in it."

She felt the breath whisper through her chest, joy and relief and question, but she couldn't say anything. Not for a moment.

And again, she didn't have to. "I found a good lawyer," he told her, and his tone had sobered, though the smile that lingered in his eyes and at the corners of his lips seemed incapable of fading. "A good lawyer with a grudge against the system, I should say. He fought like hell for me. I ended up with a suspended sentence." He was watching her carefully. "And a criminal record. And all in all, not much more than I left here with."

Cassie took one slow step around the desk. And then another. And then she was standing right in front of him, close enough to touch him, looking straight into his eyes. "No," she said. "You do have more than you left here with."

He smiled, though this time it seemed a little strained. His eyes were busy on her face and she could feel everything he was thinking, everything he was feeling; it charged the air between them like electricity. "If you mean freedom and self-respect, you're right," he agreed. "I never thought those things meant much to me. But they do."

And she shook her head slowly. "I mean," she said simply, "you have more than that. It's been here all the time."

She saw the leap in his eyes, hope or need or perhaps even fear. He looked as though he wanted to step away, or move forward, and he did neither. There was a space of about three feet between them. She could see the rise and fall of his chest and the movement of his throat when he swallowed. "Cassie..." His voice was hoarse. "I didn't come back here to— I only wanted to see you again, to tell you...well, how things were. I thought you deserved that."

She didn't move, either. Her voice was very quiet. Her heart was thudding through her chest. "I deserve more."

His eyes were mesmerized on hers. "I didn't ask you to wait for me."

"But I did."

He moved, or she moved, and they were in each other's arms. Their embrace was swift and fierce and timeless; they did not kiss but merely wrapped their arms around each other, welcoming a long-lost friend, reuniting with a missing part of themselves. The texture of his jacket was rough and cold against her cheek, his muscles beneath it hard and tight and, oh, so familiar. He smelled of all things rich and wonderful and alive, and she closed her eyes and drank of him, filling herself with him. Logan, and he was home.

She felt his lips against her hair, his cheek against her ear. His arms tightened and hurt her, and hers matched his strength. He whispered, "Cassie, I'm no good at this. I can't offer you anything. I—"

She lifted her face; she caught his hair in her hands, touching him, searching him with her eyes, reassuring herself that he was really there. And she said, ''I'm not asking you for anything.''

She moved **away** from him, just a little way, and let her hands drift to his shoulders. She saw puzzlement and uncertainty on his face. She saw vulnerability and need. And love. She whispered, ''Are you going to leave me again?''

Pain crossed his eyes. The flash of it was as physical as a touch. His voice was husky. ''No.''

''Do you want to marry me?''

There was no hesitation this time. He drew her into his arms, and the word was but a breath. ''Yes.''

She buried her face in his jacket; she let herself open to joy. He held her, and he kissed her, and the fire was kindled that would never be extinguished. Some things were meant to endure. She and Logan, together, were one of them.

And then, in the delirium of the life that was just opening up for them, Cassie touched his face and looked up at him. Her eyes were brilliant, and she was breathless from his kisses. ''Just one thing,'' she said, and he looked down at her, waiting. ''What is your name?''

His eyes crinkled with the beginnings of laughter; the sparks in them danced like embers in the night. ''It's Phillip,'' he said. ''Phillip Logan Stephens.''

Cassie felt like laughing, too. She was tingling with surprise and strangeness and the beginnings of all she had to learn about him. But all she did was step again into his embrace, wrapping her arms around his neck, pressing her cheek against his shoulder. ''Well then, Phillip Logan Stephens,'' she murmured, ''welcome home.''

The Crossing
Epilogue

They came upon it at sundown, the man and the woman, the valley where the two streams divided. They dismounted and left their horses and, arm and arm, they walked to the center of the clearing. There was plenty of hardwood for building, and rich fertile land for crops. Tomorrow they would begin felling the trees. Here they would build their home.

They stood there for a long time, leaning against each other, watching the sun set over the mountains and spread shades of color over their little valley. All the stories he had heard had been right. It was the prettiest sight you ever did see.

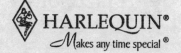

HARLEQUIN *Presents*

**The world's bestselling romance series...
The series that brings you your favorite authors,
month after month:**

Helen Bianchin...Emma Darcy
Lynne Graham...Penny Jordan
Miranda Lee...Sandra Marton
Anne Mather...Carole Mortimer
Susan Napier...Michelle Reid

and many more uniquely talented authors!

Wealthy, powerful, gorgeous men...
Women who have feelings just like your own...
The stories you love, set in exotic, glamorous locations...

HARLEQUIN *Presents*

Seduction and passion guaranteed!

HARLEQUIN®
INTRIGUE

WE'LL LEAVE YOU BREATHLESS!

If you've been looking for thrilling tales of
contemporary passion and sensuous love stories
with taut, edge-of-the-seat suspense—then
you'll love Harlequin Intrigue!

Every month, you'll meet four new heroes
who are guaranteed to make your spine tingle
and your pulse pound. With them you'll enter
into the exciting world of Harlequin Intrigue—
where your life is on the line
and so is your heart!

THAT'S INTRIGUE—
ROMANTIC SUSPENSE
AT ITS BEST!

HARLEQUIN®
Makes any time special ®

Harlequin® Historical

From rugged lawmen and valiant knights to defiant heiresses and spirited frontierswomen, Harlequin Historicals will capture your imagination with their dramatic scope, passion and adventure.

Harlequin Historicals...
they're too good to miss!